Journal of the Alamire Foundation

Journal of the Alamire Foundation

■

Volume 7 - Number 1, Spring 2015

■

General editors:
David Burn
Katelijne Schiltz

Journal of the Alamire Foundation

Volume 7 - Number 1, Spring 2015

BREPOLS

The *Journal of the Alamire Foundation* is published twice a year (spring and autumn)

General editors:
　David Burn
　Katelijne Schiltz
Editorial board:
　Barbara Haggh
　Christian Thomas Leitmeir
　Pedro Memelsdorff
　Klaus Pietschmann
　Dorit Tanay
　Giovanni Zanovello
Advisory board:
　Bonnie J. Blackburn
　M. Jennifer Bloxam
　Anna Maria Busse-Berger
　Fabrice Fitch
　Sean Gallagher
　David Hiley
　Andrew Kirkman
　Karl Kügle
　John Milsom
　Emilio Ros-Fabregas
　Rudolf Rasch
　Thomas Schmidt
　Eugeen Schreurs
　Reinhard Strohm
　Philippe Vendrix
　Rob Wegman

Coordinator:
　Stratton Bull
Music examples:
　Vincent Besson
Music font:
　Theodor Dumitrescu (CMME)

- **Subscriptions:**
　Brepols Publishers
　Begijnhof 67
　B-2300 Turnhout (Belgium)
　Tel.: +32 14448020
　Fax: +32 14428919
　periodicals@brepols.net

- **Submissions:**
　Journal of the Alamire Foundation
　c/o Prof. Dr. David Burn
　KU Leuven – Musicology Research Group
　Mgr. Ladeuzeplein 21, bus 5591
　B-3000 Leuven (Belgium)
　jaf@alamirefoundation.be

Submissions to the Journal can be sent at any time to the address listed above. For further information, including the Journal's style-sheet, see: http://www.alamirefoundation.org/en/publications/journal-alamire-foundation.

The Alamire Foundation was founded in 1991 as a collaborative venture between the Musicology Research Unit of the University of Leuven and Musica, Impulse Centre for Music. The organization is named after Petrus Alamire, one of the most important sixteenth-century music calligraphers. The Foundation aims to create an international platform for promoting research on music in or connected to the Low Countries from the earliest documents to the end of the Ancien Regime. The Foundation hopes especially to promote dialogue between the worlds of scholarship and performance. For more information, see: http://www.alamirefoundation.org/.

© 2015 Brepols Publishers NV

All rights reserved. No part of this publication may be reproduced, stored in a retrieval system or transmitted, in any form or by any means, electronic, mechanical, photocopying, recording, or otherwise, without the prior permission of the publisher.

ISBN: 978-2-503-55377-1
ISSN: 2032-5371
D/2015/0095/61

Table of Contents

Theme
Mise-en-Page in Medieval and Early Modern Music Sources II
Guest Editors: Thomas Schmidt-Beste and Hanna Vorholt

Introduction	*Thomas Schmidt-Beste and Hanna Vorholt*	9
The Layout of the Early Motet	*Oliver Huck*	11
Anachrony and Identity in the Loire Valley Chansonniers	*Jane Alden*	33
The Listening Gaze: Alamire's Presentation Manuscripts and the Courtly Reader	*Vincenzo Borghetti*	47
Printing Hofhaimer: A Case Study	*Grantley McDonald*	67

Free Papers

A King, a Pope, and a War: Economic Crisis and *Faulte d'argent* Settings in the Opening Decades of the Sixteenth Century	*Vassiliki Koutsobina*	83

Research and Performance Practice Forum

Mechanical Carillons as a Source for Historical Performance: An Artistic Reconstruction of Seventeenth-Century Carillon Music Using Historical Re-pinning Books	*Carl Van Eyndhoven*	103

Contributors to this Issue   123

Plates   127

Theme

Mise-en-Page in Medieval and Early Modern Music Sources II

Guest Editors:
Thomas Schmidt-Beste and Hanna Vorholt

Introduction

Thomas Schmidt-Beste and Hanna Vorholt

This is the second of two issues of this Journal devoted to the study of the mise-en-page—or layout—of polyphonic music books from the thirteenth to the sixteenth centuries. As with the previous issue, it takes as its point of departure the interdisciplinary research project *The Production and Reading of Musical Sources* funded by the British Arts and Humanities Research Council from 2010 to 2014 (www.proms.ac.uk). The four articles presented here are again based on papers presented in June 2013 at the project conference, hosted by the British Library and the Warburg Institute (School of Advanced Study, University of London), that brought together scholars from the United Kingdom, Europe, and the United States. The articles sit at various distances from the project's core theme of mise-en-page of polyphonic music sources around 1500 and demonstrate the wider implications of the study of layout of music sources for our understanding of medieval and early modern book production.

Oliver Huck's contribution (itself an outcome of the major research project *Organization of Knowledge in Manuscripts of Polyphonic Music from the So-Called Notre Dame Repertory* funded by the Deutsche Sonderforschungsbereich 950 Manuscript *Cultures in Asia, Africa and Europe* at the University of Hamburg) takes a systematic look at layout options for motets in thirteenth- and fourteenth-century sources. The motet, he argues, is a particularly apt genre for such scrutiny as it is continually transmitted during this time; however, the development of its mise-en-page resists simple linear narratives, instead presenting a multitude of possibilities depending on texture, number and disposition of voices, manuscript format, and scribal preference. The choirbook layout, which was to become the most common approach in polyphonic books, is by no means the endpoint of a consistent development; alternative approaches—consecutive notation, notation in two or more columns on a single page, on their own or combined with the notation of one or more voices in long lines—coexisted with choirbook layout throughout the period in question, as is most apparent in the so-called Montpellier Codex from c. 1300 (Montpellier, Bibliothèque Inter-Universitaire, Faculté de Medicine, H 196).

The contributions by Jane Alden and Vincenzo Borghetti address two of the most celebrated bodies of sources from the decades around 1500, the 'Loire Valley Chansonniers' and the Alamire codices respectively. Alden, building on her seminal monograph *Songs, Scribes, and Society: The History and Reception of the Loire Valley Chansonniers* (New York, 2010), applies to these books the concept of 'anachrony' developed by the art historians Alexander Nagel and Christopher Wood. She explores how the chansonniers' plural layers of temporality unfolded in several, only partly connected stages, ranging from their production and content (both repertorial and iconographic) to their multiple receptions and uses, with owners and readers creating their own historical and temporal references within the books. The implied reader is also at the core of Borghetti's enquiry, which investigates the network of relationships between the musical notation, the repertoire, and the decorative apparatus of the

Alamire choirbooks, in an attempt to overcome the traditional dichotomy between a book intended 'for performance' and one intended 'for display'. Borghetti argues that the visual separation of the voices is as useful for performance as it is visually striking; that the beautifully decorated initials not only serve to indicate the beginning of voice parts, but that the 'singing heads' contained in many of them can also symbolise the sound of the music itself; and that the marginal decoration can assume meaning both in relationship to the musical repertoire with which it appears as well as to the acts of reading, singing, and listening.

In the final study Grantley McDonald (drawing on research conducted within another major research project, *Early Music Printing in German-Speaking Lands*, funded by the Austrian Science Fund at the University of Salzburg) opens up an added perspective on printed books. Taking as his case study Paul Hofhaimer's *Harmoniae poeticae* published by Johannes Petreius in 1539, he examines the context of that book within the tradition of the humanist ode and within Hofhaimer's own biography, but most crucially in terms of its physical production. He also provides the first discussion of 'nested fonts' for polyphonic printing: a method of single-impression printing apparently unique to German printers, using a flexible combination of noteheads, stavelines, and other symbols. This method achieved smoother results and was more economical than the straightforward single-stave type pioneered by Pierre Attaingnant; in spite of the higher effort in setting the page, this made it attractive to printers for whom music was only a small part of their output.

The four studies assembled here thus illuminate aspects of the production and reading of a range of music sources of different types and periods. They demonstrate how such sources act not only as repositories of musical or artistic content, but also as objects whose visual composition is intrinsic to their function and to our understanding of musical and cultural history.

The Layout of the Early Motet[*]

Oliver Huck

Even the very first 'music sources' with polyphonic music have their own distinctive layouts.[1] This article will provide an outline of the history of layouts of polyphonic music in medieval manuscripts—a history that is considerably more complex than often claimed. It will focus on early motets, early double motets, the unity of a motet and a single opening or page, as well as on manuscripts with Machaut's motets.

In the manuscript F, three different ruling patterns are used: one for the two-part organa and clausulae, another for the two-part conducti, and a third for the monophonic pieces.[2] Pages for two-part organa and clausulae are ruled with groups of two staves, a five-line stave for the duplum and a four-line stave for the tenor (fols. 65r-184v). Pages for two-part conducti are ruled with groups of two five-line staves (fols. 263r-380v), and pages for monophonic pieces with single five-line staves (fols. 415r-476v). For motets, double motets, and the so-called monotextual (or conductus) motets there is no such specific ruling.[3] The motets and double motets on fols. 399r-414v are written on pages ruled in the same way as those for monophonic conducti or rotundelli. Monotextual motets are written on pages ruled in the same way as those for two-part conducti (fols. 381r-398v). The layout presents triplum and duplum in pseudo-score (parts written on top of each other but not aligned) and places the tenor at the end.[4]

Histories of layouts of polyphonic music start with the parts in succession in the earliest sources, followed by pseudo-score layout (in the Notre-Dame manuscripts), by an arrangement of the parts in 'Lesefenstern' ('reading windows', in the Ars antiqua manuscripts), and finally by choirbook layout (in the Ars nova manuscripts).[5] These

---

[*] The research for this paper was supported by the Sonderforschungsbereich 950 *Manuscript Cultures in Asia, Africa and Europe*, funded by the Deutsche Forschungsgemeinschaft at the University of Hamburg. I am grateful to Miriam Wendling, Eva Maschke, and Andreas Janke for comments on an earlier version of this paper.

[1] We can consider any manuscript with musical notation to be a 'source with music'. As 'music sources', however, I would like to label only those manuscripts in which musical notation is intended to accompany all of the texts. A real 'music source' thus requires a particular layout based on the pre-ruling of the pages with staves.

[2] For manuscript sigla see the Appendix, which also gives references to images and further reading.

[3] See Darwin F. Scott, 'The Three- and Four-Voice Monotextual Motets of the Notre-Dame School' (Ph.D. diss., University of California at Los Angeles, 1988).

[4] The same layout is used for the monotextual motets in CTr (*Agmina milicie celestis* [532]/*Agmina*, fol. 230v), Ma (*Ecclesie vox hodie* [524]/*Et florebit*, fols. 103v-104v), MüA (*Doce nos optime vite* [346]/*Docebit*, fols. B6r-6v), and W2; in Hu the tenor is placed at the bottom of the page(s) (see for example *Agmina milicie celestis* [532]/*Agmina*, fols. 90v-92r). That the monotextual motets are related to the conductus is obvious from the layout of *Veni doctor previe* [359]/*Veni sancte spiritus reple* (F, fols. 390v-392v) with all three voices in pseudo-score as in LoA (fols. 69r-71v and 84v-86r), and the monotextual motets throughout this manuscript as well as Ch, LoHa (see *Ave gloriosa mater salvatoris* [804] (*Duce creature virgine* [806])/*Domino*, fols. 9v-10r with the tenor as part of the pseudo-score and at the end as well), and Worc—manuscripts which present monotextual motets in pseudo-score similar to three-part conductus. The spelling of titles and the numbers given for tripla and motetus in square brackets follow Friedrich Ludwig, *Repertorium organorum recentioris et motetorum vetusssimi stili. Vol. 2: Catalogue raisonné der Quellen*, ed. Luther Dittmer (Hildesheim and New York, 1972) and Hendrik van der Werf, *Integrated Directory of Organa, Clausulae, and Motets of the Thirteenth Century* (Rochester NY, 1989). For all motets not included there, the spelling follows Gilbert Reaney (ed.), *Manuscripts of Polyphonic Music (c. 1320-1400)*, Répertoire international des sources musicales B IV (Munich and Duisburg, 1966-69).

[5] See Nicole Schwindt, 'Quellen', in *Die Musik in Geschichte und Gegenwart*, ed. Ludwig Finscher (Kassel etc., 1997), Sachteil 7, cols. 1946-86 at cols. 1959-60: 'sukzessive Notation der einzelnen Stimmen', 'partiturartige vertikale Anordnung von der höchsten zur tiefsten Stimme', 'separate, nebeneinanderliegende Lesefenster', and

histories, however, tend to neglect the relationship of layout and musical genre which is obvious in F. The layouts seen in F for the organum and the conductus remain stable over the entire course of their history,[6] while the only musical genre to be found with changing layouts and without interruption in sources from c. 1250 to c. 1430 is the motet.

Early Motets

Many of the compositions in the very first manuscripts that include motets are related to clausulae. Without reconsidering the interdependence between motet and clausula, I would nonetheless emphasize that, despite their shared musical substance, the layouts of the motets and the clausulae differ.[7] Like organa and conducti, clausulae are written in pseudo-score layout, while in the motets, the tenor is placed after the motetus. This layout results from the need for space in order to place the words in the motetus—the presence of text results in far fewer ligatures than in the clausulae—whereas in the tenor no words accompany the music and its repetitions can be abridged, although only some manuscripts use repeat signs in the tenor for repetitions of the entire tenor or smaller sections thereof (see ArsA, ArsB, Boul, Ca, Cl, Hu, LoB, LoC, Lyell, and MüA).[8] Abbreviations of the tenor are indicative of the ongoing transformation of that voice's function from a plainchant reference to a *color* as a structured part of the composition.

There are two different motet layouts in the early manuscripts. In the so-called Notre-Dame manuscripts (F, Ma, MüA, and W2) and some further sources (ArsA, LoC, and N), the tenor concludes—if its end does not by chance coincide with the end of the stave—on the second half of the first stave of the following motet (see Figure 1).[9] In a second and larger group of manuscripts (ArsB, Boul, Ca, Cl, Erf, Fauv, H, Hu, LoB, LoD, Lyell, Maz, MüC, R, Sab,[10] and StV[11]), the tenor ends on a stave of its own (see Figure 2). This group includes all of those manuscripts laid out in two columns, the chansonniers H and R, as well as ArsB,[12] Boul, Cl, and Fauv.

'Chorbuchnotierung'. Heinrich Besseler, 'Studien zur Musik des Mittelalters', in *Archiv für Musikwissenschaft* 7 (1925), 167-252 at 171-74, distinguishes the periods by the size of the manuscripts ('mittleres Oktavformat', 'Quartformat', and 'Foliohandschrift'), the layout with 'Lesefeldern' for each voice is related to mensural notation, in the fourteenth-century 'findet sich eine so tiefgreifende Umwälzung nicht wieder. Man geht jetzt darauf aus, das Lesefeld zu vergrößern'.

[6] That pseudo-score layout is the standard for certain genres—organum and conductus—is obvious from the use in later manuscripts, for example in *Deus in adiutorium meum intende* in Ba (fol. 62v), Da (fol. 1ar), and Mo (fols. 1r and 350r).

[7] On the relationship between the motet and clausula, see Franz Körndle, 'Von der Klausel zur Motette und zurück? Überlegungen zum Repertoire der Handschrift "Saint-Victor"', in *Musiktheorie* 25 (2010), 117-28.

[8] The repetitions of the tenor are indicated by double (or triple, etc.) bars in ArsA, Ca, Cl, LoC, and Lyell and sometimes by paratexts: 'Iterum' (e.g., *Res nova mirabilis* [582]/*Virgo decus castitatis*[583]/*Alleluya* in Cl, fol. 373v and Hu, fols. 105v-106r), 'Item' (*Maniere esgarder* [80]/*Manere* MüA, fol. A8v), 'quinquies' (*In omni fratre tuo* [197]/*In seculum* LoC, fol. 5v), and 'dicatur bis' (*O Maria Mater pia* [411]/*Go* Lyell, fols. 173v-174r).

[9] It is noteworthy that in the appendix of the third fascicle of Mo, the first staves of *Custodi nos Domine natus alma* [833]/*Custodi nos Domine* (fols. 84r-v) and *A Cambrai avint l'autrier* [857]/*Soier* (fols. 84v-85r) are prepared to include the ending of the tenor of the preceding motet as in the Notre-Dame manuscripts, but the blank space is not used in this way.

[10] *Homo quam sit pura* [231]/*Latus* (fols. 138v-140r). The second and third stanza follow after the tenor and are written out with music.

[11] The beginning of the tenor of the only motet with text *Agmina milicie celestis* [532]/*Agmina* (fols. 258r-258v) is written on a short stave in the lower margin of fol. 258r as well.

[12] The layout was planned in a two-column ruling, but the staves have been drawn across the columns. Text and music ultimately have a two-column layout.

Figure 1. Tenor ends in the second half of the first stave of the following motet

Figure 2. Tenor ends on a stave of its own

In the Notre-Dame manuscripts, the chansonniers, and most of the other manuscripts there is either no coloured initial introducing the tenor (Erf, F, Hu, Lyell, Ma, MüA, MüC, N, R, and W2), or the initial is much smaller than that of the motetus (ArsB, Cl, Fauv, H, LoB, LoC, and LoD). This layout decision conveys the impression that the tenor is considered a secondary part of the composition. However, it should be noted that in all of these manuscripts the tenor begins, wherever possible, in the middle of the same stave on which the motetus ends, making it impossible to insert an initial with the same dimensions as the one for the motetus at the beginning of the stave. On the other hand, when the tenor does happen to begin on a new stave, only Fauv provides it with a larger initial (see fols. 2v, *In mari miserie* [76]/*Manere*, and fol. 21v, *Inter amenitatis tripudia/Reverenti*).

The impression conveyed by the smaller initial—that the tenor is somehow a paratextual element of the motet—is further made evident by the layout of the motets in StS, a manuscript in which all tenors are written in the margin.[13] In some cases, a single, short four-line stave is used for this, in others there is a pair of such staves surrounded by a circle. No special layout is needed in those manuscripts that do not merely place the tenor outside the writing area but leave it out altogether (Ch throughout, sometimes Ma[14] and MüC[15]). In the chansonniers, motets written down without a notated tenor and songs must not be confused. In the R, for example, the song-section and the motet-section (fols. 205r-210r) are clearly distinguished by paratexts at their respective beginnings: 'Ci comencent li motet' (fol. 205r) and 'Ci comencent les chansons' (fol. 80r). The only difference regarding the respective layouts is that the song section contains further stanzas of text without music. In the Chansonnier du Noailles (N), the difference in the production of the respective sections is striking: whereas the motet-section can be considered as a 'music source'—all folios are ruled with twelve five-line staves before

---

[13] Some examples for tenors only indicated in the form of paratexts are *O quam sollempnis legatio* [364]/*Amoris* (Lille, fols. 32r-v, without notation but 'cujus tenuram tenet amor') and *Gaudeat devotio* [215]/*Nostrum* (Tor, fol. 140v, without notation but 'super N[ostrum]'). See also the chansonniers N and R, where sometimes the music of the tenor is not notated, but a verbal indication of the tenor is provided: examples are in N *Se j'ai ame folement* [123]/*Hec dies* (fols. 189r-v), *Se j'ai folloie* [162]/*In seculum* (fol. 190v), and *Amours ki tant ies* [566]/*Pacem* (fols. 192v-193r); in R *Onques n'amai tant con* [820]/*Sancte Germane* (fol. 205r), *Ki leiaument sert s'amie* [819]/*Letabitur* (fol. 205r), *D'amor trop lontaigne* [82]/*Manere* (fol. 205r), *Greve m'ont li maus* [385]/*Johanne* (fol. 205v), *Bien doit joie demener* [504]/*In Domino* (fol. 206r), *Main s'est levee* [252]/*Et tenuerunt* (fol. 206r), *Nus ne se doit repentir* [475]/*Audi filia* (fol. 208r), *Avueqes tel Marion* [81]/*Manere* (fol. 208v), *He douce dame pour quoi* [508]/*Et sperabit* (fol. 208v), *Je n'amerai autrui* [401]/*Pro patribus* (fols. 209r-v), *M'amie a doute ke ne* [813]/*Domino* (fol. 209v), *Mainte dame est desperee* [393]/*Johanne* (fol. 209v), *Mieuz vueill sentir* [434]/*Alleluya* (fol. 209v), *Renvoisiement i vois* [435]/*Hodie* (fol. 209v), and *A vous pens belle* [457]/*Propter veritatem* (fol. 209v).

[14] See *Ave Maria fons* [230] (fols. 105r-v), *Ad celi sublimia* [310a] (fols. 105v-106r), *Ne sedeas sortis* [248] (fols. 124v-125r), *In Bethleem Herodes* [98] (fols. 125r-v), *Homo quo vigeas* [313] (fols. 126r-v), *Flos de spina rumpitur* [437] (fols. 126v-127v), *Ad solitum vomitum* [439] (fol. 127v), *Mens fidem seminat* [495] (fols. 130v-131v), and *Alpha bovi et leoni* [762] (fol. 131v).

[15] See for example *Flos de spina rumpitur* [437] (fols. 75v-76v) and *Salve virgo nobilis Maria* [644] (fols. 79v-80r).

THE LAYOUT OF THE EARLY MOTET ■ 13

the notation of text and music—the song-section can be considered as a 'source with music' because the five-line staves were ruled after the text was written down and the length of the staves coincides exactly with the length of the text line. Sometimes the music is missing, sometimes even the staves are lacking (e.g., on fols. 231r-232v).

In two further manuscripts—the sixth fascicle of Mo[16] and E-Tc 98.28[17]—the tenor is placed at the bottom of the page in order to make the layout of the motets match that of the double motets within the same manuscripts.

Early Double Motets

When the layout is adapted for double motets, the question arises of where to place the triplum. While in the motets, the tenor follows the motetus, in the double motets triplum, motetus, and tenor can be notated in succession,[18] resulting in a layout close to that of songs in chansonniers: triplum and motetus appear as though they were individual songs. It is not surprising that most of the manuscripts comprising exclusively French motets use this layout (H, N, and R, but not V; see fol. 114v, *Diex ou porrai je trouver* [31]/*Che sont amouretes* [32]/*Omnes*). In the chansonniers H, N, and R the only difference in layout between a double motet and two motets following each other is that in the double motet, there is no tenor inserted after the triplum. The same is true for the Notre-Dame manuscripts (F, Ma, MüA, and W2) and even more so for Cl, a manuscript which, like many chansonniers, is written in columns.

---

[16] Tischler's description of the layout in the sixth fascicle of Mo, which states that 'motetus and tenor either follow one another on the page or are placed as shown in Figure 7 [i.e., motetus and tenor at the bottom of the page]' (Hans Tischler [ed.], *The Montpellier Codex* [Madison WI, 1978], vol. 1, xxix) is not precise. The end of the tenor of a number of motets is not written at the bottom of the page but on the stave on which the motetus ends; see Catherina Parsoneault, 'The Montpellier Codex: Royal Influence and Musical Taste in Thirteenth-Century Paris' (Ph.D. diss., University of Texas at Austin, 2001), 57-58. There is no motet in which the entire tenor is written consecutively after the motetus (disregarding the last motet in the fascicle, *E munnier porrai je modre* [823]/*Pretiosus*, fol. 269v). Only where the motetus of a new motet begins on the top stave of a recto page and its tenor at the beginning of the bottom stave of the same page is the layout modified for motets which begin and end on the following verso page. As a result, the tenor of *Onc voir par amours* [1039] is missing on fol. 268v because there was no space. In *Puis que belle dame m'aime* [671]/*Flos filius ejus* (fol. 259r), the tenor begins in the middle of the stave and is continued after the motetus at the end of the second to bottom stave where it is linked with a sign (://). In *Bien doit avoir joie* [151]/*In seculum* (fol. 233r), *Hui mein au douz* [122]/*Hec dies* (fol. 234v), and *La pire roe du char* [242]/*Latus* (fol. 245v), the tenor begins after the motetus on the same stave and is continued on the next (bottom) stave. Wherever there is insufficient space on the bottom stave, the tenor is continued directly after the motetus so that the tenor of the following motet begins at the beginning of the bottom stave: see *D'amors nuit et jour me lo* [826]/*Hodie* (fols. 231v-232v), *A tort sui d'amours* [241]/*Latus* (fols. 232v-233r), *Tant grate chievre* [641]/*Tanquam* (fols. 233v-234r), *En non de Deus* [271]/*Ferens pondera* (fols. 234r-v), *Biaus douz amis on ne vouz* [814]/*Domino* (fols. 240r-241r), *J'ai trove qui me veut* [167]/*In seculum* (fols. 241r-v), *Quant yver la bise* [170]/*In seculum* (fols. 255r-v), *Tout ades mi troveroiz* [153]/*In seculum* (fols. 259v-260r), *J'ai un cuer qui me* [355]/*Docebit* (fols. 260r-v), *Ja ne me souvendra de cele* [568]/*Eius* (fols. 260v-261v), *Mout sui fous quant* [489]/*Inquirentes* (fols. 262r-v), *Pensis chief enclin* [677]/*Flos filius eujs* (fol. 263v), *Quant voi la flor* [250]/*Et tenuerunt* (fols. 264v-265r), and *Pour quoi m'aves voz* [353]/*Docebit* (fols. 265v-266r). The motets in the appendix to the third fascicle (*O natio que vitiis* [337]/*Hodie perlustravit*, fols. 83v-84r, *Custodi nos Domine natus alma* [833]/*Custodi nos Domine*, fols. 84r-v, *A Cambrai avint l'autrier* [857]/*Soier*, fols. 84v-85r, and *Fole acoustumence* [45]/*Dominus*, fols. 85r-v), and the motet in the appendix of the seventh fascicle (*Laqueus conteritur venantium* [95]/*Laqueus*, fols. 347r-348r) have the same layout as those of the sixth fascicle, but only once (fol. 85r) is the tenor continued elsewhere.

[17] See *Ave gloriosa mater salvatoris* [804]/*Domino* (fols. 236v-237r), the only two-part motet in this fragment of a larger manuscript.

[18] But see the triplum after the tenor in Ca (*Chorus innocencium* [99]/*In Bethleem Herodes* [98]/*In Bethleem*, fol. 130r) and H (*Par un matin me levai* [522]/*Je ne puis plus durer* [523]/*Justus*, fols. 1r-v, as well as in N, fols. 182r-v).

Writing parts consecutively often does not allow the user(s) to read all parts at the same time, be it for performance or study; none of the manuscripts shows an interest by the scribe in keeping all parts together on the same opening. Moreover, even where the music is notated in columns, there is no evidence in the consecutive layout of a visual relationship between the triplum and the motetus or between the tenor and the upper parts. On the other hand, writing in columns is the precondition for a layout that no longer places the voices in succession, but gives each of the upper parts its own specific space—comparable to the arrangement of text and commentary in many thirteenth-century text manuscripts—and places the tenor as the foundation of the texture on a continuous stave at the bottom of the page (see Figure 3). This layout can be found in manuscripts that only contain double and triple motets (Ba, Da, MüB, Ps, Reg, Stock,[19] Tu, and the motets of Adam de la Halle in Ha), and in the seventh and eighth fascicles of Mo.

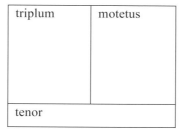

Figure 3. Upper parts in columns, tenor on the lowermost stave

The smaller size of the tenor initial in the manuscripts Ba and Ps once more visually suggests a conceptual subordination of the tenor below the triplum and motetus. From this perspective, the alphabetical ordering of the motets in Ba—in contrast to F and MüA—following the text incipits of the motetus is only consistent. In Da,[20] Fauv, Stock, and Tu, on the other hand, there is no difference in size and style between the initials of the tenor and those of the upper parts. This layout suggests an idea of three-part polyphonic writing with parts of equal importance. In Mo, finally, a significant change in layout occurs between those fascicles with older and those with more recent repertoire: smaller tenor initials in fascicles 3-5 against initials of equal size in fascicles 7 and 8.

The layout shown in Figure 3 is by no means the only part-layout that presents the voices in distinct and related reading areas for each part rather than in succession. Mo, in particular, shows a wide range of different layouts,[21] and there is a strict relationship between repertoire layers and layouts. In fascicles 3-5, double motets are laid out on an opening. The second part of the third fascicle and the entire fourth and fifth fascicles (fols. 74v-227r with the exception of fol. 111r) place the triplum on the verso, the motetus

---

[19] Stockholm, Riksarkivet, Fr 813 (with five hitherto unknown motets) and Fr 5786 containing the motets *O Maria virgo davitica* [449]/*O Maria maris stella* [448]/*Veritatem* (fols. 1r-v) as well as *Non pepercit deus filio* [260]/*Non pepercit deus nato* [261]/*Mors* (fols. 2r-v).

[20] See for example *Celi domina quam* [552]/*Ave virgo virginum ave lumen* [553]/*Et super* (fol. 3v) with its concordance in Ba (fol. 3r).

[21] Tischler's overview over the layouts in Mo (see Tischler, *The Montpellier Codex*, vol. 1, xxx) mentions neither columns of unequal width nor the layout in three columns.

on the recto, and the tenor at the bottom across both pages—a layout also found in E-Tc 98.28 and in some unica in Hu (see below). In a small number of bilingual motets with French and Latin texts—five motets at the beginning of the third fascicle—the tenor part is placed only on the rectos, below the motetus.[22]

While the opening as a visual and conceptual entity is considered a characteristic of the later so-called choirbook layout, fascicles 7 and 8 as the youngest part of Mo abandon the opening as a unit in favour of writing in columns on one page. In the seventh fascicle, apart from the previously described layout with columns for the upper parts and a continuous stave for the tenor at the bottom (Figure 3), there is also a layout in three columns for one motet where the tenor is texted—a layout also found in Ba.[23] And there are three more layouts for motets in which the triplum has more text and notes than the motetus (see Table 1):

- columns of unequal width for the upper parts with a wider column for the triplum (Figure 4), a layout also found in Tu;[24]
- the placement of the tenor only below the motetus column (Figure 5), a layout also found in Stock[25] and Vorau;[26]
- columns of unequal width for the upper parts with a wider column for the triplum and placement of the tenor only below the motetus column (Figure 6).

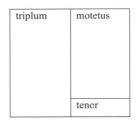
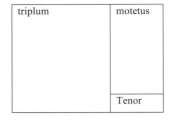

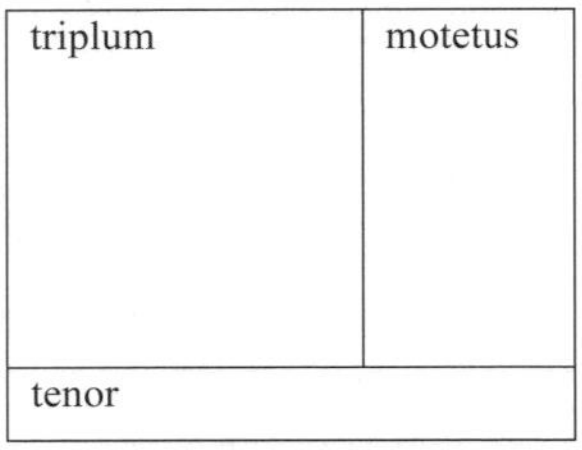

Figure 4. Columns of unequal width

Figure 5. Tenor below the motetus

Figure 6. Columns of unequal width and tenor below the motetus

---

[22] See *El mois d'avril* [318]/*O quam sancta quam benigna* [317]/*Et gaudebit* (fols. 63v-66r), *Mout me fu gries* [196]/*In omni fratre tuo* [197]/*In seculum* (fols. 66v-69r), *Doz rossignoles jolis* [541]/*Virgo gloriosa forma* [542]/*Letabitur* (fols. 68v-71r), *Povre secors* [265]/*Gaude chorus omnium* [266]/*Angelus* (fols. 71v-73r), and *Par une matinee el mois* [807]/*Mellis stilla maris stella* [808]/*Domino* (fols. 72v-75r). The need for more space in the triplum in this repertory is obvious, for example in *Doz rossignoles jolis* [541]/*Virgo gloriosa forma* [542]/*Letabitur* in Tu (fols. 32r-33v), with columns of different width. On this fascicle see Parsoneault, 'The Montpellier Codex', 41-45.

[23] *Qui amours veut maintenir* [880]/*Li dous pensers qui me* [881]/*Cis a cui je sui amie* (fols. 316r-319v) has this layout on fols. 316v-319v and a different layout on fol. 316r; in Ba (fols. 32v-34r); this motet is written in three columns throughout. The other two motets with this layout in Ba—*Entre Copin et Bourgois* [866]/*Je me cuidoie tenir* [867]/*Bele Yzabelos* (fols. 31v-32r) and *Au cuer ai un mal qui* [868]/*Ja ne m'en repentirai* [869] /*Jolietement* (fols. 32r-v)—have a different layout in Mo (fols. 277v-279r and 283v-284v) because there is no text in the tenor in Mo.

[24] See *Or voi je bien* [428]/*Eximium decus virginum* [429]/*Virgo* (fols. 1r-2v), *Entre Adam et Haniket* [725]/*Chief bien seantz* [726]/*Aptatur* (fols. 2v-3v), and *Aucuns vont souvent par* [613]/*Amor qui cor vulnerat* [614]/*Kyrie eleyson* (fols. 13r-14r).

[25] With the exception of *Non pepercit deus filio* [260]/*Non pepercit deus nato* [261]/*Mors* (fols. 2r-2v of Fr 5786) and *Dies ista celebris/Hec est dies/Manere* (fols. 1r and 2r of the second bifolium of Fr 813, but not fol. 1v with the tenor on a continuous stave below the columns and fol. 2r with the tenor below the triplum).

[26] *Entre Adam et Haniket* [725]/*Chief bien seantz* [726]/*Aptatur* (fol. 1r) by Adam de la Halle has the same layout as in Mo (fols. 280v-282r), while *Or voi je bien* [428]/*Eximium decus virginum* [429]/*Virgo* (fol. 1r) has a different layout in Mo (fols. 304r-305v). For the different layout of fol. 2r see below.

The layout in columns of unequal width for the upper parts with a wider column for the triplum and placement of the tenor only below the motetus column demonstrates that the primary aim is not the clear arrangement of 'Lesefelder'[27] ('reading areas') for the different parts on the page, but, rather, to gain more space for the triplum part (this arrangement is only found in the first four motets of the seventh fascicle[28]). This is especially, but by no means only, needed in the motets of Petrus de Cruce.

A layout placing the tenor only in the right-hand column below the motetus abandons the visual concept of the tenor as a fundament for the two upper parts in favour of a concept of highlighting the two-part texture of tenor and motetus.

In the eighth fascicle the need for even more space for the triplum can cause another modification of the layout in columns,[29] by which the triplum concludes on one or more long lines below both columns, followed by the tenor on the lowermost stave (Figure 7 and Table 1).[30]

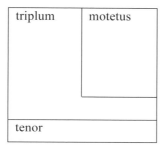

Figure 7. Triplum continued above the tenor

---

[27] See Besseler, 'Studien zur Musik des Mittelalters', 173.
[28] All with columns of unequal width but the tenor on a continuous stave in Tu (see fols. 24v-27r, 14r-15v, 11r-13r, and 20r-21r but columns of equal width on fols. 20r and 21r).
[29] See the different layouts of *Amours qui si me maistrie* [701]/*Solem justicie leticie* [702]/*Solem*, found, respectively, on fols. 328r-329v and 390r-391v.
[30] It should be noted that only one of the motets with concordances in other musical sources or quotations in treatises within the eighth fascicle uses this layout: *Virginale decus et presidium* [769]/*Descendi in ortum* [767]/*Alma*, with a different layout in Da, fol. 1br.

Table 1. Layouts in Mo with more space for the triplum than the motetus, fascicles 7 and 8

Layout	Fols.	Motet
Figure 4	286r-288r	*Bien me doisor toutes* [611]/*Je n'ai que que nus en* [612]/*Kyrie fons*
	288r-290r	*Aucun se sont loe* [834]/*Adieu quemant amouretes* [835]/*Super te*
	290v-292r	*Aucuns vont souvent par* [613]/*Amor qui cor vulnerat* [614]/*Kyrie eleyson*
	292r-293r	*Mout me fu grief* [297]/*Robin m'aime* [298]/*Portare*
	301v-022v	*Tres joliement me voell* [874]/*Imperatrix supernorum civium* [875]/*Cis a cui je sui amie*
	304r-305v	*Or voi je bien* [428]/*Eximium decus virginum* [429]/*Virgo*
	305v-307r	*Quant vient en mai* [382]/*Ne sai qe je die* [380]/*Johanne*
	307v	*Jam nubs dissolvitur* [699]/*Jam novum sydus oritur* [700]/*Solem*
Figure 5	275v-277v	*J'ai mis toute ma pensee* [609]/*Je n'en puis mais se* [610]/*Puerorum caterva*
	277v-279r	*Entre Copin et Bourgois* [866]/*Je me cuidoie tenir* [867]/*Bele Yzabelos* (on fol. 278r the tenor is written below the column of the triplum)
	280v-282r	*Entre Adam et Haniket* [725]/*Chief bien seantz* [726]/*Aptatur*
	282r-283v	*Par un matinet l'autrier* [295]/*Les un bosket vi Robechon* [296]/*Portare*
	284v-285v	*L'autre jour par un matinet* [628]/*Hier matinet trouvai sans* [629]/*Ite missa est*
	298v-300v	*Amours dont je sui espris* [858]/*L'autrier au dout mois d'avril* [859]/*Chose Tassin*
	310v-311r	*Coument se poet nul* [876]/*Se je chante mains que* [877]/*Qui prendroit a son cuer*
	330r-331v	*Nouvele amour m'asaisi* [882]/*Haute amor m'a assalli* [883]/*He dame jolie mon cuer*
Figure 6	270r-273r	*S'amoures eost point de pooir* [531a]/*Au renouveler du jolis tans* [531b]/*Ecciam*
	273r-275r	*Aucun ont trouve chant* [106]/*Lonc tans me sui tenu* [107]/*Annuntiantes*
	275v-277v	*J'ai mis toute ma pensee* [609]/*Je n'en puis mais se* [610]/*Puerorum caterva*
	277v-279r	*Entre Copin et Bourgois* [866]/*Je me cuidoie tenir* [867]/*Bele Yzabelos* (but columns of equal width on fols. 278v-79r)
Figure 7	351v-352v	*Mout ai longuement amour* [301]/*Li dous maus d'amer* [302]/*Portare*
	352v-353r	*O presul eximie* [575]/*O virtutis speculum* [576]/*Sacerdotum*
	353v-354v	*Diex comment porrai laissier* [602]/*O regina glorie spes* [603]/*Nobis concedas*
	355r-355v	*Audi mater generosa virga* [789]/*Imperatrix potentis gracie* [790]/*Neuma*
	355v-356v	*Par une matinee el moys* [896]/*O clemencie fons et venie* [897]/*D'un joli dart*
	357r-357v	*In sompnis mira dei nuncia* [851]/*Amours me commande et prie* [852]/*In sompnis*
	357v-359v	*Se je chante ce fait amour* [514]/*Bien doi amer mon ami* [515]/*Et sperabit*
	359v-361r	*Au tans nouvel que naissent* [900]/*Chele m'a tollu ma joie* [901]/*Villain lieve sus o*
	362r-363v	*Diex comment puet li cuers* [929]/*Vo vair oel m'ont* [930]
	364r-365v	*Se je sui lies* [39]/*Jolietement de cuer bonement* [40]/*Omnes*
	366r-367r	*Aucun qui ne sevent servir* [777]/*Jure tuis laudibus benivolis* [778]/*Maria*
	368v-369v	*On parole de batre* [904]/*A Paris soir et matin* [905]/*Frese nouvele muere france*
	371r-371v	*De mes amours sui souvent* [898]/*L'autrier m'estuet venue* [899]/*Defors Compiegne*
	374r-375r	*Quant se depart li* [207]/*He cuer joli trop m'aves* [208]/*In seculum*
	376v-377v	*Benedicta Marie virginis* [409]/*Beate virginis fecondat* [410]/*Benedicta*
	379r-381r	*Virginale decus et presidium* [769]/*Descendi in ortum* [767]/*Alma*
	382r-383v	*Je cuidoie bien metre vis* [703]/*Se j'ai folement ame* [704]/*Solem*
	385r-386v	*A maistre Jehan Lardier* [269]/*Pour la plus jolie* [270]/*Alleluya*
	386r-388r	*Cis a petit de bien en li* [303]/*Pluseur dient que j'aim* [304]/*Portare*
	390r-391v	*Amours qui si me maistrie* [701]/*Solem justicie leticie* [702]/*Solem*
	394v-395r	*Qui d'amours n'a riens* [577]/*Tant me plaist amour* [578]/*Virga Yesse*
	397r-397v	*La bele estoile de mer* [389]/*La bele en cuige* [388]/*Johanne*

Neither the Notre-Dame manuscripts nor the chansonniers of the same period could have been used for performance because their layout does not allow singers to read all the parts simultaneously from the same opening.[31] On the other hand, in Ars Antiqua manuscripts with a distinct reading area for each part, page turns do occur simultaneously in all the parts.[32] But in none of the thirteenth-century music sources and sources with music does the layout help to avoid page turns within a single motet. The concept of a motet as a unit on a single opening or page is not to be found before the fourteenth century.[33]

One Motet Per Opening or Page

The only music source that avoids page turns within single motets and which contains motets of thirteenth-century repertoire is Hu. But the two different layouts of motets in this codex are by no means new. The main corpus presents the two or three voices in succession, as do the earliest motet sources.[34] On the other hand, a small corpus of motets without concordances presents the upper parts on different pages of the same opening with the tenor on the lowermost stave across both pages[35]—a layout to be found in Mo as well as in E-Tc 98.28.

There is only one further manuscript that avoids page turns within a single motet and contains motets of the thirteenth-century repertoire: Fauv, a source with music. Thanks to the large format and a layout in three columns throughout most of the manuscript there is no need for page turns within a single motet.[36] Fauv shows several different motet layouts which might have been copied from their respective exemplars, including the successive presentation of the voices in columns, and layouts with distinct columns for the upper parts placing the tenor either below both columns, only below the motetus, or only below the triplum respectively (see Table 2).

---

[31] See Besseler, 'Studien zur Musik des Mittelalters', 173.
[32] It is noteworthy that the only manuscript in which the upper parts are aligned in such a way that line breaks occur simultaneously in the triplum and in the motetus is Ba.
[33] On openings as a precondition for the visual organization see Jeffrey Hamburger, 'Openings', in *Imagination, Books and Community in Medieval Europe*, ed. Constant Mews (Melbourne, 2009), 50-133.
[34] Double motets with a motetus beginning on top of the recto page have the same layout, as can be seen from the concordances: *Res nova mirabilis* [582]/*Virgo decus castitatis* [583]/*Alleluya* (fols. 105v-106r) in Cl (fol. 273v) and *Jam nubes dissolvitur* [699]/*Jam novum sydus oritur* [700]/*Solem* (fols. 120v-121r) in LoD (fols. 50v-51v) and Trier (fols. 214v-215r). For *Salve virgo virginum salve lumen* [727]/*O dulcissima virgo mater domini* [729a]/*Aptatur* (fols. 106v-107r) with an empty stave at the bottom of the verso page there is no such concordance. *Amor vincens omnia* [732]/*Marie preconio devotio* [733]/*Aptatur* (fols. 116v-117r) is the exception insofar as the incomplete tenor (as 'tenura') is inserted after the triplum, but the complete tenor occurs as 'tenor' after the motetus. This layout is the same as in Flor 122 (fols. 144v-145r). The layout of *O Maria virgo davitica* [449]/*O Maria maris stella* [448]/*Veritatem* (fols. 102v-103r) shows how a monotextual motet with the tenor at the bottom of fol. 102v becomes a new double motet through the addition of a triplum on fol. 103r. I assume that the same procedure was used for *Ave gloriosa mater salvatoris* [804]/*Salve virgo regia mater clemencie* [805]/*Domino* (fols. 100v-101r) and *Ex semine Abrahe* [483]/*Ex semine rosa* [484]/*Ex semine* (fols. 117v-118r), which have only the triplum and the tenor on the verso page; both motets are transmitted as monotextual motets elsewhere; the same applies to *Virgo parit puerum* [761a]/*Nova salus hominis* [761b]/*Benedicamus domino* (fols. 99v-100r).
[35] See fols. 119v-120r and 121v-125r.
[36] The exception is *Firmissime fidem teneamus* [530]/*Adesto sancta trinitas* [531]/*Alleluya* (fols. 43r-v).

Table 2. Double motet layouts in Fauv

Layout	Fols.	Motet
Successive presentation of the voices in columns	9v	Je voi douleur avenir car tout/Fauvel nous a fait present/Fauvel autant mest si poise arriere comme avant
	7v	Orbis orbatus oculus in die/Vos pastores adulteri/Fur non venit nisi ut furetur et mactet et perdat (layout may be intended in this way)
	15v-16r	La mesnie fauveline qui a mau fere/J'ai fait nouvelement amie/Grant despit ai je Fortune de Fauvel (layout may be intended in this way)
Distinct columns for the upper parts placing the tenor below both columns	6v	Quasi non ministerium creditum/Trahunt in precipitia qui nos/Ve qui gregi deficiunt/Displicebat ei
	11v-12r	Conditio nature defuit in filio/O natio nephandi generis/Mane prima sabbati
	13r	Facilius a nobis vitatur/Alieni boni mundia/Imperfecte canite
	44v	Garrit Gallus flendo dolorose/In nova fert animus/Neuma
	45r	Quant je le voi ou voirre cler volentiers/Bon vin doit l'en a li tirer/Ci me faut un tour de vin
Distinct columns for the upper parts placing the tenor only below the motetus	2r	Scariotis geniture vipereo/Iure quod in opere davitico/Superne matris gaudia
	3r	Nulla pestis est gravior/Plange nostra regio/Vergente ex imperfectis
	8v	Desolata mater ecclesia a filiis/Que nutritos filios/Filios enutrivi et exaltavi
	10v	Se coeurs joians jonnes jolis et gentis/Rex beatus, confessor domini/Ave
	29v	Bonne est amours ou dangier/Se mes desirs fust souhais/A
	43r-v	Firmissime fidem teneamus [530]/Adesto sancta trinitas [531]/Alleluya
Distinct columns for the upper parts placing the tenor only below the triplum	10v-11r	Servant regem misericordia et veritas/O Philippe prelustris Francorum/Rex regum et dominus dominantium
	22r	Inflammatis invidia demon/Sicut de ligno parvulus generatur/Victimae paschali laudes
	41v-42r	Tribum quem non abhorruit/Quoniam secta latronum spelunca/Merito hec patimur

There is only one thirteenth-century motet in Fauv, *Conditio nature defuit in filio/O natio nephandi generis/Mane prima sabbati*, with a layout similar to that found for the same motet in another extant manuscript (Ba, fol. 49v). The layout used in the eighth fascicle of Mo (Figure 7) reoccurs for *Super cathedram moysi latitat/Presidentes in thronis seculi/Ruina* in Fauv[37] (fol. 1v) and for the same motet as well as many others in the Cambrai fragments[38]. A related layout (Figure 8), with the tenor placed only below the column of the motetus and the end of the triplum on continuous staves below both columns, can be found twice in Mo,[39] in Fauv,[40] as well as throughout in the rotuli B-Br 19606 and F-Pn 67.

---

[37] See also Fauv, fol. 30r, *Quoniam novi probatur exitu/Heu! Fortuna subdola/Heu me! tristis est anima mea*.

[38] F-CA 165, fol. 1v. In the Cambrai fragments, the tenor begins on the same stave on which the triplum ends wherever possible. The only motets that do not show this layout are *Apta caro plumis ingenii/Flos virginum decus et species/Alma redemptoris mater* (F-CA 1328 fol. 10v-11r), which presents the voices in succession rather than in columns, and *Flos ortus inter lilia quorum radix/Celsa cedrus ysopus effecta/O quam magnus pontifex* (see below).

[39] See *Pour chou que j'aim ma dame* [622]/*Li jolis tans que je voi* [623]/*Kyrie eleyson* (fols. 344r-345v) in the seventh fascicle and *Theotera virgo geratica* [878]/*Las pour qoi l'eslonge* [879]/*Qui prendroit* (fols. 348r-349v), only fol. 348v in the appendix to the seventh fascicle. Neither motet has concordances in other manuscripts.

[40] See *Detractor est nequissima vulpis/Qui secuntur castra sunt/Verbum iniquum et dolosum abhominabitur dominus* (fol. 4r) and *Celi domina quam sanctorum/Maria virgo virginum/Porchier mieuz estre ameroie* (fol. 42v), but not in the

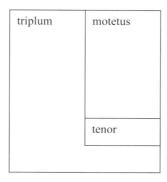

Figure 8. Triplum continued below the tenor

In contrast to Hu and Fauv, which are incommensurable and whose repertoire was never copied into other extant manuscripts, the rotuli may have had an impact on the development of layouts in fourteenth-century music sources.[41] Unlike an opening in a codex, the reading area of a rotulus does not have a fixed size corresponding to a page, but can be adjusted according to the length of each motet.[42] The layout of these rotuli, which witnesses the birth of the correspondence between the unity of the motet and the unity of the writing (and reading) area, can be found throughout in at least three fragmentary codices (F-Pn 2444,[43] F-AS 983,[44] and CH-Fcu 260[45]), as well as once in F-CA 1328 (fol. 14v, *Flos ortus inter lilia quorum radix/Celsa cedrus ysopus effecta/O quam magnus pontifex*).

  concordances with the rotuli B-Br 19606 and F-Pn 67, which have this layout throughout. See in Fauv *Tribum quem non abhorruit/Quoniam secta latronum spelunca/Merito hec patimur* (fols. 41v-42r), *Firmissime fidem teneamus* [530]/*Adesto sancta trinitas* [531]/*Alleluya* (fols. 43r-v), and *Garrit Gallus flendo dolorose/In nova fert animus/Neuma* (fol. 44v).

[41] Besides the French manuscripts discussed below, see also the layout of the earliest Italian motets in GB-Ob 112 (with the layout shown in Figure 7 instead of two columns on two pages of an opening) and in I-Vmg s.s. (with the triplum in the left column and motetus, tenor, and contratenor in succession in the right column).

[42] Not all of the Ars nova rotuli have the same layout. In PL-WRu Ak 1955/KN 195, triplum and motetus are written in columns, the tenor on a continuous stave below the columns (see e.g., *Colla iugo subdere/Bona condit cetera bonum libertatis/Libera me* current fols. 1v and 2v). This layout coincides with that of the thirteenth-century motet manuscripts (e.g., Ba), but differs insofar as each motet ends with its own continuous stave for the tenor dividing the motets visually. When the rotulus is scrolled, columns and continuous staves alternate. This layout can be found in some further, predominantly English, sources; see for example *Psallat chorus in novo* [723]/*Eximie pater et regie* [724]/*Aptatur* (West, fol. 2v, and 114ll, fol. 45v). In Da and Vorau, columns and a continuous stave alternate on the same page as well see *Benedicite dominus gustate* [741]/*Benedicite dominus edent* [740]/*Aptatur* (Da, fol. 8ar) and *Amor vincens omnia* [732]/*Marie preconio devotion* [733]/*Aptatur* (Vorau, fol. 2r). Other fragments with motets considered to have been part of English rotuli present the parts in succession; see GB-BER 55, GB-Cgc 820/810, GB-Ob 652, GB-Ob 400, and US-PRu 119.

[43] *In virtute nominum/Decens Carmen cedere/Clamor meus* (fol. 48r) and *Flos ortus inter lilia quorum radix/Celsa cedrus ysopus effecta/O quam magnus pontifex* (fol. 49r). In *O canenda vulgo per computa/Rex quem metrorum depingit/Rex regum* (fol. 48v) the triplum is not continued below the tenor, because the space in the left column fits. In *Beatius se servans liberat/Cum humanum sit peccare* (fol. 49v) the triplum is continued on the missing recto.

[44] *Tant a souttille pointure la tres gentille/Bien pert qu'en moy n'a dart point mal/Cuius pulcritudinem sol et luna mirantur* (fol. 62v). In the second motet, *Colla iugo subdere/Bona condit cetera bonum libertatis/Libera me* (fol. 62r), the triplum ends in its own column.

[45] *Li enseignement de Chaton/De touz les bien qu'amorss/Ecce tu pulchra et amica mea* (fol. 86r). In *O canenda vulgo per computa/Rex quem metrorum depingit/Rex regum* (fol. 86v), the lowest stave contains the contratenor.

Manuscripts with Machaut's Motets

It is noteworthy that there is no manuscript written after 1320 within the corpus considered here in which the unity of motet and opening (or page) is not respected. However, there is by no means only one 'Ars nova layout'. The corpus of Machaut motets alone shows five different layouts, none of which is found in manuscripts before the third quarter of the fourteenth century. Manuscripts in which the three voices follow each other in succession (Vg fols. 260v-283r, B fols. 258v-281r, and E fols. 131r-146r)[46] may be regarded as both retaining and reinventing the layout of thirteenth-century chansonniers.

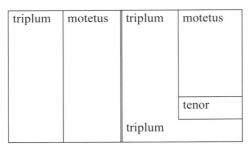

Figure 9. Layout of Machaut A and G

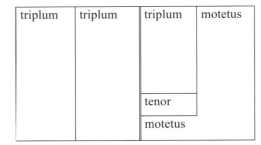

Figure 10. Layout of Machaut C and W

It seems possible that the layout found in Machaut manuscripts A (fols. 414v-437v) and G (fols. 102v-125r; Figure 9) has its ancestor in the layout found in the rotuli. In contrast, the layouts of F-CA 1328[47] and of Machaut manuscripts C (fols. 206v-225r) and W[48] (Figure 10) can be regarded as individual and isolated solutions to the need for additional space for the triplum.

I-IV 115 is the only manuscript that contains Machaut motets in choirbook layout. The motets show different layouts here that might have been taken from their respective exemplars. Most of the motets show a choirbook layout on one opening with the triplum on the verso and the motetus on the recto.[49] The position of the tenor varies

---

[46] The few motets handed down entirely in F-Pn 23190 have the same layout (fols. 2v and 3v). As in the earliest manuscripts, the tenor sometimes ends in the second half of the stave in which the next motet begins; see *Colla iugo subdere/Bona condit cetera bonum libertatis/Libera me* (fol. 2v). However, the layout of Machaut's motets *Amours qui ha le pouvoir de moy faire recevoir/Faus Samblant m'a deceü/Vidi Dominum* (fol. 3r) and *Qui es promesses de Fortune se fie/Ha Fortune trop sui mis loing de port/Et non est qui adiuvet* (fol. 3r) is ambiguous. The verso page with the triplum *Amours a qui* and the motetus *Ha Fortune trop sui mis loing de port* is lost. In manuscript Machaut E, *Ha Fortune trop sui mis loing de port* requires more space than *Faus Samblant m'a deceü*, so it is possible that *Amours qui ha le pouvoir de moy faire recevoir/Faus Samblant m'a deceü/Vidi Dominum* had a choirbook layout at the top of the page, and the inversion of the parts in *Qui es promesses de Fortune se fie/Ha Fortune trop sui mis loing de port/Et non est qui adiuvet* was the result of the available space.

[47] See *Qui es promesses de Fortune se fie/Ha Fortune trop sui mis loing de port/Et non est qui adiuvet* (fol. 16v); the standard layout in F-CA 1328 is described above.

[48] The only extant page from the motet section in Machaut W is the beginning of *Quant en moy vint premierement/Amour et biauté parfaite/Amara valde* (fol. 74v); see the same motet on fols. 206v-207r in Machaut C.

[49] Exceptions are *Ida capillorum matris/Portio nature precelentis/Ante tronum* (fols. 6v-7r) with the motetus on the verso page (as opposed to to the same motet in NL-Lu 342A, fol. 2v and F-CH 564, fols. 61v-62r), and two motets written as space fillers in the lower half of an opening: *Dantur official burse consilio/Quid scire proderit consilio/Tenor* (fols. 5v-6r) and *Quiconques vault d'amours joïr/Tenor* (fols. 6v-7r).

in the Machaut motets as well as in the manuscript in general (see Table 3). The most common layout, which presents the triplum and the motetus on opposite sides and the tenor beginning on a stave of its own below the motetus, is found in *Martirum gemma latria tiranny/Dilligenter inquiramus Quintini preconia/Christo honorato*. In *Amours qui ha le pouvoir de moy faire recevoir/Faus Samblant m'a deceü/Vidi Dominum*, the tenor begins on the same stave on which the motetus ends, although there would have been sufficient space available to write the tenor on the following blank ruled staves. In *Qui es promesses de Fortune se fie/Ha Fortune trop sui mis loing de port/Et non est qui adiuvet*, the tenor is written on the verso page beginning on the same stave on which the triplum ends.[50] The order of the voices is the same as in Machaut C, F-Pn fr. 23910, and F-CA 1328.

For a more detailed study regarding the rise of the choirbook layout,[51] one would, for example, have to look ahead to the motets ascribed to Philippe de Vitry in several fourteenth- or fifteenth-century sources.[52] Apart from I-IV 115 (see Table 3), there are only two recently discovered fragments (D-AAst 14 and D-WÜf I.10) in which the choirbook layout is found.[53] However in all three sources, the choirbook layout is not the only one used for motets.[54] Whatever layout the respective exemplars of I-IV 115 had used, the presentation of the parts in succession in *O canenda vulgo per computa/Rex quem metrorum depingit/Rex regum* is related to the succession of parts in columns in CH-Fcu 260 (fol. 86v) and F-Pn 2444 (fol. 48v), and the position of the tenor after the triplum in I-IV 115 in *Cum statua Nabucodonasor metalina/Hugo princeps invidie/Tenor* is related to the layout in F-CA 1328 (fol. 11v). However, so far nothing certain can be said about the predecessors for the four Vitry-motets in I-IV 115 in choirbook layout.

---

[50] There is already one example of this layout in the appendix to the fifth fascicle of Mo: *O virgo pia candens* [714]/*Lis ne glay ne rosier* [715]/*Amat* (fols. 227v-228r). The same motet reappears in another layout in the same source on fols. 293r-v.

[51] On choirbook layout in later manuscripts see Thomas Schmidt and Hanna Vorholt, 'Mise-en-page in Choirbooks, c. 1450-1550', in *Gazette du livre médiéval* 55 (2009), 31-42.

[52] See Karl Kügle, 'Philippe de Vitry', in *Die Musik in Geschichte und Gegenwart*, ed. Ludwig Finscher (Kassel etc., ²2007), Personenteil 17, cols. 58-67 at 60-61.

[53] *Vos quid admiramini virgines/Gratissima virginis species quam decorat/Gaude gloriosa* (D-AAst 14, fol. 1r) and *Impudenter circuivi solum/Virtutibus laudabilis moribus/Alma redemporis mater* (D-WÜf I.10a, fol. 2r), to which one may add some further fragmentary manuscripts of which only one of the two pages of an opening expected to show a choirbook layout is extant (NL-Lu 342A, fol. 1v and I-Fsl 2211, fol. 79v but not F-APT 16bis 13v-14r, where the tenor begins on the same stave on which the motetus ends), as well as for *O canenda/Rex quem metrorum/Reg regum* (GB-DRc 20, fol. 337v).

[54] In D-AAst 14 *Phi millies/O creator/Iacet granum* and *Petre clemens/Lugentium siccentur/Non est inventus similis illi* present the parts in succession (fol. 1v and 2r).

Table 3. Choirbook layouts in I-IV 115

Tenor layout	Fols.	Motet
Below motetus, begin on the same stave on which the motetus ends	1v-2r	*O Philippe Franci qui generis/O bone dux indolis optime/Tenor*
	2v-3r	*Altissonis aptatis viribus modulando/Hin principes qui presunt seculi/ Tenor* (with an additional contratenor)
	13v-14r	*Zolomina zelus virtutibus vitiorum/Nazarea que decora bonitate/Ave Maria*
	19v-20r	*A vous vierge de douçour que j'aour/Ad te virgo clamitans venio dei mater/ Regnum mundi*
	20v-21r	*Amours qui ha le pouvoir de moy faire recevoir/Faus Samblant m'adeceü/ Vidi Dominum*
	26v-27r	*Li enseignement de Chaton/De touz les bien qu'amorss/Ecce tupulchra et amica mea*
Below motetus, begin on a stave of its own	3v-4r	*Febus mundo oriens girans/Lanista viperous ibi fundens/Cornibus equivocis pascens*
	4v-5r	*Impudenter circuivi solum/Virtutibus laudabilis moribus/Alma redemporis mater*
	5v-6r	*Apta caro plumis ingenii/Flos virginum decus et species/Alma redemptoris mater*
	7v-8r	*Post missarum sollempnia divina/Post misse modulamina post verbi/Tenor*
	8v-9r	*Vos quid admiramini virgines/Gratissima virginis species quam decorat/ Gaude gloriosa*
	9v-10r	*Flos ortus inter lilia quorum radix/Celsa cedrus ysopus effecta/O quam magnus pontifex*
	10v-11r	*Martirum gemma latria tiranny/Dilligenter inquiramus Quintini preconia/ Christo honorato*
	11v-12r	*Almifonus melos cum vocibus matrem/Rosa sine culpe spina per quam patet/Tenor*
	23v-24r	*Douce playsence est d'amer loyalment car autrement/Garison selon nature/ Neuma*
	37v-38r	*Petre Clemens tam re quam nomine/Lugentium siccentur occuli plaudant/ Non est inventus*
	56v-57r	*Amer amours est l'achoison pour quoy/Durement au cuer me blece/Dolour meus*
	59v-60r	*L'amoureuse flour d'esté qui en sa novelleté/En l'estat d'amere tristour/Tenor*
Below triplum, begin on the same stave on which the triplum ends	16v-17r	*Rachel plorat filios suos Christi nuntios/Ha fratres ha vos domini cum fides/ Tenor*
	17v-18r	*Colla iugo subdere/Bona condit cetera bonum libertatis/Libera me* (same layout as in F-APT 16bis, fols. 20v-21r)
	24v-25r	*Qui es promesses de Fortune se fie/Ha Fortune trop sui mis loing de port/ Et non est qui adiuvet*
Below triplum, begin on a stave of its own	12v-13r	*Apolinis eclipsatur unquam lux/Zodiacum signis lustrantibus/In omnes terram*
	14v-15r	*Cum statua Nabucodonasor metalina/Hugo princes invidie/Tenor*
	15v-16r	*Tuba sacre fidei proprie/In arboris empiro prospere/Virgo sum*
	18v-19r	*Tant a soutille pointure la tres gentile/Bien pert qu'en moy n'a dart point mal/Cuius pulcritudinem*
	25v-26r	*Sa paour d'umbleastinance par douceatrenpance/Diex tan desir ester amés de m'amour/Concupisco*
	57v-58r	*Trop ay dure destinée mal fu/Par sauvage retenue suy tenue/Tenor*
	61v-62r	*Je comence ma chançon/Et je seray li segons/Soulés viex*

A few motets in I-IV 115 present the voices in succession.[55] Some other motets are written in columns; these include *Leis l'ormelle en la* [892]/*Main soi levat sires Garins* [893]/*Je ne chaindrai mais* (fol. 22r).[56] This motet shows a wide range of layouts in different sources, including columns of equal width in its earliest source, Tu (fol. 34r), and choirbook layout in a fragment from I-UDc 290 (with motetus and tenor on fol. 1r; the opposite verso page is missing). In F-CA 1328 (fol. 11r) the end of the triplum is written on a continuous stave below the triplum and motetus columns, followed by the tenor—the standard layout in this manuscript (see above). In I-IV 115, the position of the tenor is remarkable: the beginning of the ninth stave is indented in order to make room for the tenor initial; the text mark 'Enor' is entered, but not the initial itself, nor the music which was meant to be placed in the column below the motetus as in some pieces in the seventh fascicle of Mo. Instead, the tenor is written on a continuous stave below the triplum and motetus columns in a layout similar to Tu and the thirteenth-century motet manuscripts (e.g., Ba). The two different layouts in I-IV 115 are a late reflection of the change from thirteenth- to fourteenth-century motet layouts. In contrast to thirteenth-century manuscripts, the final layout with the tenor-based upper parts as well as the planned but not executed placement of the tenor below the motetus highlighting a two-part contrapuntal texture are confined to one single page for one motet.

The different layouts of the motet do not succeed each other in chronological order: there is neither a 'Notre-Dame layout' nor an 'Ars antiqua layout'. The consecutive presentation of the voices is found from the very beginning of the transmission of motets until the late fourteenth century, in the earliest motets as well as in some Machaut manuscripts. The presentation of the upper parts in two columns of equal width with the tenor on a continuous stave at the bottom, a format that emerges with the *liber motetorum*, is still found in the second half of the fourteenth century. The only coincidence between repertoire layers and distinct layouts is found in the more particular layouts of fascicles 7 and 8 of Mo. The choirbook layout combines the concept of a unity of motet and opening (to be found in Hu, Fauv, and the rotuli for the first time) with a disposition of the parts first to be found in the seventh fascicle of Mo, Stock, Vorau, and Fauv, but there constricted to the page as an entity.

---

[55] See fol. 55r, *O canenda vulgo per computa/Rex quem metrorum depingit/Rex regum*, and—upside down—fol. 53r, *Fortune mere a doulour et norrice/Ma doulour ne cesse pas ains est/Dolour meus*.

[56] Cf. the same layout in *Se grasse n'est a mon* [630]/*Cum venerint miseri* [631]/*Ite missa est* (fol. 21v, tenor below the motetus as in F-T 476, fol. 33v, where the end of the triplum is written on continuous staves below the columns), *Mon chant en plaint ma chancon en clamour/Qui dolereus onques n'a cogneü/Tristis est anima mea* (fols. 22v-23r, tenor below the motetus), *In virtute nominum/Decens carmen edere/Clamor meus* (fol. 55v, tenor and contratenor one after another on a continuous stave below the columns) and *Clap clap par un matin s'en aloit/Sus Robin alons au molin clap clap/ Tenor* (fol. 60v, tenor below the motetus).

Appendix. Sigla, manuscripts, images, facsimiles, and further reading

11411	Paris, Bibliothèque Nationale, Ms. lat. 11411
ArsA	Paris, Bibliothèque de l'Arsenal, Ms. 135
	<http://gallica.bnf.fr/ark:/12148/btv1b550057271.r=135.langDE>[a]
ArsB	Paris, Bibliothèque de l'Arsenal, Mss. 3517-18
	<http://gallica.bnf.fr/ark:/12148/btv1b55006913x.r=3517.langDE>
Ba	Bamberg, Staatsbibliothek, Msc. Lit. 115
	http://digital.bib-bvb.de/view/bvbmets/viewer.0.5.jsp?folder_id=0&dvs=1419232093251~258&pid=5399204&locale=de&usePid1=true&usePid2=true
	Patricia P. Norwood, 'Evidence Concerning the Provenance of the Bamberg Codex', in *Journal of Musicology* 8 (1990), 491-504
	Karl-Georg Pfändtner, 'Zum Entstehungsraum der Bamberger Motettenhandschrift Msc. Lit. 115 – kodikologische und kunsthistorische Argumente', in *Acta musicologica* 84 (2012), 161-66
B-Br 19606	Brussel, Koninklijke Bibliotheek van België, Ms. 19606
	Facsimile: *Rotulus, Brussel, Koninklijke Bibliotheek, Ms 19606* (Peer, 1990)
	Karl Kügle, 'Two Abbots and a Rotulus: New Light on Brussels 19606', in *Quomodo cantabimus canticum? Studies in Honor of Edward H. Roesner*, ed. David Butler Cannata et al. (Middleton WI, 2008), 145-85
Boul	Boulogne-sur-mer, Bibliothèque municipale, Ms. 148
	Facsimile of fol. 91r : Pierre Aubry, Les plus anciens monuments de la musique française (Paris, 1905), Plate 7
B-Tc 476	Tournai, Chapitre de la Cathédrale, Ms. 476
	Jean Dumoulin et al. (eds.), *La Messe de Tournai* (Tournai, 1988), with facsimile
Ca	Cambrai, Mediathèque municipale, Ms. A 410
	<http://www.diamm.ac.uk/jsp/Descriptions?op=SOURCE&sourceKey=270#imageList>
Ch	Châlons-en-Champagne, Archives Départementales, Ms. 3.J.250
CH-Fcu 260	Fribourg, Bibliothèque Cantonale et Universitaire, Ms. Z260
	Gabriel Zwick, 'Deux motets inédits de Philippe de Vitry et de Guillaume de Machaut', in *Revue de musicologie* 27 (1948), 28-52, with a facsimile of fol. 86v
Cl	Paris, Bibliothèque nationale, Ms. nouv. acq. fr. 13521
	<http://gallica.bnf.fr/ark:/12148/btv1b530121530.r=13521.langDE>
	Sean Curran, 'Composing a Codex: The Motets in the "La Clayette" Manuscript', in *Medieval Music in Practice: Studies in Honor of Richard Crocker*, ed. Judith Ann Peraino (Middleton WI, 2013), 219-53
CTr	Cambridge, Trinity College, Ms. O.2.1
	<http://www.diamm.ac.uk/jsp/Descriptions?op=SOURCE&sourceKey=319#imageList>
Da	Darmstadt, Universitäts- und Landesbibliothek, Ms. 3471
	<http://www.diamm.ac.uk/jsp/Descriptions?op=SOURCE&sourceKey=30#imageList>
	Friedrich Gennrich, *Die Wimpfener Fragmente der Hessischen Landesbibliothek Darmstadt: Faksimile Ausgabe der HS 3471*, Summa musicae medii aevi 5 (Darmstadt, 1958)
D-AAst 14	Aachen, Öffentliche Bibliothek, Beis E 14
	Joachim Lüdtke, *Kleinüberlieferung mehrstimmiger Musik vor 1550 in deutschem Sprachgebiet IV: Fragmente und versprengte Überlieferung des 14. bis 16. Jahrhunderts aus dem mittleren und nördlichen Deutschland*, Nachrichten der Akademie der Wissenschaften in Göttingen, Philologisch-Historische Klasse 6 (Göttingen, 2001), 6-14 and facsimile, 51-54

---

[a] All digital images online were accessed 26 July 2013.

D-WÜf I.10a	Würzburg, Bibliothek des Franziskanerklosters, Ms. I.10a
	Joachim Lüdtke, *Kleinüberlieferung mehrstimmiger Musik vor 1550 in deutschem Sprachgebiet IV: Fragmente und versprengte Überlieferung des 14. bis 16. Jahrhunderts aus dem mittleren und nördlichen Deutschland*, Nachrichten der Akademie der Wissenschaften in Göttingen, Philologisch-Historische Klasse 6 (Göttingen, 2001), 15-22 and facsimile, 55-58
Erf	Erfurt, Universitätsbibliothek, CA 2°169
E-Tc 98.28	Toledo, Archivio y Biblioteca Capitulares de la Catedral Metropolitana, Ms. 98.28
F	Firenze, Biblioteca Medicea Laurenziana, Ms. Pluteo 29.1
	Facsimile: Luther Dittmer (ed.), *Florence, Biblioteca Mediceo-Laurenziana, Pluteo 29.1*, Publications of Mediaeval Musical Manuscripts 10-11 (Brooklyn, 1966)
	Barbara Haggh and Michel Huglo, 'Magnus liber, maius munus: The Origin and Fortune of the *F*-Manuscript', in *Revue de musicologie* 90 (2004), 193-230
	Catherine A. Bradley, 'Ordering in the Motet Fascicles of the Florence Manuscript', in *Plainsong and Medieval Music* 22 (2013), 37-64
Fauv	Paris, Bibliothèque nationale, Ms. fr. 146
	<http://gallica.bnf.fr/ark:/12148/btv1b8454675g.r=146.langDE>
	Emma Dillon, *Medieval Music-Making and the Roman the Fauvel* (Cambridge, 2002)
F-APT 16bis	Apt, Cathédrale Ste Anne, Trésor, Ms. 16bis
F-AS 983	Arras, Bibliothèque municipale, Ms. 983
F-CA 165 and 1328	Cambrai, Médiathèque municipale, Inc. B 165 and B 1328
	<http://www.diamm.ac.uk/jsp/Descriptions?op=SOURCE&sourceKey=266#imageList>
	<http://www.diamm.ac.uk/jsp/Descriptions?op=SOURCE&sourceKey=271#imageList>
	Irmgard Lerch, *Fragmente aus Cambrai: ein Beitrag zur Rekonstruktion einer Handschrift mit spätmittelalterlicher Polyphonie*, Göttinger musikwissenschaftliche Arbeiten 11 (Kassel etc., 1987)
F-CH 564	Chantilly, Musée Condé, Ms. 564
	Facsimile: Yolanda Plumley and Anne Stone (ed.), *Chantilly Codex, Bibliothèque du Chateau de Chantilly, Ms. 564* (Turnhout, 2008)
Flor 122	Firenze Biblioteca Nazionale Centrale, Ms. II.I.122
F-Pn 2444	Paris, Bibliothèque nationale, Ms. nouv. acq. lat. 2444
F-Pn 23190	Paris, Bibliothèque nationale, Ms. nouv. acq. fr. 23190
	<http://gallica.bnf.fr/ark:/12148/btv1b8451108d.r=23190.langDE>
	Lawrence Earp, *Guillaume de Machaut: A Guide to Research* (New York etc., 1990), 122-23
F-Pn 67	Paris, Bibliothèque nationale, Ms. Coll. de Piccardie 67
GB-BER 55	Berkeley, Castle Archive, Select Roll 55
GB-Cgc 820/810	Cambridge, Gonville and Caius College, Ms. 820/810
GB-DRc 20	Durham, Cathedral Library, Ms. C.I.20
	<http://www.diamm.ac.uk/jsp/Descriptions?op=SOURCE&sourceKey=363#imageList>
GB-Ob 112	Oxford, Bodleian Library, Ms. Canon. Class. Lat. 112
	<http://www.diamm.ac.uk/jsp/Descriptions?op=SOURCE&sourceKey=501#imageList>
GB-Ob 400	Oxford, Bodleian Library, Ms. Rawl. C 400
GB-Ob 652	Oxford, Bodleian Library, Ms. Bodl. 652

H	'Herentals Fragment' (Leuven, Universiteitsbibliotheek, lost)
	Photographs preserved in Göttingen, Niedersächsische Universitäts- und Landesbibliothek, Ludwig Nachlass, IX,14.
	Facsimile: Eugeen Schreurs (ed.), *Anthologie van muziekfragmenten uit de lage landen (Middeleeuwen-Renaissance)* (Peer, 1995), 3-6
Ha	Paris, Bibliothèque nationale, Ms. fr. 25566
	<http://gallica.bnf.fr/ark:/12148/btv1b6001348v.r=+25566+.langDE>
Hu	Burgos, Monasterio de las Huelgas, Ms. IX
	Facsimile: *Codice musical de Las Huelgas Reales de Burgos* (Madrid, 1997).
	Nicolas Bell, *El códice musical de Las Huelgas: Un estudio complementario del facsimile*, Colección Scriptorium 7 (Madrid, 2004)
I-Fsl 2211	Firenze, Biblioteca Medicea Laurenziana, Archivio Capitolare di San Lorenzo, Ms. 2211
I-IV 115	Ivrea, Biblioteca Capitolare, Ms. 115
	Facsimiles of fol. 9r and fol. 21r: Alfonso Professione, *Inventario dei manoscritti della Biblioteca Capitolare di Ivrea* (Alba, 1967), Plates 4 and 5
	Karl Kügle, *The Manuscript Ivrea, Biblioteca Capitolare 115: Studies in the Transmission and Composition of Ars nova Polyphony* (Ottawa, 1997)
	Andrew Tomasello, 'Scribal Design in the Compilation of Ivrea Ms 115', in *Musica Disciplina* 42 (1988), 73-100
I-Udc 290	Udine, Biblioteca Comunale Vincenzo Joppi, Ms. 290
	<http://www.diamm.ac.uk/jsp/Descriptions?op=SOURCE&sourceKey=188#imageList>
	Pierluigi Petrobelli, 'Due mottetti francesi in una sconosciuta fonte udinese', in Collectanea historiae musicae 4 (1966), 201-14
I-Vmg s.s.	Venezia, Monastero di St. Giorgio Maggiore, s. s.
	F. Alberto Gallo, 'Da un codice italiano di mottetti del primo Trecento', in *Quadrivium* 9 (1968), 25-36, with facsimile.
Lille	Lille, Bibliothèque municipale, Ms. 316
	Adam de La Bassée, *Ludus super Anticlaudianum*, ed. Paul Bayart (Tourcoing and Lille, 1930), with facsimile.
LoA	London, British Library, Ms. Egerton 2615
	Mark Everist (ed.), *French Thirteenth-Century Polyphony in the British Library* (London, 1988), with facsimile
LoB	London, British Library, Ms. Egerton 274
	Pamela Whitcomb, 'The Manuscript London, British Library, Egerton 274: A Study of its Origins, Purpose, and Musical Repertory in Thirteenth-Century France' (Ph.D. diss., University of Texas at Austin, 2000), with facsimiles of fols. 43r and 45r
LoC	London, British Library, Ms. Add. 30091
	<http://www.diamm.ac.uk/jsp/Descriptions?op=SOURCE&sourceKey=388#imageList>
	Mark Everist (ed.), *French Thirteenth-Century Polyphony in the British Library* (London, 1988), 1-40
LoD	London, British Library, Ms. Add. 27630
	Wolfgang Dömling (ed.), *Die Handschrift London, British Museum, Add. 27630 (LoD)*, Das Erbe deutscher Musik 52 (Kassel etc., 1972), with facsimile
LoHa	London, British Library, Ms. Harley 978
	<http://www.diamm.ac.uk/jsp/Descriptions?op=SOURCE&sourceKey=434#imageList>
Lyell	Oxford, Bodleian Library, Ms. Lyell 72
Ma	Madrid, Biblioteca Nacional, Ms. 20486
	Facsimile: Luther Dittmer (ed.), *Facsimile Reproduction of the Manuscript Madrid 20486*, Publications of Mediaeval Musical Manuscripts 1 (Brooklyn NY, 1957)

Machaut A	Paris, Bibliothèque Nationale, Ms. fr.,1584 <http://gallica.bnf.fr/ark:/12148/btv1b84490444.r=1584.langDE> Lawrence Earp, *Guillaume de Machaut: A Guide to Research* (New York etc., 1990), 87-89
Machaut B	Paris, Bibliothèque nationale, Ms. fr. 1585 <http://gallica.bnf.fr/ark:/12148/btv1b8449032x.r=1585.langDE> Lawrence Earp, *Guillaume de Machaut: A Guide to Research* (New York etc., 1990), 85-87
Machaut C	Paris, Bibliothèque Nationale, Ms. fr. 1586 <http://gallica.bnf.fr/ark:/12148/btv1b8449043q.r=1586.langDE> Lawrence Earp, *Guillaume de Machaut: A Guide to Research* (New York etc., 1990), 77-79
Machaut E	Paris, Bibliothèque nationale, Ms. fr.,9221 <http://gallica.bnf.fr/ark:/12148/btv1b6000795k.r=9221.langDE> Lawrence Earp, *Guillaume de Machaut: A Guide to Research* (New York etc., 1990), 92-94
Machaut G	Paris, Bibliothèque Nationale, Ms. fr.,22546 <http://gallica.bnf.fr/ark:/12148/btv1b6000793r.r=22546.langDE> Lawrence Earp, *Guillaume de Machaut: A Guide to Research* (New York etc., 1990), 90-92
Machaut Vg	Cambridge, Corpus Christi College, Ferrell-Vogüé Ms. <http://www.diamm.ac.uk/jsp/Descriptions?op=SOURCE&sourceKey=3774#imageList> Lawrence Earp, *Guillaume de Machaut: A Guide to Research* (New York etc., 1990), 84-85
Machaut W	Aberystwyth, National Library of Wales, Ms. 5010C Facsimile: Andrew Wathey, *The British Isles, 1100-1400*, Répertoire international des sources musicales, B 4, 1-2, Suppl. 1 (Munich etc., 1993), 101 Lawrence Earp, *Guillaume de Machaut: A Guide to Research* (New York etc., 1990), 79-84
Maz	Paris, Bibliothèque Mazarine, Ms. 307
Mo	Montpellier, Faculté de Médecine, Ms. H 196 <http://manuscrits.biu-montpellier.fr/vignettem.php?GENRE[]=MP&ETG=OR&ETT=OR&ETM=OR&BASE=manuf> Mary Elizabeth Wolinski, 'The Compilation of the Montpellier Codex', in *Early Music History* 11 (1992), 263-301 Catherina Parsoneault, 'The Montpellier Codex: Royal Influence and Musical Taste in Thirteenth-Century Paris' (Ph.D. diss., University of Texas at Austin, 2001)
MüA	München, Bayerische Staatsbibliothek, Cod. gall. 42 and Berlin, Staatsbibliothek zu Berlin, Preußischer Kulturbesitz, Musikabteilung, 55 Ms. 14 <http://daten.digitale-sammlungen.de/~db/0006/bsb00065719/images/index.html> Martin Staehelin, *Kleinüberlieferung mehrstimmiger Musik vor 1550 in deutschem Sprachgebiet I: Die Notre-Dame-Fragmente aus dem Besitz von Johannes Wolf*, Nachrichten der Akademie der Wissenschaften in Göttingen, Philologisch-Historische Klasse 6 (Göttingen, 1999)
MüB	München, Bayerische Staatsbibliothek, Clm. 16444 <http://daten.digitale-sammlungen.de/~db/0006/bsb00069136/images/>
MüC	München, Bayerische Staatsbibliothek, Clm. 5539 <http://daten.digitale-sammlungen.de/~db/0004/bsb00042722/images/index.html> Marie Louise Göllner, *The Manuscript Cod. lat. 5539 of the Bavarian State Library*, Musicological Studies and Documents 43 (Neuhausen, 1993), with facsimile of fol. 72r

N	Paris, Bibliothèque nationale, Ms. fr. 12615 <http://gallica.bnf.fr/ark:/12148/btv1b60007945.r=12615.langDE>
NL-Lu 342A	Leiden, Bibliotheek der Rijksuniversiteit, Fragment L.T.K. 342A Facsimile: Eugeen Schreurs (ed.), *Anthologie van muziekfragmenten uit de lage landen (Middeleeuwen-Renaissance)* (Peer, 1995), 12-15
PL-WRu Ak 1955/ KN 195	Warszawa, Biblioteka Uniwersytecka, Ak 1955/KN 195 Charles E Brewer, 'A Fourteenth-Century Polyphonic Manuscript Rediscovered', in *Studia musicologica Academiae Scientiarum Hungaricae* 24 (1982), 5-20, with facsimile
Ps	Paris, Bibliothèque nationale, Ms. lat. 11266<http://gallica.bnf.fr/ark:/12148/btv1b8432482r.r=11266.langDE>
R	Paris, Bibliothèque nationale, Ms. fr. 844 <http://gallica.bnf.fr/ark:/12148/btv1b84192440.r=844.langDE>
Reg	Roma, Biblioteca Apostolica Vaticana, Ms. Reg. lat. 1543
Sab	Roma, Archivio dei Dominicani di Santa Sabina, Ms. XIV L3 Heinrich Husmann, 'Ein Faszikel Notre-Dame-Kompositionen auf Texte des Pariser Kanzlers Philipp in einer Dominikanerhandschrift (Rom, Santa Sabina XIV L 3)', in *Archiv für Musikwissenschaft* 24 (1967), 1-23, with facsimile of fol. 140r
Stock	Stockholm, Riksarkivet, Fr 813 and Fr 5786 Gunilla Björkvall, Jan Brunius, and Anna Wolodarski, 'Flerstämmig musik från medeltiden', in *Nordisk tidkrift för bok- och biblioteksväsen* 83 (1996), 129-55 with facsimile of Fr 813 Jan Brunius, *From Manuscripts to Wrappers: Medieval Book Fragments in the Swedish National Archives* (Stockholm, 2013), with facsimile of Fr 5768 (Plate 16)
Sts	Stary Sącz, Biblioteka Klasztoru SS. Klarysek, Ms. Muz. 90 Miroslaw Perz, 'The Oldest Source of Polyphonic Music in Poland. Fragments from Stary Sącz', in *Polish Musicological Studies* 1 (1977), 9-57 Katarzyna Grochowska, 'Tenor Circles and Motet Cycles: A Study of the Stary Sącz Manuscript [Pl-SS Muz 9] and its Implications for Modes of Repertory Organization in 13th-Century Polyphonic Collections' (Ph.D. diss., University of Chicago, 2013), with facsimile
StV	Paris, Bibliothèque nationale, Ms. lat. 15139 <http://gallica.bnf.fr/ark:/12148/btv1b8432457p.r=15139.langDE> Fred Büttner (ed.), *Die Klauseln der Handschrift Saint-Victor (Paris, BN, lat. 1539)* (Tutzing, 1999), 9-25
Tor	Tortosa, Biblioteca de la Catedral, Ms. 97
Trier	Trier, Stadtbibliothek, Ms. 322
Tu	Torino, Biblioteca Reale, Ms. Vari 42 Antoine Auda, *Les 'Motets Wallons' du manuscrit de Turin: Vari 42* (Brussels, 1953), with facsimile
US-PRu 119	Princeton, University Library, Ms. Garrett 119
V	Rome, Biblioteca Apostolica Vaticana, Ms. Reg. lat. 1490
Vorau	Vorau, Bibliothek des Augustiner Chorherrenstifts, Fragm. 118D Rudolf Flotzinger, 'Die Vorauer Motettenfragmente', in *Annäherungen. Festschrift für Jürg Stenzl zum 65. Geburtstag*, ed. Ulrich Mosch et al. (Saarbrücken, 2007), 88-99, with facsimile of fol. 2r Rudolf Flotzinger (ed.), *Musik in der Steiermark. Katalog der Landesausstellung 1980* (Graz, 1980), 110 with facsimile of fol. 1r
W2	Wolfenbüttel, Herzog August Bibliothek, Cod. Guelf. 1099 Helmst. <http://diglib.hab.de/wdb.php?dir=mss/1099-helmst&distype=thumbs-img&imgtyp=0&size=> Mary Wolinski, 'Drinking Motets in Medieval Artois and Flanders', in *Yearbook of the Alamire Foundation* 6, ed. Bruno Bouckaert and Eugeen Schreurs (Leuven-Neerpelt, 2008), 9-20

West	London, Westminster Abbey, Ms. 33327 Facsimile: Luther Dittmer (ed.), *Worcester Add. 68, Westminster Abbey 33327, Madrid, Bibl. Nac. 192*, Publications of Mediaeval Musical Manuscripts 5 (Brooklyn, 1959)
Worc	Worcester, Dean and Chapter Library, Ms. Add. 68, Frag. XVIII <http://www.diamm.ac.uk/jsp/Descriptions?op=SOURCE&sourceKey=615#imageList>

Abstract

As the only genre to be found in sources from c. 1250 to c. 1430, the motet is the perfect subject for a study of layouts of music in medieval manuscripts. The variety of sources in which medieval polyphonic music can be found ranges from manuscripts with occasional musical notation over sources with music to music sources. The formats and layouts of these manuscripts differ significantly. The different layouts of the motets do not occur in chronological order, there is neither a Notre-Dame layout nor an Ars antiqua or an Ars nova layout. The presentation of the voices one after another is found from the very beginning of the transmission of motets until the late fourteenth century, with the earliest motets as well as in some Machaut manuscripts. The presentation of the upper parts in two columns of equal width with the tenor on a continuous stave at the bottom, which emerges with the *liber motetorum*, is still found in the second half of the fourteenth century. The only coincidence between repertoire layers and distinct layouts is found for the more particular layouts of fascicles seven and eight of Mo.

Anachrony and Identity in the Loire Valley Chansonniers

Jane Alden

An inventory of the property belonging to Amadeus, Prince of Piedmont (1412-31), son of Amadeus VIII, duke of Savoy, lists the objects this young nobleman kept by his bedside. Along with a *Roman de la rose*, various other *romans*, some devotional and liturgical books (in expensive bindings), card games, and a mappa mundi, the list includes 'ung *livre de chanczons* notées en papier'.[1]

Even though bedchambers in the fifteenth century were less private than modern-day bedrooms, finding a chansonnier among the prince's possessions suggests that, at least for this young man, a songbook might have been an object for private contemplation. Night-time was recommended for the reading of devotional texts: for example, an anonymous text (included among the treatises of Jean Gerson) in a manuscript from the early fifteenth century suggests to the reader that 'the most profitable hour for you and us would be midnight, after sleeping, after the digestion of food, when the labours of the world have been separated and left behind and when also the neighbors will not see us, nor will anyone see us but God…' ('l'eure la plus prouffitable a vous et a nous seroit de mynuyt apres dormir, apres la digestion de la viande, quant les labours du monde sont separez et delaissez, et quant aussi les voisins ne nous verront point et que nulz ne nous regardera fors Dieu').[2] We might imagine the young prince reading from his chansonnier, perhaps recalling musical performances, during the quiet, nocturnal hours.

Most of the items in the inventory contain some description of the binding materials (e.g., 'couvert de cuir rouge'). Since the 'livre de chanczons' lacks any such description, it is possible that this book remained unbound, perhaps with the intention that more songs would be added. The inventory does specify that it was copied on paper. Although parchment was more usual, a number of songbooks survive on paper from the early- and mid-fifteenth century (see Table 1). The prince's chansonnier, for example, might have resembled the near-contemporary PC II, an octavo manuscript copied in the Veneto.[3]

---

[1] The full inventory appears in Sheila Edmunds, 'The Medieval Library of Savoy (II): Documents', in *Scriptorium* 25 (1971), 253-84 at 267-68.
[2] Paris, Bibliothèque de l'Arsenal, Ms. 2176, fol. 109v, translated by Robert L. A. Clark, in 'Constructing the Female Subject in Late Medieval Devotion', in *Medieval Conduct*, ed. Kathleen M. Ashley and Robert L. A. Clark (Minneapolis, 2001), 175.
[3] Hans Schoop, *Entstehung und Verwendung der Handschrift Oxford Bodleian Library, Canonici misc. 213*, Publikationen der Schweizerischen musikforschenden Gesellschaft 2nd ser. 24 (Bern, 1971), 72-77, argues that the manuscript of which PC II was once part may have been an exemplar for Ox213; see Appendix for source information for all manuscripts cited here with sigla abbreviations.

Table 1. Comparison of songbooks, 1400-60

Siglum	Date	Material
C5943	c. 1400	paper
PragueU	c. 1415	paper
Pz	1420s	parchment
PC II	c. 1428	paper
Rei	c. 1430	paper
Ox213	c. 1427-36	paper
NYB	c. 1430	parchment
M902	1430s	parchment
RU1411	before 1450	parchment
Cop17	after 1450	paper
Tr93	c. 1450-56	paper
Tr90	by 1456	paper
Porto	1450s	parchment
EscB	1450s; additions in 1460s	paper
M9659	c. 1460	paper
Tr88	1456-60/62	paper
Schedel	1456-63	paper
Bux	c. 1460; later additions	paper
Pav	early 1460s	paper
Tr89	1460-65; additions c. 1468	paper

Demand for both polyphonic and monophonic chansonniers dramatically increased in the later fifteenth century. Although the ravishingly beautiful heart-shaped songbook (Cord) was apparently prepared in Savoy, for Jean de Montchenu, papal protonotary and bishop of Viviers, scribal activity seems to have been focused in the Loire Valley region, at least until the 1480s.[4] With the French royal court based in this area, there was a ready market of aspiring bibliophiles. Of particular interest to these bourgeois professionals were books that were personal, intimate, petite, and exquisitely crafted. The presence in Tours of the renowned artist Jean Fouquet (c. 1425-c. 1480), and his atelier, ensured that many of these were finely illustrated.[5]

The five so-called 'Loire Valley Chansonniers', dating from the 1470s (with later additions), are the earliest examples of elaborately decorated polyphonic songbooks in white (void) notation.[6] Like the books produced in Fouquet's workshop, they are characterized by their small dimensions and tiny copying spaces (see Table 2). Nonetheless, they represent substantial collections, the largest (Dij) containing as many as 161 songs.[7]

---

[4] For a deluxe facsimile of Cord, see *Chansonnier de Jean de Montchenu* (Valencia, 2007) and David Fallows, *Chansonnier de Jean de Montchenu (ca. 1475): Commentary to the Facsimile of the Manuscript Rothschild 2973 (I.5.13) in the Bibliothèque Nationale de France* (Valencia, 2008).

[5] See Stephen C. Clancy, 'A New "Fouquet Workshop" Book of Hours at the Beinecke Library', in *Manuscripta* 35 (1991), 206-28.

[6] The Loire Valley Chansonniers are all available online; study is further aided by the copious information presented by Peter Woetmann Christoffersen on <http://chansonniers.pwch.dk/>.

[7] These manuscripts are discussed in detail in Jane Alden, *Songs, Scribes, and Society: The History and Reception of the Loire Valley Chansonniers* (New York, 2010).

Table 2. The Loire Valley chansonniers: a brief summary

Siglum	Measurements	No. of folios	No. of scribes	No. of pieces
Cop	170 x 116 mm; writing space 107 x 70 mm	49	1 main scribe, 1 later	34
Dij	173 x 125 mm; writing space 107 x 70 mm	204	1 main scribe, 2 later	161
Niv	190 x 133 mm; writing space 132 x 85 mm	77	1 main scribe, 3 later	66
Lab	126 x 92 mm; writing space 92-96 x 57-60 mm	151	2 main scribes, 3 later	106
Wolf	148 x 104 mm; writing space 106-109 x 62-65 mm	70	1 main scribe, 3 later	56

That the Loire Valley Chansonniers were intended for individual rather than communal use is evident from their small size and lavish presentation. Initials are decorated with grotesques, dragons, swans, *putti*, fish, snails, cameo heads, and full-length figures. There are knights in armour, courtiers, jesters, peasant-like figures, and exotic-looking bearded men; ladies wear a variety of courtly head-dresses, including the Burgundian steeple-cap (*hennin*) and rustic hats. The initials are sometimes supported by intricate foliage and acanthus-leaf decoration. Marginalia rarely relate specifically to the texts they accompany, but rather hint at the reception context for these manuscripts. Alongside the 'H' for *Helas que pourra* in the Dijon Chansonnier (see Plate 1), a noble couple is shown dancing; the man's pointed shoe (*poulaine*) mirrors the bow of the 'h', while a butterfly rests on top of the letter. On the facing recto leaf, the tenor initial presents a man in a red gown with a black *chaperon* (band of material) over his shoulder.

A similarly attired man is found in the Laborde Chansonnier (see Plate 2). This was the dress code of royal secretaries. Its enduring 'legibility' is attested to by the appearance in 1587 of a painting by Jan Coessaet of the Opening Session of the Parliament of Mechelen under Charles the Bold (on 3 January 1474; see Plate 3). Documenting an event that took place over a century earlier, the court positions are indicated by dress. On the left, standing in the middle of the floor, are four secretaries, also identified by name (J. or L. Coule, P. De Pullen, P. Poulaert, and G. Batault).[8]

Why would secretaries be included in the iconographic vocabulary of chansonniers from the 1470s? As David Fallows revealed, the dedicatee of the Wolfenbüttel Chansonnier was 'Etiene Petit', royal notary and secretary.[9] Mysterious inscriptions featuring the word 'fumee' on the flyleaves of the Laborde Chansonnier similarly link this manuscript to a bourgeois, rather than an aristocratic, family: the Fumée family was in royal service from the mid-fifteenth to the late sixteenth century.[10] They were part of a group of

---

[8] I am grateful to Dr. Wim Hüsken of the Museums Department of the city of Mechelen for supplying this image and for his assistance reading the names.
[9] David Fallows,"'Trained and Immersed in All Musical Delights": Towards a New Picture of Busnoys', in *Antoine Busnoys: Method, Meaning, and Context in Late Medieval Music*, ed. Paula Higgins (Oxford, 1999), 42-43.
[10] For further biographical details on the Fumée family, see Jacques-Xavier Carré de Busserolle, *Dictionnaire géographique, historique et biographique d'Indre-et-Loire et de l'ancienne province de Touraine* (Tours, 1880), 145-46, 180-82; the link between the Fumée family and the Laborde Chansonnier is made in Alden, *Songs, Scribes, and Society*, 206-10.

families who profited from the royal presence in this city in order to move from local business into the service of the monarchy.[11]

The Petit and Fumée families were new nobility—'of the robe', as distinct from the inherited nobility 'of the sword'. Typical of the newly gentrified, they were tremendous bibliophiles and collectors of manuscripts. The Fumée most likely to correspond to the Laborde inscription would have been Adam Fumée, a doctor in royal service from 1457 to 1494. According to the bibliographer Louis Jacob de Saint-Charles (1608-70), who wrote a treatise on all the most celebrated libraries in the world, Adam Fumée had one of the most splendid libraries of his day.[12]

Books of love songs may have had particular appeal for notaries and secretaries, in evoking the leisurely pursuits of courtly society. But these readers were also interested in, and indeed participated in, new literary trends. A surviving inventory of Etienne Petit's library shows a strong humanist influence, with many texts by Latin authors, alongside books of grammar, rhetoric, logic, physics, natural philosophy, metaphysics, history, medicine, theology, and law.[13] Petit owned a large illustrated version of the *Chroniques de France*, a version of Jehan Mansel's revision of the *Fleur des histoires*, and various classics of French literature, including a *Roman de la rose* decorated in azure and gold, the royal colours.

In the Fumée and Petit family libraries it would not have been unusual to find historical texts alongside contemporary works, and indeed manuscripts whose illustrations 'modernize' past events. Temporal juxtapositions, and the contraction of historical time, characterize reading materials from this era, as a way of of idealizing the present. In an influential study relating to Renaissance art-historicity, Alexander Nagel and Christopher Wood propose the term 'anachronic' in order to describe a work of art 'when it is late, when it repeats, when it hesitates, when it remembers, but also when it projects a future or an ideal'.[14] By their reasoning, works of art do not have a fixed temporal reality, but a plural relationship to time. To call a work of art 'anachronistic' is to grasp it not as art, but as a witness to its times.[15] On the other hand, to label a work of art as 'anachronic' is to describe what the artwork *does*, as art. Of course, works were made, or designed, by an individual or by a group at a precise moment in time, but they also reach back to earlier precedents and forward to the object's future recipients, each in their own temporality.[16] Nagel and Wood are hardly the first authors to address the issue of time in art; they borrow the term 'anachronies' from the French philosopher Jacques Rancière and acknowledge their debts to Erwin Panofsky, Aby Warburg, Walter Benjamin, and Georges Didi-Huberman.[17] But it is their usage of anachronic, and plural temporalities, that most readily offers a new way of understanding the complexities of the Loire Valley Chansonniers.

---

[11] For detailed discussion of the history of these 'grandes familles' of Tours, and their rise to power, see Bernard Chevalier, *Tours, ville royale (1356-1520): Origine et développement d'une capitale à la fin du moyen âge* (Leuven, 1975), 471-507.

[12] Louis Jacob de Saint-Charles, *Traicté des plus belles bibliothèques publiques et particulières qui ont esté, et qui sont à présent dans le monde* (Paris, 1644), 588.

[13] Charles Beaulieux, 'Un fragment de l'histoire de la bibliothèque du collège d'Autun à Paris', in *Revue des bibliothèques* 22 (1912), 62-103 and 334-51.

[14] Alexander Nagel and Christopher S. Wood, *Anachronic Renaissance* (New York, 2010), 13. The word 'anachronic' derives from the the Greek *anachronizein*, 'to be late or belated', 'to linger'.

[15] Anachronism has been much studied by French scholars; see, in particular, Nicole Loraux's influential 'Éloge de l'anachronisme en histoire', in *Le genre humain* 27 (1993), 23-39, and Georges Didi-Huberman, *Devant le temps: histoire de l'art et anachronisme des images* (Paris, 2000), 9-55.

[16] Nagel and Wood, *Anachronic Renaissance*, 9.

[17] Jacques Rancière, 'Le concept d'anachronisme et la vérité de l'historien', in *L'Inactuel: Psychanalyse et culture* 6 (1996), 53-68, cited by Nagel and Wood, *Anachronic Renaissance*, 370 n. 18. On the burgeoning topic of time and art, see Marvin

A central plea of Nagel and Wood's *Anachronic Renaissance* is for a 'substitutional' rather than an 'authorial' model of artistic production. According to this view, the old and the new borrow from each other. As rising nobility, the patrons of books like the Loire Valley Chansonniers sought works that functioned precisely as 'types' or tokens, substituting for the objects patronized by the ancient nobility. As Plates 1 and 2 show, a secretary could now appear in his manuscript just across the page from icons connoting the aristocracy.

The first scribes of the Copenhagen, Laborde, and Wolfenbüttel Chansonniers made no composer attributions. In line with Nagel and Wood's substitution model, ownership superseded individual authorship. Likewise, the figures, creatures, and objects that decorate all five of these chansonniers draw from an anachronic repertoire of established types. They present, or re-present, characters seen elsewhere, in other kinds of books. As the art historian Anne D. Hedeman explains, the 'rhetoric of costume drew on a visual vocabulary that artists, authors, and audiences shared and understood'.[18]

The lovers who are the subjects of the chansonniers' poetic texts are similarly universalized, their songs paying homage to the cultural heritage of *fin'amors*. The malleability of time, and the practices of equivalence and exchangeability may have had particular appeal for new bibliophiles. Personal identification with the historical, mythical, or allegorical characters represented in *romans* was a long-entrenched practice among the aristocracy. For newer readers, chansonniers made possible a two-fold process of identification—with past bibliophiles and with the timeless poetic subjects of the texts contained. Adroit substitution enabled new nobility to participate in a literary and musical version of the world to which they sought entry.

Whatever the original intentions might have been for the Loire Valley Chansonniers, whoever their original patrons or intended owners were, the first commissions all seem to have fallen through. But their stories did not stop there: each chansonnier was reconceived, and additional pieces added. The chaotic manner in which these collections were reappropriated is further revealing of their polytemporality. This relates to Nagel and Wood's notion that 'the work of art is a message whose sender and destination are constantly shifting'.[19]

Dramatic differences in the histories of the five Loire Valley Chansonniers become all the more intriguing in light of the fact that three of them were, in part, copied by the same scribe. I have dubbed this person the Dijon Scribe, on account of his longest project, the Dijon Chansonnier.[20] His appearance in both Cop, for which he was the primary scribe, and his extensive contributions to Lab suggest that only a small number of scribes had the requisite expertise, and resources, to prepare chansonniers in the 1470s. A total of 216 songs (across Cop, Dij, and Lab) were copied by the Dijon Scribe.

Trachtenberg, *Building in Time: From Giotto to Alberti and Modern Oblivion* (New Haven, 2010), and Keith Moxey, *Visual Time: The Image in History* (Durham, 2013).

[18] Anne D. Hedeman, 'Presenting the Past: Visual Translation in Thirteenth- to Fifteenth-Century France', in *Imagining the Past: History in Manuscript Painting, 1250-1500*, ed. Elizabeth Morrison and Anne D. Hedeman (Los Angeles, 2010), 69-85 at 78.

[19] Nagel and Wood, *Anachronic Renaissance*, 9.

[20] See Alden, *Songs, Scribes, and Society*, 66; the Dijon Scribe's contributions are discussed at various points throughout the book. Since chansonnier scribes most likely gained their musical expertise in cathedral *maîtrises*, I use the masculine pronoun.

This is an impressive legacy, almost four times more than any other song scribe of the fifteenth century (see Table 3).[21]

Table 3. Scribal hands in the Loire Valley chansonniers

Scribe	No. of songs copied	Notes
Dijon Scribe	216	Includes his work in Cop, Dij, and Lab
Dijon Scribe 2	3	Scribal concordance with FR2794
Dijon Scribe 3	1	
Dijon index corrections		This person erased 36 of the original ordinals
Laborde Scribe 1	60	
[Laborde Scribe 2]	[26]	= the Dijon Scribe (see above)
Laborde Scribe 3	5	Scribal concordance with FR2794
Laborde Scribe 4	9	
Laborde Scribe 5	9	
Laborde Index-Scribe 1		= the Dijon Scribe
Laborde Index-Scribe 2		Added 12 attributions and entries to the index
Laborde Index-Scribe 3		Added 1 entry to the index
Nivelle Scribe 1	58	
Nivelle Scribe 2	6	
Nivelle Scribe 3	1	
Nivelle Scribe 4	1	
Wolfenbüttel Scribe 1	52	
Wolfenbüttel Scribe 2	2	One of these has text by Wolfenbüttel Scribe 3
Wolfenbüttel Scribe 3	1	
Wolfenbüttel Scribe 4	1	

Nagel and Wood find anachronicity in 'the ability of the work of art to hold incompatible models in suspension without deciding...the artwork is more than the sum of its own original myths'.[22] This provides a useful lens through which to understand the complicated history of Lab. The manuscript must have been deemed complete after Scribe 1 had finished his work since it was then sent for decoration. The only stage remaining after that should have been binding. The manuscript comprised twelve gatherings, making it already larger than the final versions of Cop, Wolf, and Niv. The Dijon Scribe's involvement, at this stage, was slight: he had added just three pieces to the end of Gathering 8. But for reasons unknown, Lab almost doubled in size, with the addition of eight newly ruled gatherings.[23] The Dijon Scribe added twenty-three songs to these gatherings and then passed the manuscript to two new artists for decoration. Some time later, Scribes 3, 4, and 5 copied a further twenty-three songs (approximately a fifth of the total contents). They clearly anticipated decoration, leaving guide letters and omitting the first initials of texts, but their songs all remain undecorated.

What the Laborde Chansonnier comprises today is a conjunction of histories, bearing the traces of various different stages of completion. The initial twelve-gathering manuscript may have contained a sign of ownership on its first leaf since this was

---

[21] For discussion of the Dijon Scribe's editorial initiatives, see Alden, *Songs, Scribes, and Society*, 159-66.
[22] Nagel and Wood, *Anachronic Renaissance*, 18.
[23] The structure of Lab is discussed in detail in Alden, *Songs, Scribes, and Society*, 77-93.

subsequently removed. A change of ownership seems likely when the manuscript expanded to twenty gatherings and acquired attributions, a table of contents, foliation, and further decoration. Coats of arms, presumably belonging to the new owner, were added in several places. Some time later, a modified coat of arms and the initials 'M' and 'I' or 'J' were added to the first surviving leaf. But many gatherings still remained blank. Scribes 3 and 4, who also made corrections to certain earlier songs, worked in a third phase of preparation; further additions were made to the index (Index-Scribes 2 and 3 in Table 3), and the manuscript eventually passed to Scribe 5, after which collation labels were added and it was finally bound, in a modest, soft leather binding.

Each layer is distinct, pointing up changes in patronage, variable scribal roles, different aesthetic priorities, and the availability of certain kinds of repertory. There is a generational shift between composers copied by Scribe 1 (predominently from the Du Fay/Binchois generation) and those added by Scribes 3, 4, and 5 (Hayne, Compère, Agricola, and Prioris, etc.). But the other modifications—the inclusion of attributions, decoration, tables of contents, etc.—are no less significant.

A manuscript's ability to adapt to a series of shifting realities depended on the flexibility of its scribe(s). The Dijon Scribe demonstrates remarkable adaptability in his various encounters with these manuscripts. Although he supplied both Dij and Lab with indexes, the presentation, intention, and function of each index is quite different. In spite of their ubiquity in later book history, indexes were still the exception, rather than the norm, in the fifteenth century, particularly in secular manuscripts.[24] An index, strictly speaking, is an alphabetical arrangement, whereas a table of contents need only present the works in manuscript order. The term 'index' is often used in this broader sense, but the distinction is relevant in that a manuscript's contents can only be collated alphabetically after it has been copied. A table of contents, on the other hand, can be compiled as works are added, reflecting simply the order of copying. There is a third category—a quasi-alphabetical index—where songs are grouped under the appropriate letter, but in order of occurrence in the manuscript. Both Dij and Lab fall in this category.[25]

In terms of presentation, the Laborde index, in two columns, like calendar pages in Books of Hours (see Figure 1), has titles on the left and foliation on the right; first initials are decorated with gold; subsequent initials alternate red and blue, complemented by red and brown text lines. The Dijon index, on the other hand, was copied in an unruled gathering, with only one column per page and a single ink colour; the reference numbers (ordinals, not folios) follow immediately after the incipits. The first initial for each group of letters is a little larger in size than the running text, but none is decorated or illuminated (see Figure 2).

Leaving almost no space between letters suggests that the scribe added the Dijon index after this manuscript's completion, by which time he knew its entire contents. His intervention with the Laborde Chansonnier was rather different: the manuscript already

---

[24] The subject is discussed by Margaret Bent, 'Indexes in Late Medieval Polyphonic Music Manuscripts: A Brief Tour', in *The Medieval Book: Glosses from Friends and Colleagues of Christopher de Hamel,* ed. James H. Marrow, Richard A. Linenthal, and William Noel (Houten, 2010), 196-207; on the late-medieval development of the table of contents, see Mary A. Rouse and Richard H. Rouse, 'Concordances et index', in *Mise en page et mise en texte du livre manuscrit,* ed. Henri-Jean Martin and Jean Vezin (Paris, 1990), 219-28.

[25] Other surviving chansonnier indexes, such as FR2356, MC871, RCas, P12744, and FC2349, mostly conform to this third category.

Figure 1. Laborde Chansonnier, fol. 4v, Index N-O

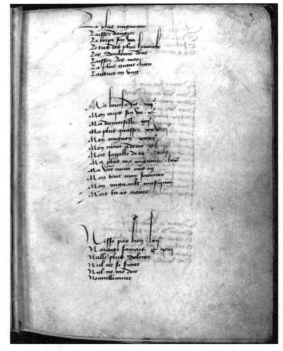

Figure 2. Dijon Chansonnier, fol. 3r, Index L-N

contained the sixty songs copied by Scribe 1 when the Dijon Scribe first encountered it. He was therefore able to enter all of these songs into the index, as well as the pieces he added to the manuscript. Knowing that the manuscript was still not complete, he provided an additional fifty-two lines with initials, to be filled in with song titles at a later date (Figure 1 shows spaces left for four further 'N' and five further 'O' songs). The Dijon Scribe's deep knowledge of the chanson repertoire is suggested by the relationship between the number of spaces he afforded each letter and the number of surviving songs beginning with those letters, which are directly proportional.[26] The Dijon Scribe had the expertise, as well as pragmatic sense, to cater to the new book market, which included providing his readers with 'finding devices' such as indexes.

Work on the Dijon Chansonnier, like Laborde, took place in fits and starts. That the various stages of its completion are still visible provides a rare insight into manuscript preparation. Dij's Gatherings 1, 2, 3, 4, 5, 7, and 10 have calligraphic brown initials embellished with inked line drawings (see Figure 3), which, in Gatherings 1, 2, 7, and 10, are fully coloured (see Figure 4).[27] In Gatherings 6, 8, 9, and the first two leaves of Gathering 11, on the other hand, the calligraphic letters remain unadorned (see Figure 5). Hereafter there seems to have been a drastic change in the terms of patronage, which resulted in the rest of the manuscript being left without decoration. The Dijon Scribe apparently hoped the situation would improve, since he continued to fill the leaves, and continued to omit the first initial of each text, in case decorated initials might one day be added.

It is extraordinary to have evidence of this scribe at work in three different situations, as witnessed by his surviving sources (Cop, Dij, and Lab). Subtle differences in the character of his hand suggest that they represent different kinds of commissions. While in Dij the scribe's writing is highly flourished, his script in Cop is notable for its neat precision. Lab lies somewhere between Dij and Cop, notwithstanding the additional challenge of fitting songs into the smallest of copying spaces. Unlike the fragmented evolutions of Dij and Lab, Cop seems to have been prepared without any major interruptions. This seems also to be his latest offering.

Whereas books of liturgical chant depended on set sequences, there was no fixed order for collections of *forme fixes* songs. Earlier miscellanies, such as the trouvère manuscripts K and L, or the Squarcialupi Codex (Sq), grouped works by author/composer. The Dijon Scribe could have done similarly, since he had in his possession many songs by the leading composers of the 1470s, Ockeghem and Busnoys.[28] But instead of concentrating their works within a single section, he copied songs by these two composers on the first and second openings of gatherings, and on the middle leaves, surrounding them with less well-known repertory.[29] This suggests a new aesthetic,

---

[26] Of the 273 songs transmitted in the Loire Valley Chansonniers, the most popular first letters of incipits are 'I'/'J', 'L', 'P', and 'S'; the least well represented letters are 'B', 'F', 'G', and 'H'. The Laborde index provides eighteen, seventeen, eleven, and twelve initialled lines for song titles beginning with, respectively, 'I'/'J', 'L', 'P', and 'S', and only two lines each for 'B', 'F', 'G', and 'H'.

[27] The initials on the central bifolio of Dij's Gathering 10 were not inked with the two-prong stylus, but instead formed by the decorative figures themselves. This style, closely resembling the initials in Cop and Wolf, does not appear anywhere else in Dij.

[28] For the view that the Dijon Scribe worked in the orbit of St. Martin, Tours, see Alden, *Songs, Scribes, and Society*, ch. 3.

[29] Songs by Busnoys, almost all attributed, are found, in the Dijon Chansonnier, on the second openings of Gatherings 1, 3, 4, 5, 6, 7, 8, 13, and 23; see Andrea Lindmayr-Brandl, *Quellenstudien zu den Motetten von Johannes Ockeghem*

Figure 3. Dijon Chansonnier, fol. 22v, *Bel acueil*

Figure 4. Dijon Chansonnier, fol. 12v, *Les desleaulx*

Figure 5. Dijon Chansonnier, fol. 44v, *Mort j'appelle*

focusing on the readers' experience of the whole collection. Vernacular miscellanies gained popularity in the thirteenth century; the trend continued through to the sixteenth century in intellectual circles around universities and among professional classes, including notaries and secretaries.[30]

Even more than other anthologies, the Loire Valley Chansonniers present arresting juxtapositions—esteemed composers alongside minor authors, decorated leaves next to incomplete calligraphy, works by different generations, and a considerable variety of hands. Some of these juxtapositions were planned, while others resulted from the apparently dramatic changes in patronage. We see the Dijon Scribe adapting and reconceptualizing Dij and Lab as anachronic objects.

The process of collecting involved multiple actions—acquiring, amassing, selecting, omitting, creating, and presenting—which in turn depended on a web of connections between the maker, editor, compiler, patron, and reader, all of which take place in time. Nagel and Wood draw attention to art's capacity to both escape from and belong to time. The collaboration between composers, artists, patrons, and audiences that created the Loire Valley Chansonniers also generated a community of readers who would have seen the past as an integral part of the present. These manuscripts use

---

(Laaber, 1990), 43-45. Indeed, the only gathering in the early part of the manuscript not to have a song by Busnoys in the second opening, gathering 2, may be due to scribal error: perhaps the Dijon Scribe mistook the song he copied here, the anonymous *Mon corps s'en va*, for Busnoys's similarly titled *Le corps s'en va*.

[30] On medieval miscellanies more generally, see the influential Jacqueline Cerquiglini, 'Quand la voix s'est tue: la mise en recueil de la poésie lyrique aux XIVe et XVe siècles', in *La présentation du livre: Actes du colloque de Paris X-Nanterre*, ed. Emmanuèle Baumgartner and Nicole Boulestreau, Littérales 2 (Nanterre, 1987), 313-27.

rhetorical devices to keep the past alive and relevant to the fifteenth-century present, particularly in the context of performance.

Part of the 'drama' of performing *formes fixes* songs involves the unfolding and repetition of structural units. This 'performance' could take place on the page, at some remove from a live event, in the spatial separation of distinct sections. Although most songs were made to fit onto a single opening, in the Loire Valley Chansonniers, virelais were better suited than rondeaux to being copied over two, since the reader only has to turn the page twice (once before and once after the short strophes of the *b* section (*A*-[turn]-*b*-*b*-[return]-*a*-*A*). There was the added advantage that virelais across two openings drew attention to the musical distinction between the *prima* and *secunda pars*. Cognisance of the ability to represent form visually is suggested by the Dijon Scribe spacing the notes differently (generally more widely) for a *secunda pars*. This suggests that material presentation was not seen as separate from 'the music'; rather, the identity of a piece could be connected to the means of its representation.

While the vast majority of the virelais in Dij (22/27) are copied across two openings, five have just a single opening. Included among these is Busnoys' *Au gré de mes yeulx*, for which Dij is the unique source (see Figure 6). There is no contratenor part for the *secunda pars*, but it was not lack of space that forced a reduction from a three-voice texture to a discantus-tenor duet. The Dijon Scribe's contratenor clef is further indented than contratenor clefs on any of the surrounding leaves, further even than the tenor clef; moreover, the notes of this contratenor part are less condensed than those in many other songs. From the Dijon Scribe's skilled planning of space elsewhere, we can be certain that he did not omit the contratenor's couplet through lack of foresight: this textural reduction was pre-planned. *Au gré de mes yeulx* already stands apart from Busnoys's other pieces. With only five syllables per line, it is so short that there is hardly time to miss a third voice in the *secunda pars*. Since the tenor drops down into the contratenor range, the texture sounds complete in just two voices. As always in this repertoire, the tenor-discantus duet is harmonically complete.

Subtle performance considerations may have been among the factors that contributed to the popularity of chansonniers in the later fifteenth century, but these deluxe songbooks are characterized by the variety of materials they offered to potential readers. The Loire Valley Chansonniers were ideally suited to piecemeal reading, rather than following a single linear narrative. They functioned as portable musical libraries that could be visited regularly, for different amounts of time, in a variety of circumstances. Choosing to hear the musical notation, browse the poetic texts, or simply feast on the elaborate initials and borders, readers could select their own type and level of engagement. The multiple modes of access help us to understand the cultural context of this music, and of its patrons.

Nagel and Wood question how historical time is addressed by a work of art. For them, 'the time of art, with its densities, irruptions, juxtapositions, and recoveries, comes to resemble the topology of memory itself'.[31] Although in terms of portability and visual elegance the Loire Valley Chansonniers may seem to be a world apart from

---

[31] Nagel and Wood, *Anachronic Renaissance*, 45. On the construction of musical memory, see Anna Maria Busse Berger, *Medieval Music and the Art of Memory* (Berkeley, 2005), esp. ch. 6, 'Visualization and the Composition of Polyphonic Music', 198-251.

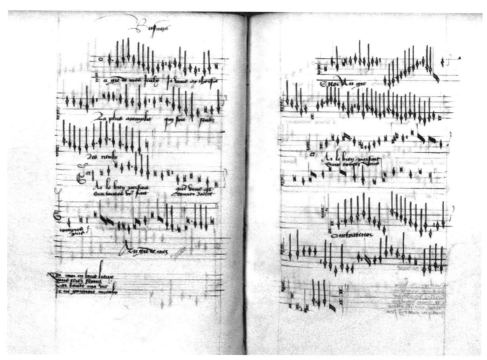

Figure 6. Dijon Chansonnier, fols. 113v-114r, *Au gré de mes yeulx*

the major song collections of the early fifteenth century, such as Rei or Ox213, they are rooted in the same tradition of *amour courtoise* and vernacular music-making. Self-conscious referentiality, catering to the new readership, contributes to the timelessness of these manuscripts. They show us not what the past sounded like but that the past is also in the present.

Appendix. Source abbreviations

Siglum	Location
Bux	Munich, Bayerische Staatsbibliothek, Cim. 352b (formerly Mus. Ms. 3725)
C5943	Cambridge, University Library, Ms. Add. 5943, fols. 161-72
Cop	Copenhagen, Det Kongelige Bibliotek, Ms. Thott 291, 8°
Cop17	Copenhagen, Det Kongelige Bibliotek, Ms. Fragmenter 17, I (inv. 2400-2406)
Cord	Paris, Bibliothèque nationale de France, Rothschild 2973 (I.5.13)
Dij	Dijon, Bibliothèque municipale, Ms. 517
EscB	Real Monasterio de San Lorenzo del Escorial, Biblioteca y Archivo de Música, Ms. IV.a.24
FC2439	Florence, Biblioteca del Conservatorio di Musica Luigi Cherubini, Ms. Basevi 2439
FR2356	Florence, Biblioteca Riccardiana, Ms. 2356
FR2794	Florence, Biblioteca Riccardiana, Ms. 2794
K	Paris, Bibliothèque de l'Arsenal, Ms. 5198
L	Paris, Bibliothèque nationale, Ms. fr. 765
Lab	Washington, Library of Congress, Ms. M2.1.L25 Case

Appendix (continued)

Siglum	Location
M902	Munich, Bayerische Staatsbibliothek, Cod. gall. mono 902 (formerly Mus. Ms. 3192)
M9659	Munich, Bayerische Staatsbibliothek, Mus. Ms. 9659
MC871	Montecassino, Biblioteca dell'Abbazia, Ms. 871
Niv	Paris, Bibliothèque nationale, Département de la Musique, Rés. Vmc. Ms. 57
NYB	New York, private collection of Stanley Boorman (parchment bifolium from an octavo manuscript)
Ox213	Oxford, Bodleian Library, Ms. Canon. misc. 213
P12744	Paris, Bibliotheque Nationale de France, Ms. f. fr. 12744
Pav	Pavia, Biblioteca Universitaria, Ms. Aldini 362 (formerly 131.A.17)
PC II	Paris, Bibliothèque nationale de France, Ms. nouv. acq. fr. 4379, fols. 43-60
Porto	Porto, Biblioteca Publica Municipal, Ms. 714
PragueU	Prague, Národní Knihovna (formerly Státní Knihovna SSR-Universitní Knihovna), Ms. XI E 9, fols. 247-251 and fols. 257v-261r
Pz	Paris, Bibliothèque nationale de France, Ms. nouv. acq. fr. 4917
RCas	Rome, Biblioteca Casanatense, Ms. 2856 (formerly O.V.208)
Rei	Paris, Bibliothèque nationale de France, Ms. nouv. acq. fr. 6771
RU1411	(Rome), Vatican City, Biblioteca Apostolica Vaticana, Urb. lat. 1411
Schedel	Munich, Bayerische Staatsbibliothek, Cod. germ. mono 810 (formerly Mus. Ms. 3232 and Cim. 351a)
Sq	Florence, Biblioteca Medicea Laurenziana, Med. Pal. 87
Tr88	Trento, Castello del Buonconsiglio, Monumenti e Collezioni Provinciali (formerly Museo Provinciale d'Arte), Ms. 88 (now 1375)
Tr89	Trento, Castello del Buonconsiglio, Monumenti e Collezioni Provinciali (formerly Museo Provinciale d'Arte), Ms. 89 (now 1376)
Tr90	Trento, Castello del Buonconsiglio, Monumenti e Collezioni Provinciali (formerly Museo Provinciale d'Arte), Ms. 90 (now 1377)
Tr93	Trento, Museo Diocesano, Ms. 'BL', commonly known as Trent 93
Wolf	Wolfenbüttel, Herzog August Bibliothek, Ms. Guelf. 287 Extrav.

Abstract

Polyphonic chansonniers originating in the Loire Valley are linked to a new market for luxury books that emerges in the later fifteenth century among the class of rising nobility working in the orbit of the French royal court. Theories advanced by Alexander Nagel and Christopher Wood are used to show how chansonniers serve a substitutional role, standing in for, and evoking, the noble world to which their bourgeois owners sought entry. Various elements within these manuscripts, including their illustrations and thematic content, draw from a shared repertoire of established types. The practice of universalizing would have fed the cultural aspirations of the notaries and secretaries who counted among their patrons. Nagel and Wood's articulation of multiple temporalities also serves to help contextualize the disrupted preparation of the Loire Valley Chansonniers. The interventions of a certain copyist (the 'Dijon Scribe'), who took on an unusual variety of editorial responsibilities, enabled these anachronic objects to stay current.

The Listening Gaze:
Alamire's Presentation Manuscripts and the Courtly Reader[*]

VINCENZO BORGHETTI

The so-called presentation manuscripts produced by Petrus Alamire and his predecessors at the Habsburg court in the Low Countries in the early sixteenth century rate among the most precious music books of their time. Made as gifts for sovereigns and members of the ruling classes or commissioned by them, they have long attracted the attention of musicologists, both for the music they contain and for their sumptuous elegance. However, although these manuscripts featured among the sources studied by nineteenth-century music historians,[1] it is only since the 1950s, with the work of Herbert Kellman and Martin Picker,[2] that they have been the object of an increasing volume of ever more specialized research, culminating in two important publications: the catalogue of the exhibition *The Treasury of Petrus Alamire* of 1999 and, four years later, the proceedings of the related conference hosted by the Alamire Foundation, both of which constitute a benchmark for subsequent research in this field.[3]

Despite some research on the production context of the Alamire 'scriptorium', these presentation manuscripts have been investigated primarily as vehicles of music, or in some cases of art, and their musical and visual components have been associated either with performance or with display.[4] There are exceptions: both in the *Proceedings* (2003) and in

---

[*] The term 'Alamire's presentation manuscripts' refers here to all the luxury manuscripts produced at the Habsburg-Burgundian court, and thus not only to those copied out by or under the supervision of Petrus Alamire, but also to those produced in the years prior to his activity in the workshop of 'Scribe B'.
[1] Ambros, for example, highlights their rich decoration ('jene reich ausgestatteten Codices'); see August Wilhelm Ambros, *Geschichte der Musik*, 3 vols. (Leipzig, ²1880-81), vol. 3, 239. Vander Straeten knew some of the manuscripts as well, and published various documents concerning the activity of Alamire as copyist for the Habsburgs; see Edmond Vander Straeten, *La musique aux Pays-Bas avant le XIXe siècle*, 8 vols. (Brussels, 1867-88), vol. 7, 340-44.
[2] Herbert Kellman, 'The Origins of the Chigi Codex: The Date, Provenance, and Original Ownership of Rome, Biblioteca Vaticana, Chigiana, C VIII 234', in *Journal of the American Musicological Society* 11 (1958), 6-19; Herbert Kellman, 'Josquin and the Courts of the Netherlands and France: The Evidence of the Sources', in *Josquin des Prez. Proceedings of the International Josquin Festival Conference (Held at the Julliard School in New York City, 21-25 June 1971)*, ed. Edward Lowinsky and Bonnie J. Blackburn (London-New York, 1976), 181-216; Martin Picker (ed.), *The Chanson Albums of Marguerite of Austria: MSS 228 and 11239 of the Bibliothèque Royale de Belgique, Brussels* (Berkeley, 1965). Among the precedents for these studies in the twentieth century we must certainly mention Georges Van Doorslaer, 'Calligraphes de musique à Malines, au XVIe siècle', in *Bulletin du Cercle Archéologique, Littéraire et Artistique de Malines* 33 (1928), 91-101; Georges Van Doorslaer, 'La chapelle musicale de Philippe le Beau', in *Revue Belge d'Archéologie et d'Histoire de l'Art* 4 (1934), 21-57, 139-65; Charles Van den Borren, 'Inventaire de manuscrits de musique polyphonique qui se trouvent en Belgique', in *Acta Musicologica* 5 (1933), 66-71, 120-27; and idem. 6 (1934), 116-21; Karl Erich Roediger, *Die geistlichen Musikhandschriften der Universitäts-Bibliothek Jena*, 2 vols. (Jena, 1935).
[3] Herbert Kellman (ed.), *The Treasury of Petrus Alamire: Music and Art in Flemish Court Manuscripts 1500-1535* (Ghent-Amsterdam, 1999) (hereafter *Treasury*); Bruno Bouckaert and Eugeen Schreurs (eds.), *The Burgundian-Habsburg Court Complex of Music Manuscripts (1500-1535) and the Workshop of Petrus Alamire*, Yearbook of the Alamire Foundation 5 (Leuven-Neerpelt, 2003) (hereafter *Alamire Proceedings*).
[4] See Stanley Boorman, 'The Purpose of the Gift: For Display or for Performance?', in *Alamire Proceedings*, 107-15; Honey Meconi, 'The Function of the Habsburg-Burgundian Court Manuscripts' in *Alamire Proceedings*, 117-24; Dagmar Thoss, 'Flemish Miniature Painting in the Alamire Manuscripts', in *Treasury*, 53-62; Dagmar Thoss, 'Initialien und Bordüren in den Musikhandschriften des burgundisch-habsburgischen Hofes', in *Alamire Proceedings*, 149-60. For an example

more recent essays, some scholars have tried to go beyond the traditional opposition between 'display' and 'performance'. Pursuing different lines of enquiry, Brigitte Dekeyzer, Bonnie Blackburn, and Honey Meconi have shown the importance of the decorative elements in these sources.[5] In an article on the typology of manuscripts of polyphonic music between 1480 and 1550, Thomas Schmidt-Beste has also contributed to this line of enquiry, emphasizing the problematic status of a 'straightforward one-to-one relationship between the basic functional context of a book of polyphonic music and its external appearance or the repertoire it contains'.[6] More in general, for several decades now, various fields of medieval and early modern studies have pursued research perspectives of particular relevance for those manuscripts that, like Alamire's codices, make use of different codes of communication.[7] Such studies of decorated manuscripts take into account their multiplicity of meanings and uses as 'texts' determined by the interaction of all verbal, musical, and visual elements. In spite of the importance of their results and the substantial methodological enrichment they have produced, these studies have still not borne their rightful fruits in studies devoted to Alamire and his presentation manuscripts.

In this article I wish to return to the presentation manuscripts of Alamire and, in the light of this recent literature and new approaches to the study of medieval and early modern manuscripts, pay particular attention to the dynamics and cultural significance of the use of these presentation manuscripts as books and, specifically, as music books. It is precisely the importance of the decorative devices that prompts reflection not only

---

of a recent return to the binary opposition of 'display' versus 'performance' in relation to the Alamire codices see Zoe Saunders, 'Manuscripts in the Age of Print: Production, Function, and Destination of the Alamire Manuscripts', in *Books in Transition at the Time of Philip the Fair: Manuscripts and Printed Books in the Late Fifteenth and Early Sixteenth Century Low Countries*, ed. Hanno Wijsman (Turnhout, 2010), 181-212.

[5] Brigitte Dekeyzer, 'The Decoration of the Alamire Music Manuscripts: Function and Meaning', in *Alamire Proceedings*, 125-48; Bonnie J. Blackburn, 'Messages in Miniature: Pictorial Programme and Theological Implications in the Alamire Choirbooks', in *Alamire Proceedings*, 161-84; Honey Meconi, 'Margaret of Austria, Visual Representation, and Brussels, Royal Library, Ms 228', in this *Journal* 2 (2010), 11-36.

[6] Thomas Schmidt-Beste, 'Private or Institutional – Small or Big? Towards a Typology of Polyphonic Sources of Renaissance Music', in this *Journal* 1 (2009), 13-26.

[7] The literature on communication through books in the late Middle Ages is vast; what follow are only the titles which I have principally used in the preparation of this article: Stephen G. Nichols, 'Philology in a Manuscript Culture' in *Speculum* 65 (1990), 1-10; Mary J. Carruthers, *The Book of Memory: A Study of Memory in Medieval Culture* (Cambridge, 1990); Michael Camille, *Image on the Edge: The Margins of Medieval Art* (London, 1992); Sylvia Huot, *The 'Romance of the Rose' and its Medieval Readers: Interpretation, Reception, Manuscript Transmission* (Cambridge, 1993), especially ch. 8 ('Sacred and Erotic Love: The Visual Gloss of MS Bibl. Nat. fr. 2556'), 273-322; Joyce Coleman, *Public Reading and the Reading in Public in Late Medieval England and France* (Cambridge, 1996); Andrew Taylor, 'Into his Secret Chamber: Reading and Privacy in Late Medieval England', in *The Practice and Representation of Reading in England*, ed. James Raven, Helen Small, and Naomi Tadmor (Cambridge, 1996), 41-61; Kathryn Kerby-Fulton and Denise L. Despres, *Iconography and the Professional Reader: The Politics of Book Production in the Douce 'Piers Plowman'* (Minneapolis-London, 1998), especially the introduction, 1-14, and ch. 5 ('Visualizing the Text: The Heuristics of the Page'), 119-46; Laurel Amtower, *Engaging Words: The Culture of Reading in the Later Middle Ages* (New York, 2000); Emma Dillon, *Medieval Music-Making and the 'Roman de Fauvel'* (Cambridge, 2002); Andrew Taylor, *Textual Situations: Three Medieval Manuscripts and Their Readers* (Philadelphia, 2002); Sylvia Huot, 'Polytextual Reading: The Meditative Reading of Real and Metaphorical Books', in *Orality and Literacy in the Middle Ages: Essays on a Conjunction and its Consequences in Honour of D.H. Green*, ed. Mark Chinca and Christopher Young (Turnhout, 2005), 203-22; Eamon Duffy, *Marking the Hours: English People and their Prayers, 1240-1570* (New Haven, 2006); Joyce Coleman, 'Aural Illumination: Books and Aurality in the Frontispices to Bishop Chevrot's *Cité de Dieu*', in *Orality and Literacy in the Middle Ages*, 223-52; Jane Alden, 'Reading the Loire Valley Chansonniers', in *Acta Musicologica* 79 (2007), 1-31; Jane Alden, *Songs, Scribes, and Society: The History and Reception of the Loire Valley Chansonniers* (Oxford-New York, 2010); Cynthia J. Brown, *The Queen's Library. Image-Making at the Court of Anne of Brittany, 1477-1514* (Philadelphia-Oxford, 2011), especially the introduction, 1-14; Emma Dillon, *The Sense of Sound: Musical Meaning in France, 1260-1330* (Oxford-New York, 2012), especially ch. 6 ('Sound in Prayer Books'), 186-242; Virginia Reinburg, *French Book of Hours: Making an Archive of Prayer, c. 1400-1600* (Cambridge, 2012).

on more complex and differentiated typologies of reading and use than the ones implied by the binary opposition of performance versus display, but also of the multiple meanings of the two terms when speaking of artefacts like these.

I shall begin with some general considerations concerning music books at the time of Alamire, and then analyze some features of his presentation manuscripts with respect to other music manuscripts of this period, and the possible motivations for these features. Finally, I shall consider the potential relevance of my interpretation for larger issues concerning the uses and meanings of luxury music books in the fifteenth and sixteenth centuries.

Music Books at the Time of Alamire: Forms and Meanings

In a recent essay Emma Dillon observes that commentators 'from Isidore of Seville to Roman Ingarden suggest a drastic distinction between inscription and performance: music exists in sound, and writing (on the page, or in Isidore's case, in the memory) is a representation removed from musical reality'.[8] In spite of their partial nature, music manuscripts can nonetheless tell us quite a lot about this reality, Dillon goes on, 'particularly if we consider not just what they transmit, but also how they do so'.[9] The so-called 'new philology' teaches us that it is possible to consider manuscripts not just as vehicles of texts, but as texts in their own right, whose physical characteristics are the outcome of specific choices on the part of those who made them, oversaw their production or commissioned them.[10] All these characteristics contribute to the meaning of the music they transmit, enabling us to reflect on the forms of cultural representation of this music. 'Forms', as Dillon says, paraphrasing Donald F. Mackenzie, 'effect meaning'.[11] What link is there, then, between polyphony and the books in which it was written down in the fifteenth and sixteenth centuries? In particular, what is the relationship between the books and the music as sound in the presentation manuscripts of Alamire? Or, in other words, how do forms and meaning influence each other in these manuscripts?

By the age of Alamire, the choirbook format was the standard for written polyphony. Whether as an individual fascicle or a larger book makes little difference: the different parts are distributed on the opening next to one another. This layout is justified by the requirements of performance: each singer reads from a clearly defined and separate area on the page. However, there is more to the relationship between the choirbook format and the sounding music. One of the most interesting clues in this regard is found in the *Compendium musices* by the theoretician Lampadius (1537), which provides one of the first descriptions of the *tabula compositoria* with a ten-line system (*scala decemlinealis*) as a compositional aid. According to the author, this had been in use since the time of Josquin (Figure 1a).[12] This is a sort of condensed score in which the four parts of a very short

---

[8] Emma Dillon, 'Music Manuscripts', in *The Cambridge Companion to Medieval Music,* ed. Mark Everist (Cambridge, 2011), 291.
[9] Dillon, 'Music Manuscripts', 291.
[10] Dillon, 'Music Manuscripts', 317-18.
[11] Dillon, 'Music Manuscripts', 292. See Donald F. McKenzie, *Bibliography and the Sociology of Texts,* The Panizzi Lectures 1985 (Cambridge, 1986), 1-7.
[12] Lampadius, *Compendium musices* (Bern, 1537), sig. Fvijr-v (a digital reproduction of this text can be found here: <http://imslp.org/imglnks/usimg/f/f7/IMSLP228255-PMLP373514-lampadius_compendium_musices.pdf>). On

composition are notated concurrently. Lampadius's *tabula* is followed by the phrase *Sequitur Resolutio*, and on the verso the same music is written out again in an embryonic choirbook format: the verticality of the *tabula* is broken down into separate parts written out one below the other on the same page (Figure 1b). In Lampadius' time the term *resolutio* was customarily used for the resolution of canons: a *resolutio* offered a graphic representation of how the music sounded when performed according to the indications of the canon (as, for example, in some of the books of masses printed by Petrucci at the turn of the sixteenth century).[13] As is the case with canons, Lampadius' *resolutio* has a practical purpose: it makes the example from the *tabula* performable because in the choirbook format singers could read and sing it in the way they were used to. Nevertheless, Lampadius' testimony also helps us to understand the conceptual difference between the two ways of committing music onto the written page: in using the term *resolutio* to indicate the transition from the *tabula* to the final version, he identified the choirbook format, like the writing *in extenso* of the canon, as presenting the composition in a form closer to the 'real thing' or, in other words, closer to how it actually sounds. The choirbook format, then, was viewed not simply as a useful tool for performance, but also as a graphic counterpart of the music as sound: the individual parts are set out so as to reproduce on the page the individuality of sound sources located in different, albeit contiguous, places. Lampadius suggests a certain type of relationship between the mise-en-page in choirbook format and the musical event, and this relationship is particularly significant for the analysis of the presentation manuscripts of Alamire, as we shall see.

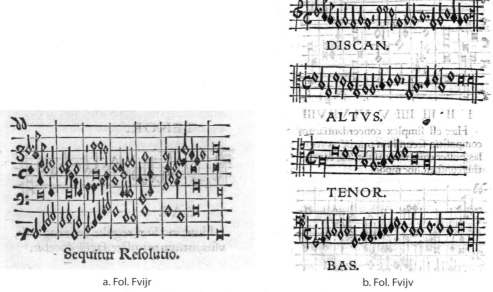

a. Fol. Fvijr   b. Fol. Fvijv

Figure 1. Lampadius, *Compendium musices* (Bern, 1537)

Lampadius and his *tabula* see Jessie Ann Owens, *Composers at Work: The Craft of Musical Composition 1450-1600* (Oxford-New York, 1997), 26-29. See also Vincenzo Borghetti, 'Il suono e la pagina. Riflessioni sulla scrittura musicale nel Rinascimento', in *La scrittura come rappresentazione del pensiero musicale*, ed. Gianmario Borio (Pisa, 2004), 103-6.

[13] See for example the books of masses by Josquin (1502), Obrecht, and La Rue (both 1503).

If we now focus on Alamire's presentation manuscripts themselves, we can say that, although the layout of the parts on the page here is the same as in many contemporary sources, the *forms* (in Mackenzie's sense of the word) of this layout are nonetheless specific to them. Manuscripts that are similar in dimensions and repertory can be very different in appearance. When comparing one of Alamire's presentation manuscripts with a non-presentation manuscript produced around the same time, the differences become quite clear.[14] We can see this if we look at one of the manuscripts copied in Modena for use in the cathedral there (ModD 10, datable to 1520-30) against one of the presentation manuscripts made in Alamire's scriptorium for Friedrich of Saxony (JenaU 3, probably made in 1518-20) (see Plates 4 and 5).[15] Their dimensions are similar (560 x 410 millimetres and 557 x 380 millimetres respectively), and both contain exclusively polyphonic masses. However, the former is on paper, with uniformly ruled, generally quite crowded, pages (ten staves per page), that use ink of the same colour for staves, music, text, rubrics, and cadels. The latter is a parchment manuscript, with a variable number of staves per page in relation to the music copied, with ample margins around the text and, in several cases, also between the individual parts, using ink of different colours and, above all, denoting the beginning of each composition with rich decoration, featuring margins and historiated or calligraphic initials. Here I have deliberately set a manuscript created for use by the singers in a cathedral alongside one of Alamire's most luxurious creations, produced for one of the sovereigns of his day. These sources differ in terms of the *modalities* by which the music is committed to the written page: they vary according to the financial resources involved, the standing of the donors or recipients, and the purposes for which the manuscripts were commissioned, conceived, made, and used.

The generous layout and the decoration of the pages from JenaU 3 are characteristic of the opening of a composition in Alamire's presentation manuscripts, especially those placed at the beginning of the book. While in many cases, the practice of leaving some space between different parts was also adopted for subsequent openings,[16] it is primarily (sometimes exclusively) on those initial openings that Alamire's presentation manuscripts diverge from non-presentation ones: here, we find the richest decorative apparatus and

---

[14] For general studies on the material features of music manuscripts in the fifteenth and sixteenth century in relation to their uses and functions see Schmidt-Beste, 'Private or Institutional – Small or Big?'; Vincenzo Borghetti, 'Il manoscritto di musica tra Quattro e Cinquecento', in *Il libro di musica. Per una storia materiale delle fonti musicali in Europa*, ed. Carlo Fiore (Palermo, 2004), 89-114; Stanley Boorman, 'Sources, MS I. Introduction', in *New Grove Dictionary of Music and Musicians*, ed. Stanley Sadie and John Tyrell (London, ²2001), vol. 23, 792-803 (also in *Grove Music Online*, <http://www.oxfordmusiconline.com/subscriber/article/grove/music/50158pg1>, accessed 25 november 2013); Nicole Schwindt, 'Quellen', in *Die Musik in Geschichte und Gegenwart*, ed. Ludwig Finscher (Kassel etc., ²1997), Sachteil 7, cols. 1946-86; Heinrich Besseler and Hans Albrecht, 'Chorbuch', in *Die Musik in Geschichte und Gegenwart*, ed. Friedrich Blume (Kassel, 1952), Sachteil 2, cols. 1332-54; Martin Just, 'Chorbuch', in *Die Musik in Geschichte und Gegenwart*, ed. Ludwig Finscher (Kassel etc., ²1995), Sachteil 2, cols. 863-82.
[15] For the bibliographic details of all the manuscripts mentioned, see the list of sources in the Appendix. On the manuscripts of Modena cathedral in general see David Crawford, 'Vespers Polyphony at Modena's Cathedral in the First Half of the Sixteenth Century' (Ph.D. Dissertation, University of Illinois at Urbana-Champaign, 1967); see also Herbert Kellmann and Charles Hamm (eds.), *Census-Catalogue of Manuscript Sources of Polyphonic Music 1400-1550*, 5 vols. (Neuhausen-Stuttgart, 1979-1988), vol. 2, 156-61. On JenaU 3 see Eric Jas, 'JenaU 3', in *Treasury*, 87. All the Jena choirbooks are available at <http://www.digitalesthueringen.de> (search for 'Chorbuch').
[16] For some examples of non-ruled space between the parts see JenaU choirbooks 2-4, 7-9, 20. When the page has been completely ruled the layout is often 'generous', with some staves left blank so as to avoid a crowded aspect. To give one example see JenaU 7, in particular fols. 1-29 (respectively *Missae de Sancta Anna* by Pierre de la Rue, and *Ave Maria* by Antoine de Févin).

the most generous layout. However, these *forms* of layout and decoration are more than accessories to the music they transmit. They serve a rhetorical function as well: through them, the music that they surround communicates in specific ways, and therefore has specific meanings. This does not mean that a presentation manuscript cannot be useful for performers; but there is no doubt that these forms exceed the practical purpose of singing—indeed, they are generally missing from manuscripts conceived and realized primarily for singing, as the pages from ModD 10 show.

At this point it seems worthwhile to look more closely at Alamire's presentation manuscripts, focussing on the features that characterize them when compared with other music manuscripts of the time. Contrary to initial appearances, listing such features will help us to question the dichotomy between display and performance—indeed, it will help us problematize the very meanings of these terms.

Seeing and Reading Music

Alamire's presentation manuscripts generally adopt a mise-en-page which visually clarifies the distinctiveness of the different voices. Such emphasis on the separation of voices is characteristic of luxury manuscripts even before Alamire. One eloquent example of this differentiation is to be found in the intarsia work of the studiolo of Federico da Montefeltro in Urbino, dating from 1476. On the northern wall, among other closed books and next to some musical instruments, there is a chansonnier opened to an anonymous three-voice *J'ay pris amours*. This source could have been used in practical music-making, as the presence of instruments bears out (Figure 2). On the western wall, among the precious objects of what may be termed a *Schatzkammer*, another music book is depicted, displaying *Bella gerit*, an anonymous motet celebrating Duke Federico (Figure 3). The dimensions of the two books are similar. However, there is one feature that differentiates the motet codex from the chansonnier: the clarity of the layout. In the motet codex, each part has its own well-defined space, with an empty stave separating adjacent parts. In contrast to the chansonnier, the layout of the book that features among the precious objects shows particular attention to the codes of visual communication: the parts do not compactly fill up all the free space (as is the case in the chansonnier), but are set out in an order which makes the composition musically meaningful also for the beholder, distinguishing the four voices by giving each of them a clearly separate space. These four sections act like graphic counterparts of four different sources of sound, even though in that moment the aural re-creation of the music is absent—a re-creation which the layout of the chansonnier, where the voices are not as clearly separate, appears to take for granted. By analogy with the intarsia work in Urbino, in Alamire's presentation manuscripts the layout alone clarifies the polyphony of the music they contain, highlighting its 'aural spatialization'.[17]

---

[17] On the musical intarsia-work in Urbino see Nicoletta Guidobaldi, *La musica di Federico. Immagini e suoni alla corte di Urbino* (Florence, 1995); in particular on the different statuses of the two books, see Laurenz Lütteken, 'Motette', in *Die Musik in Geschichte und Gegenwart*, ed. Ludwig Finscher (Kassel etc., ²1997), Sachteil 6, cols. 514-15; Laurenz Lütteken, *Musik der Renaissance. Imagination und Wirklichkeit einer kulturellen Praxis* (Kassel-Stuttgart, 2011), 30-31; Borghetti, 'Il manoscritto di musica', 111-12.

Figure 2. Urbino, Studiolo, detail from the northern wall

There are other ways, however, in which the association between the written music on the page and the sounding music is made as immediate as possible. The pages of Alamire's presentation manuscripts not only enhance the individual identity of the separate parts, but are often also full of 'voices': illuminators made a point of reminding the reader of the aural quality of the music by presenting possible or actual utterances on the page itself, before the readers' very eyes and, in a sense, ears.[18] An example of this is the addition of human faces to the initial letters of the individual parts, as if to highlight the literally 'polyphonic' substance of the content as the product of several human voices performing together. In many cases these initials feature human faces depicted in the act of singing: there are various types, ranging from tiny faces drawn in pen inside the cadels or even in the underlaid text itself, to the more elaborately painted initials with

---

[18] On the visual presence of sound in medieval manuscripts and particularly in prayer books see Dillon, *The Sense of Sound*, 186-242.

drolleries which include those defined by Dagmar Thoss as 'derb-komische Männerköpfe'.[19] The act of vocal production is shown in various ways: with an open mouth (Figure 4), as a caricature of the act of singing (Figure 5), through emphasis on the depiction of the breath which may involve cartoon-like touches (Figure 6),[20] through elaborations of the letter-shapes (Figure 7, where the horizontal stroke of the 'E' issues directly from the mouth of the profile), or as a graphic link between an open mouth and the musical notation (Figure 8). The 'vocal' nature of the content of the manuscripts reinforced through the use of singing heads is also highlighted when voices are silent. This is the case, for example, in JenaU 2, fol. 93r, where the 'tacet' indication for the 'Pleni' in the contratenor part is personified by a face with a closed mouth, followed by the indication 'Pleni non aperuit os suum' (Figure 9).[21]

Even if initials of these types constitute a widespread form of decoration, they nonetheless make a meaningful contribution to situating the music in a polyphonic and performing context, since heads, particularly the singing ones, highlight the affinity of the written music with the music as sound. Recent media theory, however, allows us to go one step further. These kinds of decoration and mise-en-page make explicit the act of remediation on the part of the manuscripts, since the written page is, in the terms of media theorists Jay David Bolter and Richard Grusin, 'opaque' with regard to the event it is mediating: it does not try to hide its mediating function, it is not 'transparent', but, on the contrary, it highlights such a function.[22] This means that

Figure 3. Urbino, Studiolo, detail from the western wall

---

[19] Thoss, 'Initialen und Bordüren', 158.
[20] The 'sonorous' quality of this initial is further reinforced by the singing head's enormous ears. I wish to thank Bonnie Blackburn and Leofranc Holford-Strevens for pointing out this interesting additional 'audio' detail.
[21] For an analysis and catalogue of the indications of 'tacet' in the Alamire manuscripts, see Bonnie J. Blackburn, 'The Eloquence of Silence: Tacet Inscriptions in the Alamire Manuscripts', in *Citation and Authority in Medieval and Renaissance Musical Culture: Learning from the Learned*, ed. Suzannah Clark and Elizabeth Eva Leach (Woodbridge-Rochester, 2005), 206-23.
[22] See Jay David Bolter and Richard Grusin, *Remediation: Understanding New Media* (Cambridge, MA, 1999).

Figure 4. JenaU 2, fol. 75v

Figure 5. JenaU 3, fol. 74r

Figure 6. JenaU 3, fol. 92r

Figure 7. VienNB 1783, fol. 4v

Figure 8. JenaU 2, fol. 34r

Figure 9. JenaU 2, fol. 93r

presentation manuscripts not only emphasize the connection between music as written and music as sound, but also promote themselves as the medium through which this connection is made explicit. This kind of explicit, self-conscious remediation, which Bolter and Grusin have famously termed 'hypermediation', enriches the sensory experience of looking at the written page: doing so is promoted as, in a sense, even 'richer' than 'just' listening.[23]

As already stated, drolleries with heads or singing heads are not found in all of Alamire's presentation manuscripts. At the same time, they are not confined to Alamire's books: they recur in earlier and contemporary manuscripts, such as those of the Sistine Chapel (see, e.g., VatS 14), chansonniers from the second half of the fifteenth century (e.g., DijBM 517), and liturgical chant-books (e.g., BrusBR 11.3633).[24] But such evocations of the aurality of the content, while certainly an element of late-medieval book culture, are not omnipresent: the manuscripts produced at the court of Frederick the Wise of Saxony for use in his chapel at around the same time as Alamire made his, for example, bear no trace of such decoration (e.g., JenaU 30-36).[25] What is more, in some of the Alamire codices—for example, the chansonnier BrusBR 228, some of the Vienna manuscripts, and most of the Jena choirbooks—this type of 'performative' decoration becomes almost an obsession; and, as Dagmar Thoss has shown, the size, variety, and quantity of these initials constitute a distinctive characteristic of the Alamire manuscripts. They have a pictorial, visual, and I would say theatrical prominence that is unequalled elsewhere; and the singing heads in particular were one of the hallmarks of his workshop.[26]

At the same time, it is not only the initials which highlight the 'aural' or 'performative' nature of the music in Alamire's manuscripts. As is well known, on the first opening of a composition the musical text is often decorated with miniatures or historiated initials featuring sacred scenes and portraits of the donor or recipient depicted at prayer. The presence of these images reinforces the construction of the

---

[23] See Bolter and Grusin, *Remediation*, 53.
[24] The Vatican manuscript and the Dijon chansonnier are available online at <http://digi.vatlib.it/view/MSS_Capp.Sist.14> and <http://patrimoine.bm-dijon.fr/pleade/img-viewer/MS00517/viewer.html?ns=FR212316101_CITEAUX_MS00517_000_01_PS.jpg> respectively. For examples of the heads in the initials of a gradual produced in the Low Countries in the early decades of the sixteenth century, see BrusBR 11.3633, reproduced in Maurits Smeyers and Jan Van der Stock (eds.), *Flemish Illuminated Manuscripts, 1475-1550* (Ghent, 1996), 153.
[25] On these manuscripts see Jürgen Heidrich, *Die deutschen Chorbücher aus der Hofkapelle Friedrichs des Weisen. Ein Beitrag zur mitteldeutschen geistlichen Musikpraxis um 1500* (Baden-Baden, 1993).
[26] See Thoss, 'Initialen und Bordüren', 158.

written music as utterance, albeit in a different way than the initials considered above. The musical composition that follows these images is thus construed both as the concrete effect of the prayer depicted (as if the prayer itself had been collected and registered on the page), and as the instrument through which the act of devotion can be musically expressed (that is, through which the prayer depicted in the image can be performed). Often, moreover, the donor is shown contemplating the holy scene with an open book: in this way not only the music but also the book as a whole is construed and conveyed as the cause and at the same time the effect of prayer.[27] The polyphonic composition and, more generally, the characteristics of the book chosen for its mediation thus become both instrument of and testimony to the construction of the identity of the donors depicted: they artfully convey their *pietas* as good Christians while at the same time highlighting their social standing.

This relationship between prayer and book, and more generally between medium and mediated event, was fundamental for late medieval European culture and predated Alamire's presentation manuscripts, particularly in books of hours.[28] In books of hours, especially those dating from the fifteenth century, miniatures showing the patron at prayer appear frequently, thereby 'staging' a performance both of the texts with which the miniatures are associated and of the book in which they are presented.[29] Well-known examples of this include: LonBL Harley 2900, fol. 200r, where the patron is kneeling before the Virgin and Child, holding a scroll inscribed with 'O intemerata et in eternum', the incipit of the prayer which the image accompanies; BalW W.267, fols. 13v-14r, where the patroness is shown kneeling on the prie-dieu with an open book, between the archangel Gabriel and the Virgin at the moment of the Annunciation (the archangel is holding a scroll between the patron and the Virgin proclaiming 'Ave gratia plena dominus tecum', from the prayer that initiates the Hours of the Virgin); and VienNB 1857, fol. 14v, where a figure often identified as Mary of Burgundy is depicted reading her prayers, seated in a room with a window which leads into the interior of a church, where we see her praying in front of the Virgin with child.[30] These examples illustrate various ways in which books could function both as a requisite and as a mirror: the act of reading, and thus of devotion, is made possible, fostered and at the same time mirrored in the representation of this act expressed in the miniatures. Such representations are a 'user's manual', a guide for the beholder, but also a 'staging' of the devotional act, in an interplay of theatrical mirroring or a mise-en-abyme of prayer in and through the book.[31]

---

[27] On scenes of prayer decorating the Alamire manuscripts and their possible meanings see Bonnie J. Blackburn, 'For Whom Do the Singers Sing?', in *Early Music* 25 (1997), 593-609.

[28] On the resemblance between Alamire's codices and books of hours see Blackburn, 'Messages in Miniature'; Blackburn, 'For Whom Do the Singers Sing?'; Dekeyzer, 'The Decoration of the Alamire Music Manuscripts'. Though not mentioning Alamire, there are interesting observations on the relations between music books and books of hours in Alden, 'Reading the Loire Valley Chansonniers', 3-13.

[29] On the iconography of reading see Amtower, *Engaging Words*, 51-77.

[30] Reproductions and analyses of the three miniatures described can be found, respectively, in Dillon, *The Sense of Sound*, 214-15; Roger S. Wieck, *Time Sanctified. The Book of Hours in Medieval Art and Life* (New York-Baltimore, 1988), 43-44; and Amtower, *Engaging Words*, 72-77.

[31] On these aspects see in particular Amtower, *Engaging Words*, 45-77.

Luxury Music Books and Courtly Readers

The range of types of aurality and performativity observed in Alamire's presentation manuscripts raises another question: why was it so important in this type of music book to notate polyphony in a way that left open the possibility of situating it in a performative context? Like books of hours, these manuscripts were primarily made for the élite of the times: for what I call 'courtly readers'. These readers were familiar with polyphonic music, but they were not musically literate in a professional sense, or at least not necessarily so (in the same way as they were familiar with Latin but not necessarily proficient in it). Alamire's music books were created to suit these patrons, ensuring various types of use beyond performance—like the books of hours, which were not exclusively tied to devotional practice.[32] This comparison with the books of hours helps place Alamire's presentation manuscripts in the context of late Medieval book culture and reading practices, not only of a musical nature. It is now generally accepted that, thanks to the decorations often present in manuscripts, in the Middle Ages 'reading', as Sylvia Huot has argued, 'could be an intensely visual experience'.[33] Similarly to what happened with books of hours and other types of Medieval illuminated books, then, the decoration of Alamire's presentation manuscripts made them more versatile than books 'simply' designed for music making. How could this happen?

Presentation manuscripts could serve for music-making, of course, in the same way as books of hours could serve for reading prayers, and other decorated books could serve for reading texts in the literal sense: the clarity of the layout and the richness of the decoration would have aided such uses. However, these elements also made a fundamental contribution to the magnificence of the worship and, on a more general level, of the rituals of the ruling classes during which such books could be employed: display was a crucial element of the performance of these books as objects rather than only of the performance of the music they contained. Significantly, this fluidity between 'display' and 'performance' has long been observed for book of hours—which, thanks to their preciousness and notwithstanding their small size, were not confined to private, solitary use, as Lawrence R. Poos has pointed out: 'Books of Hours reflect at the same time lay religious piety, and the pride, or possibly conspicuous acquisitivness, of ownership. It is not too cynical to point out that medieval piety incorporated a substantial element of public display'.[34] Similarly, display can be considered a crucial element of the performance of Alamire's presentation manuscripts, and not a mode of use necessarily opposed to performance.

The decorative richness of the Alamire manuscripts also suggests an enhanced range of ways in which they could be related to music making, once more when compared to books of hours. For example, the different kinds of 'performative' miniatures allowed the courtly reader to follow or mentally re-enact an actual performance of polyphonic music just by gazing at the written page. As I have mentioned above, thanks to books of hours this courtly reader was familiar with books that use texts, images, and other

---

[32] On the different ways that books of hours were used, their public, and the literacy of that public, see Virginia Reinburg, 'Prayer and the Book of Hours', in Wieck, *Time Sanctified*, 39-44; Reinburg, *French Books of Hours*, 84-128; Amtower, *Engaging Words*, 32-37.

[33] Huot, *The 'Romance of the Rose'*, 279.

[34] Lawrence R. Poos, 'Social History and the Book of Hours', in *Time Sanctified*, ed. Roger S. Wieck, 34; on this argument, see also Duffy, *Marking the Hours*, 53-60; Reinburg, *French Books of Hours*, 53-83; Dillon, *The Sense of Sound*, 186-242.

graphic devices during rituals or to foster recollection or mental representation. Thus, like other sumptuous books of the same period, Alamire's manuscripts could enhance the experience of music during its performance and help to recall or imagine it.[35] In the case of sacred music, this was an expression of personal devotion of a high-born personage, while in the case of secular music, of refined and moral pastimes.

Thus, by means of the decoration Alamire not only alluded to possible performative contexts for notated music, but also construed the music itself as something which was valuable to recollect or meditate on: the contemplation of the page could sustain and encourage further meditation on its contents.[36] The borders and decorated initials situated the polyphony in a garden of delights filled with an array of precious and beautiful objects including flowers, fruits, jewels, and animals: all elements which identified the works they accompanied, making them singularly memorable, as Mary Carruthers, Anna Maria Busse Berger, and Jane Alden have observed.[37]

This splendid decoration served to emphasize the value of the music itself, as a treasure on a par with the flowers, the fruits, and the other beautiful and precious objects. At the same time, however, the decoration was also a reminder of the transient nature of music: flying and ephemeral creatures such as birds and butterflies, as well as flowers and fruits, all underlined the evanescence of sound. They implicitly invited the reader to grasp and cherish it, and to preserve it in the mind even when the physical sound was past.[38] These manuscripts also feature many venatorial images of capturing or captured prey: for example, a crane catching a snake (Figure 10); a bird catching a caterpillar (Figure 11); and a monkey trying to capture a bird with a basket, yet distracted by a butterfly as another potential prey (Figure 12). Such images occur frequently, as Mary Carruthers has shown, in medieval manuscripts.[39] However, it is significant that in Alamire's presentation manuscripts we find particularly idiosyncratic images depicting the capture of music as sound. For example, we find a bird snatching 'musical' utterances from singing faces (Figures 13 and 14; note in the latter the features of the breath). Perhaps the most surprising image of all shows an arrow shot directly into the open mouth of a singing head (Figure 15). These venatorial images thus remind the readers of the specific nature of the books they were using, books that contain music that is transient in nature: if it was not grasped with due solicitude, it was in danger of being lost forever. As a matter of fact, not all the drolleries are able or willing to sing properly: in some cases the 'singers' are depicted with a padlock sealing their lips, a pincer blocking their nose, not paying attention to the music, or with their mouth closed (see Figures 16-18).[40]

At times, the decoration also provided a warning about the potential dangers of making incorrect use of these magnificent books. For example, pictures of monkeys

---

[35] On music books and their various relations with music making see Alden, 'Reading the Loire Valley Chansonniers', 18-29; Alden, *Songs, Scribes, and Society*, 167-78; on the meaning of the decorative apparatus in relation to medieval reading habits see Carruthers, *The Book of Memory*, 255-57.

[36] See Carruthers, *The Book of Memory*, 255-57.

[37] See Carruthers, *The Book of Memory*, 246-47; Anna Maria Busse Berger, *Medieval Music and the Art of Memory* (Berkeley-Los Angeles, 2005), 198-251; Alden, 'Reading the Loire Valley Chansonniers', 28-29; Alden, *Songs, Scribes, and Society*, 167-78.

[38] See Carruthers, *The Book of Memory*, 246-47.

[39] See Carruthers, *The Book of Memory*, 246-47.

[40] In this respect, it is interesting to note that quite a few initials show two heads, of which one has his mouth open, the other one closed. This underlines the 'sonority' of the written music, while at the same time pointing to the danger of silence, as can bee seen in Figure 6.

Figure 10, VienNB 15497, fol. 1v

Figure 11, MechAS s.s., fol. 16v

Figure 12, JenaU 9, fol. 2r

Figures 13, VienN 1783, fol. 11v

Figure 14, JenaU 3, fol. 60r

Figure 15, JenaU 12, fol. 99r

Figure 16, VienNB 15497, fol. 56v

Figure 17, JenaU 8, fol. 26r

Figure 18, JenaU 4, fol. 103r

appear frequently. Monkeys are a common feature in many manuscripts from this period, with a variety of potential meanings; but one strong iconographic tradition going back to classical antiquity, transmitted to the Middle Ages in texts like the *Physiologus*, and then disseminated and vulgarised through bestiaries, attributed sinful and even diabolical meanings to the monkey.[41] Late medieval manuscripts, in particular books of hours, frequently contain depictions of monkeys, often shown aping human activities. As well as being objects of ridicule, monkeys thus highlighted the secular, potentially sinful activities they were engaged in. In the Alamire manuscripts we can find various representations of monkeys, either depicted as such (as in VerBC 756), or, more often, occupied in various human activities ranging from making music, as in the Chigi Codex (VatC C VIII 234), to hunting (see Figure 14).

If in many cases the representations of monkeys can be seen as conveying moral warnings to the reader, one is of particular interest because it provides an explicit allusion to the morality of the text and a correct use of the book. On fol. 1v of the chansonnier of

---

[41] On the iconography and meanings of the monkey, see Horst Waldemar Janson, *Apes and Ape Lore in the Middle Ages and the Renaissance* (London, 1952); see also Amtower, *Engaging Words*, 57. Monkeys are not the only negative symbols found in the Alamire manuscripts. For example, flies occur as well, symbolizing immodesty and low instincts; see Louis Charbonneau-Lassay, *Il bestiario del Cristo. La misteriosa emblematica di Gesù Cristo* (Rome, 1994), vol. 2, 531-34.

Margaret of Austria (BrusBR 228) we see a monkey admiring itself in a mirror (see Plate 6 for the first opening of the chansonnier, and Plate 7 for the detail with the monkey). The monkey is depicted in the bottom left-hand corner of the page facing the portrait of Margaret herself. Margaret is praying from a book, apparently seeing the vision of the Virgin depicted across the opening, as the object of her prayers (the words 'Memento mei' are issuing from her mouth): on fol. 1v we see a representation of the Virgin in the Sun, the Immaculate, which the medieval tradition defines as 'Speculum sine macula'. While Margaret looks at herself in the stainless spiritual mirror of the immaculate Virgin, the monkey instead looks at itself in a wordly mirror, which by contrast is 'cum macula'. In fact, one can see at the centre of its mirror a black stain which is at the same time the monkey's reflection and the allegorical 'macula', the result of non-virtuous activity generally characteristic of the earthly condition. Significantly, to underline the distance between the two scenes of 'mirroring', the monkey is placed not only on the page facing the portrait of Margaret, but also in the lower margin, in a position corresponding to the low moral level of its activity. Furthermore, it turns its back to the objects around it including a cross that is precious both in a material and a spiritual sense.[42]

But there is more. The monkey is accompanied by another symbol of primitive, imperfect humanity, which reinforces its meaning. On the extreme right of the lower margin of fol. 1v, we see a naked child playing with whatever is at hand in the garden where he is situated (he sits astride a branch holding a bird with its wings spread).[43] Like the monkey, the playing child can be considered as another example of purposeless pleasure: both creatures are unaware of what they are doing or of the moral value of their physical surroundings.[44] The monkey and the child depicted on the first opening of the book, and in the opposite corner to the portrait of Margaret of Austria, are thus designed as an admonishment to Margaret herself not to cede to the temptation of merely 'playing' or taking pleasure in her beautiful chansonnier, but to engage properly with the beautiful and precious objects it contains, including, of course, the music. Otherwise the book's noble purpose would be debased to a level of futility and sinfulness equivalent to that of the monkey and the child. This miniature calls attention not just to the moral purpose but also to the importance of the visual approach to the book itself.[45]

The clarity of the layout and lavishness of the decoration in the manuscripts of Alamire were intended to guide the courtly reader in understanding the compositional

---

[42] On the iconography and the symbolism of the Immaculate Virgin with special reference to BrusBR 228, see Bonnie Blackburn, 'The Virgin in the Sun: Music and Image for a Prayer Attributed to Sixtus IV', in *Journal of the Royal Musical Association 124 (1999)*, 157-95. On the mirror as symbol for the Immaculate Virgin, see James Hall, *Dictionary of Subjects and Symbols in Art* (New York, 1979), 328 ('Virgin Mary 5'); Emile Male, *Religious Art in France – The Late Middle Ages: A Study of Medieval Iconography and Its Sources* (Princeton, 1972), 200-2; Gustav Friedrich Hartlaub, *Zauber des Spiegels* (Münich, 1951) 147-48; Sabine Melchior-Bonnet, *The Mirror: A History* (New York, 2002), esp. 101-245.

[43] Unlike the monkey, to my best knowledge this figure is unique in the decorations in Alamire's books.

[44] On the medieval theoretical tradition considering childhood as a pre-rational and senseless phase of human development, see Pierre Riché/Danièle Alexandre-Bidon, *L'enfance au Moyen Âge* (Paris, 1994), esp. 12-23.

[45] One of Erasmus's *Colloquia*, the dialogue of the 'Abbot and the Learned Lady', shows particular affinities with the decoration of BrusBR 228's opening pages. According to Anne-Marie Legaré, the Lady in this dialogue 'exemplifies the thinker's position on the subject of the education of young ladies: books alone can save them from the snares of laziness and the vanities of this world'. Although there probably were contacts between Margaret and Erasmus, we do not know whether the latter's thought influenced this chansonnier's conception. However, BrusBR 228's opening pages, as a guide and a warning to the proper use of the whole book, seem to be a sort of distillation of Erasmus's thought on the morality and correct conduct of female reading. See Anne-Marie Legaré, '"La librairye de Madame": Two Princesses and their Libraries', in *Women of Distinction: Margaret of York/Margaret of Austria*, ed. Dagmar Eichberger (Leuven, 2005), 218.

features of the music itself: when trained on complex manuscripts like these, the listening gaze could achieve levels of considerable insight. For example, as I have argued elsewhere, it was possible to highlight the presence, and the structural and ideological importance, of a cantus firmus through coats of arms (even when strict cantus firmus treatment was not employed, in some of these choirbooks the tenor is the voice deemed worthy of representing the donor/recipient in the contrapuntal edifice, and hence of carrying his/her most representative coat of arms).[46] By use of superimposed mensural signs, the composition's imitative structure could be revealed at a glance, giving whoever looked at a manuscript considerable help in understanding this very structure; a famous example is the *Missa prolationum* as transmitted in the Chigi Codex.[47] It is significant that, as this case shows, Alamire's presentation manuscripts adopt a kind of mise-en-page which can recall Lampadius' *tabula compositoria* discussed above: although in choirbook format, the *Missa prolationum* in the Chigi Codex embraces the principle of superimposition (one written part becomes two voices thanks to two different mensuration signs), that very principle which, according to Lampadius, characterizes the compositional process, when visual control of all the voices is important.

The notation and the mise-en-page could also allude to the subtle symbolic play involved in a cantus firmus mass. In the case of the *Missa Hercules dux Ferrarie* by Josquin in BrusBR 9126 (here as *Missa Philippus rex Castilie*), the first appearance of the cantus firmus is written in red ink, and thus visually differentiated from the rest of the polyphony, as if it were a fragment of liturgical chant. The effect is aided by the fact that it comprises a sequence of breves. In the manuscript JenaU 3, featuring the same mass (here as *Fridericus dux Saxonie*), the text beneath the first appearance of the cantus firmus in the superius is in blue ink, the same colour as the background of the initial of the tenor, to underline the special link between the cantus firmus and the tenor (structurally the *fundamentum relationis*, and as such the ideologically most appropriate site for the musical symbols of the prince celebrated by the piece, as mentioned above).[48] Colour could also be used to draw the attention of courtly readers and/or performers to a specific detail for reasons difficult to gauge today: for example the red ink that suddenly appears in the tenor in the 'Osanna' of Matthaeus Pipelare's *Missa Fors seulement* in JenaU 2 (fol. 75v).

I would like to devote some final considerations to the complex relationship between the decoration of Alamire's presentation manuscripts, their dimensions, and their potential uses. Use in performance was possible, and perhaps even encouraged, by the large dimensions of these books, but, as the different types and sizes of decoration suggest, this use was not the only one for which the books were suitable: despite the considerable size of the pages, part of the decoration is visible only at very close quarters, and therefore not necessarily even to the singers performing from these sources on a lectern (for example, the small heads within initials or letters of the underlaid text). Here, Jean Froissart offers useful evidence for understanding the different potential modes of

---

[46] For a few examples, see the following manuscripts: JenaU 4, fol. 15v; JenaU 12, fol. 18v; MechAS s.s., fol. 1v (a digital reproduction of this manuscipt can be found here: <http://www.diamm.ac.uk/jsp/Descriptions?op=SOURCE&sourceKey=1159#imageList>); VerBC 756, fol. 1v; VienBN 15495, fol. 1v; VienNB 1547, fol. 10r. For an interpretation, see Vincenzo Borghetti, 'Music and the Representation of Princely Power in the Fifteenth and Sixteenth Century', in *Acta Musicologica* 80 (2008), 208-14; Vincenzo Borghetti, 'Il manoscritto di musica tra Quattro e Cinquecento', 113-14.
[47] See Vincenzo Borghetti, 'Il suono e la pagina', 116-24.
[48] On the ideological use of the tenor as *fundamentum relationis* see references in n. 46.

consumption of Alamire's manuscripts. In one of his chronicles, Froissart recounts presenting one of his manuscripts to Richard II of England. On receiving it, the King appraised the various aspects of this gift, and put the book to different uses: reading one part out loud, admiring the miniatures and other elements of its manufacture (the binding in red velvet, the finely worked golden clasps, and so on), before having it taken to his private apartments. In her commentary of this passage, Jane Alden has highlighted the various uses that were fostered and made possible by a luxury object like the book Froissart presented to the English King (reading aloud from the book in a 'public' situation, reading through the images, admiring the preciousness of the book as an object, and engaging further with it in private spaces and situations), connecting them with richly decorated music books such as the Loire Valley chansonniers.[49] In view of all the characteristics we have analyzed, some or all of these uses may well have applied to the Alamire manuscripts, which, in spite of or because of their size, are suited to being read and used in a variety of ways and contexts, both public and private, and in various venues, whether spacious or intimate, from the chamber to the chapel. Beyond their obvious appeal due to their preciousness and their social and ritual value, this is probably a further reason underpinning their fame and fortune.

Conclusions

In the Alamire presentation manuscripts the layout, the decoration, and the mise-en-page visually convey the musical content in ways that went well beyond the requisites of manuscripts conceived 'only' for music making (or 'only' for display). This means that these manuscripts presupposed, encouraged, and embodied typologies of use and reading processes so diverse that the supposedly contrasting categories of 'for display' and 'for performance' come to overlap. The display in the Alamire manuscripts was itself performance, and performance was itself display: even when these manuscripts were used for actual music making, display was an important factor, as for other courtly objects, because the splendour of the manuscripts underlined that of the music they contain, pointing metonymically to the magnificence of their owner/user (whether of the music or of the books). At the same time, the 'mere' display of the presentation manuscripts did not exclude performance: they were meaningful not only as precious objects but also as precious books of music. As I have shown, given the way in which these manuscripts mediate music, they made a point of highlighting, in various ways, the aural nature of the written pages and the reading processes they fostered. In other words, they invited the reader to listen to the written page, which recalled or referred to past, present, or possible performance, and the various meanings and purposes of this performance. Lastly, through the interaction of their visual, material, and aural components, they reminded the reader of the various modalities and goals of listening, while emphasizing the social privilege associated with their possession and use. In sum, the presentation manuscripts of Alamire were precious books because, even when 'merely' looked at, they had many ways of being musically meaningful. In a sense, gazing at their pages was already an act of listening.

---

[49] See Alden, *Reading the Loire Valley Chansonniers*, 13-14.

Appendix. List of sources

1. Music Manuscripts

BrusBR 228	Brussels, Bibliothèque royale de Belgique, Ms. 228
BrusBR 9126	Brussels, Bibliothèque royale de Belgique, Ms. 9126
BrusBR 11.3633	Brussels, Bibliothèque royale de Belgique, Ms. 11.3633
DijBM 517	Dijon, Bibliothèque Municipale, Ms. 517
JenaU 2	Jena, Thüringer Universitäts- und Landesbibliothek, Ms. 2
JenaU 3	Jena, Thüringer Universitäts- und Landesbibliothek, Ms. 3
JenaU 4	Jena, Thüringer Universitäts- und Landesbibliothek, Ms. 4
JenaU 7	Jena, Thüringer Universitäts- und Landesbibliothek, Ms. 7
JenaU 8	Jena, Thüringer Universitäts- und Landesbibliothek, Ms. 8
JenaU 9	Jena, Thüringer Universitäts- und Landesbibliothek, Ms. 9
JenaU 12	Jena, Thüringer Universitäts- und Landesbibliothek, Ms. 12
JenaU 20	Jena, Thüringer Universitäts- und Landesbibliothek, Ms. 20
JenaU 30	Jena, Thüringer Universitäts- und Landesbibliothek, Ms. 30
JenaU 31	Jena, Thüringer Universitäts- und Landesbibliothek, Ms. 31
JenaU 32	Jena, Thüringer Universitäts- und Landesbibliothek, Ms. 32
JenaU 33	Jena, Thüringer Universitäts- und Landesbibliothek, Ms. 33
JenaU 34	Jena, Thüringer Universitäts- und Landesbibliothek, Ms. 34
JenaU 35	Jena, Thüringer Universitäts- und Landesbibliothek, Ms. 35
JenaU 36	Jena, Thüringer Universitäts- und Landesbibliothek, Ms. 36
MechAS s.s.	Mechelen, Archief en Stadsbibliotheek Ms. s.s.
ModD 10	Modena, Biblioteca e Archivio Capitolare, Ms. Mus. X
VatC 234	Vatican City, Biblioteca Apostolica Vaticana, Ms. Chigi C VIII 234 ('Chigi Codex')
VatS 14	Vatican City, Biblioteca Apostolica Vaticana, Ms. Cappella Sistina 14
VerBC 756	Verona, Biblioteca Capitolare, Ms. 756
VienNB 1783	Vienna, Österreichische Nationalbibliothek, Handschriftensammlung, Ms. 1783
VienNB 15495	Vienna, Österreichische Nationalbibliothek, Musiksammlung, Ms. Mus. 15495
VienNB 15497	Vienna, Österreichische Nationalbibliothek, Musiksammlung, Ms. Mus. 15497

2. Other Manuscripts

BalW W.267	Baltimore, Walters Art Museum, Ms. W.267
LonBL Harley 2900	London, British Library, Ms. Harley 2900
VienNB 1857	Vienna, Österreichische Nationalbibliothek, Handschriftensammlung, Ms. 1857

Abstract

The presentation manuscripts produced by the scriptorium of Petrus Alamire at the Habsburg court in the Low Countries rate among the most precious music books of their time. Commissioned by sovereigns and members of the ruling classes or as gifts for them, they have long attracted the attention of musicologists. However, Alamire's presentation manuscripts have up to now been investigated essentially as vehicles of music (or in some cases of visual art). Less attention has been paid to them as books, that is, as objects constructed through the interaction of different modes of communication. This is all the more surprising given that in these manuscripts the musical text goes hand in hand with very conspicuous visual devices.

In this article I consider the dynamics and cultural significance of the use of the Alamire manuscripts as 'books' and, specifically, as 'music books'. I analyze features of his presentation manuscripts with respect to other musical manuscripts of the age, and the possible reasons for these characteristics. The conclusion considers the relevance of my interpretation for larger issues concerning the uses and meanings of luxury music books in the fifteenth and sixteenth centuries.

Printing Hofhaimer: A Case Study[*]

Grantley McDonald

This article presents a case study of the issues of mise-en-page involved in printing a collection containing both literary and musical material: the posthumously published *Harmoniae poeticae* of Paul Hofhaimer (Nuremberg: Johannes Petreius, 1539 [RISM B/I 1539[26]; VD16 H 4960]).[1] A detailed examination of this edition reveals much about the ways in which the initial conception of this collection determined factors such as layout and page format, and much also about Petreius' methods of typesetting single-impression type.

Some information about the genesis of this publication is contained in Johannes Stomius's dedication of the collection to cardinal Matthaeus Lang, archbishop of Salzburg.[2] Stomius, first attested as rector of a private Latin school at Salzburg in 1530, wrote in this dedication that the aging Paul Hofhaimer (1459-1537) had entrusted him with the task of publishing a collection of literary testimonials to his fame as imperial organist, collected over the course of some three decades. Stomius had requested in turn that Hofhaimer write a series of quantitative settings of poems by Horace, and a number of hymns by Prudentius. The inclusion in the *Harmoniae poeticae* of a poem in praise of Hofhaimer's settings by Franciscus Paedoreus, one of Stomius's students, suggests that these pieces were used in Stomius's school. The scoring—often three high voices and one baritone voice—lends itself to school use, since the upper parts could be sung by boys and the lowest part by the teacher or cantor.[3] The texts by Horace were taken from Glareanus's 1533 edition.[4] Unless Stomius altered the text for the posthumous publication, this detail can be taken as a *terminus post quem* for the composition of Hofhaimer's settings.

When Hofhaimer died in 1537, he had not yet finished setting the hymns of Prudentius, and Stomius had not yet collected the testimonials together for publication. Hofhaimer's heirs, disappointed and angry at the meagre legacy left them in his will, did

---

[*] Research for the present article was carried out in the course of the project *Early Music Printing in German Speaking Lands (Früher Notendruck in deutschsprachigen Ländern: Studien zur Entwicklung von Drucktechnik und Repertoire)*, based at the University of Salzburg and funded by the Austrian Science Fund (FWF, Projekt P24075). My thanks are due to Andrea Lindmayr-Brandl and Elisabeth Giselbrecht, my co-workers on this project.

[1] VD16 numbers refer to the standard bibliography of sixteenth-century German printed books, *Verzeichnis der im deutschen Sprachbereich erschienenen Drucke des 16. Jahrhunderts* (<www.gateway-bayern.de/index_vd16.html>).

[2] Edition and translation in Paul Hofhaimer, *Harmoniae poeticae (1539)*, ed. Grantley McDonald, Denkmäler der Musik in Salzburg 15/3 (Munich, 2014), 2-5. The standard work by Hans Joachim Moser, *Paul Hofhaimer, ein Lied- und Orgelmeister des deutschen Humanismus* (Stuttgart, 1929; Hildesheim, ²1966), is problematic in many respects; it will be replaced by my forthcoming biography. On Stomius, see Helmut Wagner, 'Johannes Stomius vulgo Mulinus (1502-1562)', in *Ostbairische Grenzmarken* 18 (1976), 63-72; Ulrike Baumann, *Ioannes Stomius, Prima Ad Musicen Instructio: Edition, Übersetzung, Kommentar* (Bern, 2010).

[3] Hofhaimer, *Harmoniae*, ed. McDonald, 18-27.

[4] *Q. HORA ||TII FLACCI POEMA ||TA OMNIA, STVDIO AC DILI ||GENTIA HEN. GLAREANI P.L. || recognita, eiusdemq; Annotationibus illustrata* […] (Freiburg im Breisgau: Johann Faber Emmeus, 1533 [VD16 H 4855 / P 1548]). Glareanus' text and his presentation of the metre of each ode is based on the 1514 edition of Benedetto Riccardini (Benedictus Philologus Florentinus), first published as: *Q: Horatii Flacci poemata* (Florence: Filippo Giunta, 1514). Hofhaimer (or Stomius) adapted Glareanus' presentation of the metre of each poem. However, it is clear that Hofhaimer did not use Riccardini's edition, but that of Glareanus, which departs from its model in a number of minor details. For example, at *Ode* II.2.17, Riccardini has *Phraotes*, while Glareanus has *Phraoten*; Hofhaimer follows Glareanus' reading. At *Ode* I.8.2-7, Riccardini has a series of indirect questions in the subjunctive, while Glareanus has direct questions in the indicative; again, Hofhaimer follows Glareanus. Moreover, Hofhaimer consistently follows Glareanus' preference for the archaic ending *-eis* for the accusative plural of the third declension, a preference that Riccardini does not share.

nothing to provide for the publication of his final compositions or the collection of literary testimonia, and it took the intervention of the Salzburg court procurator Georg Teisenperger to wrest the papers out of their grasp. Beside the daily demands of teaching, Stomius took up the task of editing the material for the press, and gathering a number of tributes to the late master.

Nothing is known about the way the edition was financed. There is no evidence that the dedicatee, Matthaeus Lang, Hofhaimer's former employer, offered any funding up-front. Petreius may have covered the printing costs in whole or in part and kept some of the copies with the expectation of turning a profit. Alternatively, it is possible that Stomius paid the initial costs from his own pocket, taking possession of the printed copies in order to sell them to his students, or to pass them on to Hofhaimer's friends and admirers as a kind of memorial volume. In either case, the fact that Stomius dedicated the edition to Lang, a connoisseur who had received the dedication of luxury editions such as the *Liber selectarum cantionum* (Augsburg: Grimm and Wyrsung, 1520 [RISM B/I 1520⁴; VD16 S 5851]), suggests that he intended to produce a book that would attract a reward large enough to cover at least the costs of printing.

The first part of the collection, described on the title page as a 'small book full of testimonies by most learned men to the said Herr Paul' ('libellus plenus doctissimorum virorum de eodem D. Paulo testimoniis'), comprises poems and letters that Hofhaimer had been collecting for some three decades. This *libellus* was printed as a self-standing booklet with its own title page and its own gathering signatures (a-b8, c4). Some of these testimonials were written as spontaneous expressions of esteem, in some cases by people who had never met Hofhaimer, such as the Venetian statesman Fantin Memo, brother of Hofhaimer's student Dionisio Memo.[5] Others—notably the extended *laudatio* by Joachim Vadianus—had been actively solicited by Hofhaimer, as revealed by the correspondence between Hofhaimer and Vadianus preserved in St. Gallen.[6] Hofhaimer's letters to Vadianus reveal him as a complex personality, confident of his artistic ability, but gnawed by feelings of social inferiority and obsessed by a desire that his fame should outlast his physical body.

The four partbooks accompanying the *libellus* present thirty-five settings by Hofhaimer, and eleven further settings by other composers: nine by Ludwig Senfl, one by Hofhaimer's assistant organist Gregor Peschin, and one anonymous. It is not entirely clear whether these latter settings were composed after Hofhaimer's death by way of tribute, or represent a musical exchange between the composers written while Hofhaimer was still alive.

The selection of tenors and texts suggests that the collection was conceived as a contribution to the tradition that began with the *Melopoiae* of Petrus Tritonius and Conrad Celtis (Augsburg: Oeglin, 1507 [RISM A/I T 1249; VD16 M 4465]) and continued in Senfl's *Varia carminum genera* (Nuremberg: Formschneider, 1534 [RISM A/I S 2806; VD16 ZV 26802]). Hofhaimer knew Conrad Celtis, who had written a poem in praise of the organist, later included in the *libellus*. Furthermore, Hofhaimer was resident in Augsburg when the *Melopoiae* was published, so there is good reason to suppose that

---

[5] Hofhaimer, *Harmoniae*, ed. McDonald, 18-27.
[6] Hofhaimer, *Harmoniae*, ed. McDonald, 6-13. St. Gallen, Kantonsbibliothek, Vadianische Sammlung Ms. 30, letters 60, 61, 67, 65, 116; Ms. 31, letters 188, 190, 192, 208, 236. These letters are edited by Emil Arbenz, *Die Vadianische Briefsammlung der Stadtbibliothek St. Gallen* (St. Gallen, 1891-1913), letters 57, 59, 68, 64, 114, 392, 394, 396, 406, and 427.

he was aware of the collection.[7] If he did not own his own copy, there was one in the library of St. Peter's monastery in Salzburg, with which he was closely associated.[8] It is unknown if Hofhaimer possessed a copy of Senfl's *Varia carminum genera*, but once again there is some reason to suppose that he knew the collection, since he set twenty-five of the thirty-one texts set by Senfl in the *Varia carminum genera*. Aside from the well-known poems of Horace, Hofhaimer set a number of much less familiar texts, notably the hymns *O summe rerum conditor* and *Rerum creator maxime* by the humanist Philipp Gundelius, a former student of Vadianus who had served as advisor to Matthaeus Lang in the years around 1530. The only printed source in which Hofhaimer could have found the text of Gundelius' hymns was Senfl's *Varia carminum genera*, though of course it is also possible that he received the poems directly from Gundelius or a third party.[9] Hofhaimer's letters to Vadianus show that he and Senfl knew each other well in the second and third decades of the sixteenth century, and it is not unreasonable to imagine that they were still in contact when composing their respective sets of *harmoniae* in the 1530s. But there is a further link between the *Varia carminum genera* and the *Harmoniae poeticae*: just as Senfl's 1534 settings of Horace were reharmonizations of Tritonius's 1507 tenors, three of Senfl's 1539 settings are reharmonizations of his own tenors from the *Varia carminum genera*.[10] A line of descent may thus be traced from the *Melopoiae* to the *Varia carminum genera* and thence to the *Harmoniae poeticae*.

Once Stomius had prepared the *libellus* and the *harmoniae* for publication, he had to decide on a printer. Stomius already had a business relationship with the Augsburg printer-publisher Philipp Ulhart, who had published his edition of selections from Lucian of Samosata (1536), as well as his own music treatise (1537). The relationship did not end there; in 1553 Ulhart would print Stomius's edition of Gregory of Nazianzus.[11] However, Ulhart did not have any music type, and the musical examples in Stomius's 1537 treatise, cut from woodblocks, are not very elegant. It was probably for this reason that Stomius decided to send Hofhaimer's ode-settings instead to Johannes Petreius in Nuremberg, who by the late 1530s had two music fonts of different sizes. Stomius may have seen Petreius's small type in publications such as Sebald Heyden's *Musicae, id est artis canendi, libri duo* (Nuremberg: Petreius, 1537 [VD16 H 3380]). Petreius also had a handsome Greek type, which was required for the *libellus*.[12]

---

[7] Manfred Schuler, 'Paul Hofhaimer in seinen Beziehungen zu Augsburg', in *Musik in Bayern* 50 (1995), 11-21.

[8] The binding of a copy of *Melopoiae* (Salzburg, Universitätsbibliothek, F II 475, not registered in RISM), bound with Franchinus Gaffurius, *Practica musicae utriusque cantus* (Venice: Augustinus de Zannis, 1512), is stamped with tools from a workshop associated with St. Peter's monastery in Salzburg. On Hofhaimer's connections with the monastery, see Lothar Hoffmann-Erbrecht, 'Paul Hofhaimer in Salzburg', in *Festschrift Heinrich Besseler zum 60. Geburtstag* (Leipzig, 1961), 211-14.

[9] Further, see Franz Joseph Worstbrock, 'Gundel (Gündl, Gundelius, Gundeli, -ly, -elli), Philipp', in *Die deutsche Literatur des Mittelalters: Deutscher Humanismus 1480-1520*, ed. Franz Joseph Worstbrock, 3 vols. (Berlin, 2009-13), vol. 1, 992-1010.

[10] See Grantley McDonald, 'Notes on the Sources and Reception of Senfl's *harmoniae*', in *Senfl-Studien II*, ed. Stefan Gasch, Birgit Lodes, and Sonja Tröster, Wiener Forum für Ältere Musikgeschichte 7 (Tutzing, 2013), 623-34.

[11] LVCIANI SA ||MOSATENSIS INSOMNI ||VM, SEV VITA. AD LIBE ||ralium disciplinarum studia || commendanda plurimum || conducens. || Item Dialogus Eiusdem (Augsburg: Philipp Ulhart the Elder, January 1536 [VD16 L 3042 / L 2958]); Stomius's involvement in this edition is deduced from the presence on the title page of a poem by one of his pupils, Franciscus Paedoreus; Johannes Stomius, PRIMA AD || MVSICEN INSTRVCTIO, || eaque simplicissima, pro artis || huius tirunculis conge ||sta per Ioannem || Stomium [...] (Augsburg: Philipp Ulhart the Elder, 1537 [VD16 S 9280]); GREGORII || NAZANZENI POE ||MATA DISTICHA || ET TETRASTICHA || MORALIA (Augsburg: Philipp Ulhart the Elder, 1553 [VD16 G 3083]).

[12] Donald Krummel, 'Early German Partbook Type Faces', in *Gutenberg Jahrbuch* 60 (1985), 80-98 esp. 83-84; for a detailed description of each of Petreius's editions, see Mariko Teramoto and Armin Brinzing, *Katalog der Musikdrucke des*

The most elegant but technically most demanding way to print music from type was through multiple impression, a technique first seen in a *Graduale* printed perhaps at Constance in about 1473. This remained the most common way to print chant books for decades to come.[13] The multiple-impression technique was adapted for polyphony by Ottaviano Petrucci in around 1500, and was subsequently picked up by a number of printers in Germany: Oeglin, Mewes, Schöffer (later in partnership with Apiarius), Vietor, Grimm and Wyrsung, and Ruff.[14] While multiple impression permitted useful and attractive variations such as rubrics, red staff lines, initials, and notes, it also demanded careful alignment of the successive impressions, achieved by mounting the page on pins. It also took longer to produce, since each page had to go through the press two or even three times, depending on the exact process: once for the black type, once again for the red type; or once for the staves, and again for the notes, clefs, and text. Although the firm of Peter Schöffer and Mathias Apiarius was still using double impression until the end of the 1530s to produce its beautiful editions of polyphony, this same decade saw most German printers switch to single-impression type: Hieronymus Formschneider in Nuremberg (1534), Christian Egenolff in Frankfurt (1535), Georg Rhau in Wittenberg (1538), Hans Varnier (1538) and Hans Zurel (1539) in Ulm, and Melchior Kriegstein in Augsburg (1540).[15] When Petreius cut (or commissioned) his small music font in 1537, and his larger music font in 1538, he was following this trend for single-impression type.

Single-impression music type is quicker and easier to use than double-impression type, though less elegant and in some ways more limited. It is of two kinds: full-staff and nested. In full-staff single-impression fonts, each piece of type (or 'sort') has a note, clef, or accidental plus five lines. This kind of type was quick and relatively uncomplicated for the compositors, and when set well it could produce good results. However, it had two major disadvantages. Firstly, a full-staff single-impression font required a large initial outlay. Cutting each punch required several hours of a skilled worker's time, and the number of sorts in such a font was considerable. A printer would therefore have to be sure that he was going to print music regularly to justify the investment. It is no coincidence that amongst German printers who produced polyphony in the 1530s, full-staff type was only used by Egenolff, Rhau, and Formschneider, who positioned themselves to some extent as specialist music printers. The other disadvantage of full-staff type, which became clear over time, was that the gaps between the individual pieces became visible as the type wore down or was set too loosely, thus breaking up the horizontal continuity of the staff lines.

Nested single-impression fonts work a little differently. Each sort has a clef, an accidental, or a note head (with a stem where required) attached to two, three, or four staff lines, and sitting either on a staff line or in a space. The only pieces of type covering five staff lines are generally those for bar lines. The compositors aligned these sorts vertically with non-printing spacers half the height of one staff line, which allowed the staff lines on each sort to line up. Blank sections of staff were filled in with rule lines of varying lengths, inserted in the gaps between the sorts as required, and kept in place by the non-printing

---

Johannes Petreius in Nürnberg, Catalogus Musicus 14 (Kassel, 1993).
[13] Mary Kay Duggan, *Italian Music Incunabula: Printers and Type* (Berkeley, 1992), 13-14.
[14] On Petrucci, see Stanley Boorman, *Ottaviano Petrucci: A Catalogue Raisonné* (Oxford, 2006).
[15] It should however be noted that many printers who had no music type continued to print music from woodcut. This list adds two printers not named in Krummel, 'Early German Partbook Type Faces': Varnier and Zurel.

spacers. Johann Winterburger (Vienna) and Melchior Lotter the Elder (Leipzig) had been using this technique to print chant from at least 1509. Using nested type produced smoother results than full-staff type, since the empty staff lines were longer—sometimes much longer—than a single note's width, and the gaps in the lines consequently fewer in number. Nested type also allowed the compositor to set two or more symbols (say a note surmounted by a fermata or a sharp sign) in the same vertical axis, something that was practically impossible to achieve with full-staff type. Furthermore, cutting a font of nested type was less expensive than cutting full-staff type: polyphonic white notation could be set with a font comprising fewer than half the number of sorts as were required for a full-staff type. This meant a smaller initial outlay and smaller risk, useful if a printer was not sure how much music he was likely to produce in future. The only real down side of nested type was that it was fiddly—the compositor had to set the pieces vertically as well as horizontally. Despite this inconvenience, nested type was quite popular amongst German printers for whom polyphonic music comprised a relatively small percentage of their total output: Petreius (eleven titles during the decade 1531-40), Kriegstein (four editions during the same period, using Petreius's type), Hans Varnier (one edition), and Hans Zurel (one edition). Even over the course of Petreius's entire working life, music played a relatively marginal role: out of the 652 titles assigned to him in VD16, only twenty-one contain music. Using nested type permitted Petreius to produce an elegant result without investing too much in the initial cost of a full-staff music font.

A close examination of the typesetting of a sample page of Hofhaimer's *Harmoniae poeticae* reveals much about the printer's working method (see Figures 1-4, where each change of type in the first system is indicated). Once each page had been printed for its respective partbook, the compositor did not redistribute the type into its cases, but untied the page cord holding the forme together, and changed only what was absolutely necessary to set up the forme for the next partbook. Since the rhythm in a metrical *harmonia* is identical in every voice part, the compositor could keep the nested type in place if a given note was in the same position on the staff as it had been in the previous partbook. Sometimes he adjusted the spacing between the systems to avoid collisions between the notes and the underlaid text. For example, when fol. a2v of the *media vox* was being set up as fol. aa2v of the *alta vox*, the compositor removed a single spacer one staff line high (or perhaps two spacers, each half a staff line high) above the third system, and added the same space above the fourth system to allow for a brevis on the top line of the staff. This altered the distance between the staves, avoiding unsightly crowding of notes and text, but leaving the total printed area of the page unchanged. The only other change the compositor needed to make was to alter the signatures for each partbook: fol. a1r in the *media vox* partbook became aa1 in the *alta*, A1 in the *infima*, AA1 in the *suprema*, and so forth. Following all such changes from one partbook to the next reveals that they were printed in the following order: *media vox, alta vox, infima vox*, and finally *suprema vox*.

Errors in the *media vox* which were subsequently corrected in the other partbooks show that the compositors treated the *media vox* as a galley proof. Rather than running off a single copy of each sheet and handing it over to the corrector before continuing the run, the press men avoided this delay by letting the correctors check each sheet of the *media vox* while they printed the next one; any corrections that had to be made were introduced only in the *alta vox*. Besides emendations suggested by the corrector, the printers sometime introduced inadvertent corruptions of the text. For example, on line 16 of fol. a2v, the first

Figure 1. Paul Hofhaimer, *Harmoniae poeticae* (1539), *media vox*, fol. a2v. Universitätsbibliothek Salzburg 2369 I Rarum. With permission

Figure 2. Paul Hofhaimer, *Harmoniae poeticae* (1539), *alta vox*, fol. aa2v. Universitätsbibliothek Salzburg 2369 I Rarum. With permission

Figure 3. Paul Hofhaimer, *Harmoniae poeticae* (1539), *infima vox*, fol. A2v. Universitätsbibliothek Salzburg 2369 I Rarum. With permission

Figure 4. Paul Hofhaimer, *Harmoniae poeticae* (1539), *suprema vox*, fol. AA2v. Universitätsbibliothek Salzburg 2369 I Rarum. With permission

two letters of 'damæ' dropped out of the forme after the *media vox* was printed, perhaps when the page cord was untied. When setting up the *alta vox*, the compositor accidentally replaced these letters upside-down. This error was evidently pointed out to him by the corrector, and he rectified it when setting up the *infima vox* partbook.

Besides the corrections made during the print run, the extant copies of the *Harmoniae poeticae* include a small number of 'in-house corrections' made by hand in dark grey ink by a corrector in Petreius's workshop after the print run was finished, but before the copies were sold.[16] These were usually made by hand, though in one case an incorrect note value was corrected with an inked piece of type used as a stamp.

When planning the book, Petreius had to decide a number of factors of mise-en-page which would affect the way in which the book was perceived and used. It is unknown how much input Stomius had in this part of the process. Two fundamental decisions were page format and the choice between choirbook layout or partbooks. Before Senfl's *Varia carminum genera*, all printed collections of quantitative ode settings had appeared in choirbook layout. The first of these was Tritonius's *Melopoiae* (Figure 5).

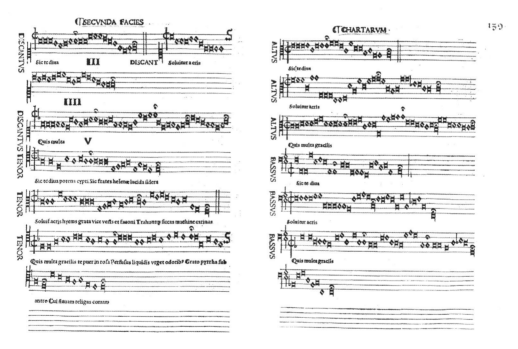

Figure 5. Petrus Tritonius, *Melopoiae* (Augsburg: Erhard Oeglin, 1507 [VD16 M 4465]), fols. 3v-4r. Munich, Bayerische Staatsbibliothek, Rar. 291. With permission

---

[16] For example, *alta vox*, bb4r: C2 clef in the second system corrected by hand in dark grey ink to a C1 clef; *infima vox*, C4v: custos at the end of the third system corrected in dark grey ink from *d* to *f*; *suprema vox* CC5r, flat added in dark grey ink just after the second *e* breve.

With its impressive folio format, two full-page woodcuts and its elegant double impression music type, *Melopoiae* is visually appealing as an object, and would have appealed to humanistic collectors.[17] However, it poses two problems for the singers. Firstly, there are many errors in the musical text. Secondly, the choirbook layout and large page format cause problems of orientation: since these pieces are quite short, Oeglin placed several of them on each opening. He numbered each piece with Roman numerals, but the numbers are not placed above each piece, as one would expect, but below, which can cause confusion to the singers, who must orient themselves with less ambiguous cues like text underlay (limited to incipits in all voices but the tenor), clefs, and custodes. Perhaps as a result of this unsuccessful experiment, no printer ever used folio format again for ode settings. When Oeglin reprinted Tritonius's Horace settings later the same year, under the title *Harmonie Petri Tritonii super odis Horatii Flacci* (Augsburg: Oeglin, 22 August 1507 [RISM A/I T 1250; VD16 H 4954]), he not only corrected the errors in the music, but also chose quarto format, which allowed him to dedicate an entire opening to each setting, thus avoiding the problems of orientation that had made the folio edition so awkward to use. It also gave him space to include the description of each of Horace's metres, borrowed from Nicolo Perotti's *De generibus metrorum*, first published in 1471 and often reprinted (Figure 6).

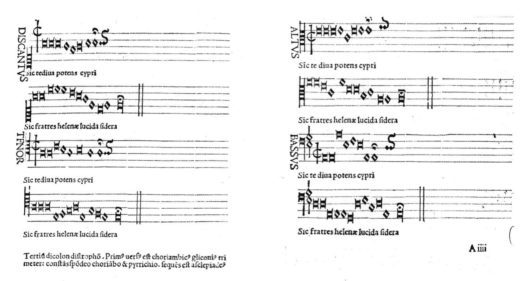

Figure 6. *Harmonie Petri Tritonii super odis Horatii Flacci* (Augsburg: Oeglin, 1507 [RISM A/I T 1250; VD16 H 4954]), fols. A3v-A4r. Munich, Bayerische Staatsbibliothek, 4 Mus. pr. 89. With permission

---

[17] The decision to print the *Melopoiae* in folio format may have been determined in part by the desire to include the two large woodcuts. The woodcut of Apollo playing the *lira* or fiddle on fol. A2r had apparently been cut for Celtis at least five years before the *Melopoiae* was printed, but had not yet been used in any of his publications. It is one of a pair of woodcuts cut by the same hand, and based on illuminations by Giampietro Birago (Wolfenbüttel, Herzog August Bibliothek, Cod. Guelf. 277.4 Extrav., fols. 1v and 23r). It is likely that both woodcuts were made together, by 1502 at the latest, since the other woodcut of the pair (Apollo and Daphne) was printed in Celtis's *Quatuor libri amorum* (Nuremberg: Sodalitas Celtica, 1502 [VD16 C 1911]). Further, see Peter Luh, *Kaiser Maximilian gewidmet: Die unvollendete Werkausgabe des Conrad Celtis und ihre Holzschnitte* (Frankfurt, 2001), 210-38.

An opening of a book in quarto format could hold a complete ode-setting in choirbook layout, underlaid with one strophe of the text. This could usually be managed in a book printed in octavo, provided that the setting was not too long (Figure 7).

Figure 7. Sebastian Forster and Lucas Hordisch, *Melodiae Prudentianae* (Leipzig: Faber, 1533 [VD16 ZV 17301]), fols. A3v-A4r. London, British Library, K.8.b.14. With permission

If the setting was a little longer, one voice part sometimes ran over to the next opening. This made it impossible for four people to sing at sight from the same copy (Figure 8).

Figure 8. Sebastian Forster and Lucas Hordisch, *Melodiae Prudentianae* (Leipzig: Faber, 1533 [VD16 ZV 17301]), fols. A6v-A7r. London, British Library, K.8.b.14. With permission

In such a case, a group of singers sight-reading would have required at least two copies in order to allow the bass to turn the page while the others remained on the previous opening. Thus the choirbook format belies what is in effect a partbook, or perhaps a repository from which individual voice parts could be copied out by hand.

Figure 9. Sebald Heyden, *Catechistica summRegensburg, Staatliche Bibliothek Regensburg*, Staatliche Bibliothek, 999/Past.173 (angeb. 3). With permission

Figure 10. Sebald Heyden, *Catechistica summula fidei Christianae* (Nuremberg: Petreius, 1538), fols. b6v-b7r. Regensburg, Staatliche Bibliothek, 999/Past.173 (angeb. 3). With permission

Figure 11. Sebald Heyden, *Catechistica summula fidei Christianae* (Nuremberg: Petreius, 1538), fols. b7v-b8r. Regensburg, Staatliche Bibliothek, 999/Past.173 (angeb. 3). With permission

When a printer tried to squeeze long ode-settings with multiple strophes onto octavo pages while maintaining choirbook layout, problems of mise-en-page could become acute (Figures 9-11). At the end of Sebald Heyden's *Catechistica summula fidei Christianae* (Nuremberg: Petreius, 1538 [VD16 ZV 7913]), a précis of Lutheran doctrine, Petreius printed Senfl's quantitative settings of Heyden's own school hymns *Ades pater benigne* and *Deus o pater optime magni*. Petreius had run out of room at the end of the volume, and evidently did not wish to add another gathering. He thus attempted instead to economize on space. As a result of this makeshift solution, the layout of these pieces is initially quite confusing. The first setting has three stanzas of text, but there was not enough space to underlay all three stanzas under each of the voices. Instead, Petreius underlaid stanza 1 under the discantus, stanza 2 under the tenor, and stanza 3 under the altus and bassus, providing the singers with some orientation by placing the numerals 1 to 3 in the margin, but offering no further explanation. At first sight, the piece looks as though the three texts are to be sung simultaneously. Singers could even be forgiven for concluding that these are separate monophonic melodies with different texts. It takes some figuring out to realize exactly what the singers are supposed to do. In the second hymn-setting, the singers are once again faced with the awkward necessity of singing their parts to words written beneath another voice-part for three out of the four stanzas. While this layout saved space and money, it is distinctly unfriendly to sight-reading. However, neither of Petreius's reprints of these pieces (1543 and 1548), nor those by Berg und Neuber (1545), Philipp Ulhart (c. 1560), or Michael Manger (1578), made any attempt to remedy these difficulties. The practical problems of using this book suggest either that those who used it learned the music and text thoroughly and sang at least in part from memory, or that they used the printed book to copy out their own voice parts by hand.

Figure 12. Ludwig Senfl, *Varia carminum genera* (Nuremberg: Formschneider, 1534 [RISM A/I S 2806, VD16 ZV 26802]), cantus secundus, fols. A1v-A2r. Munich, Bayerische Staatsbibliothek, Mus.pr. 35 Beibd.2. With permission

By contrast with the frequently cramped appearance of choirbook layout in octavo format, Senfl's *Varia carminum genera* appeared in partbooks, in oblong octavo (Figure 12). In the first half of the sixteenth century, German printers usually used oblong format for polyphonic partbooks, most commonly in quarto or octavo, but sometimes even in sexto, the format favoured by Oeglin and Schöffer for their polyphonic *Liederbücher*.[18] In Senfl's *Varia carminum genera*, the music is presented on the left side of each opening, fully underlaid, with the subsequent stanzas on the facing page. Formschneider used this same page format and mis-en-page for his anthologies of German songs.[19]

Figure 13. Paul Hofhaimer, *Harmoniae poeticae* (Nuremberg: Johannes Petreius, 1539 [RISM B/I 1539[26], VD16 H 4960]), media vox, fols. a1v-a2r. Salzburg, Universitätsbibliothek, 2369 I Rarum. With permission

[18] Donald W. Krummel, 'Oblong Format in Early Music Books', in *The Library*, 5th series, 26 (1971), 312-24.
[19] Further on Formschneider as a printer, see Royston R. Gustavson, 'Hans Ott, Hieronymus Formschneider, and the *Novum et insigne opus musicum* (Nuremberg 1537-38)', (Ph.D. diss., University of Melbourne, 1998).

The spacious appearance of Senfl's book may have prompted Stomius (or Petreius) to present the *Harmoniae poeticae* in a similarly elegant and user-friendly way, far from the impractical layout of Heyden's *Catechistica summula fidei Christianae*. However, there is one difference: the partbooks of the *Harmoniae poeticae*, uniquely for their time and place, are printed in *upright* octavo, a format which by the fourth decade of the sixteenth century had become standard for literary works and school text books, but which was unknown for music books (Figure 13). This suggests that the person responsible for determining the format, whether Stomius or Petreius, considered the literary testimonia collected in the *libellus* at least as important as the music, if not more important.

In summary, the mise-en-page of Hofhaimer's *Harmoniae poeticae* reveals much about the conception and intended function of this book, as a literary collection as much as a musical one. The experience of printing Senfl's two ode settings in Sebald Heyden's *Catechistica summula* in 1538 had taught Petreius that choirbook layout works badly on octavo pages if the settings are too long to fit on a single opening. By contrast, inspecting Senfl's *Varia carminum genera* may have shown Petreius and Stomius that partbooks are a better solution for a repertoire in which each piece could fit on a single page or a single opening. Tracing the minor changes in the Latin text from one partbook of the *Harmoniae poeticae* to the next permitted us to determine the order in which the partbooks were printed. This in turn revealed that Petreius's compositors did not redistribute the music type after printing each sheet of each partbook, but left as much type in place as possible. An intensive examination of the details of an individual edition, especially when compared with similar editions, thus reveals much about the possibilities offered—and constraints imposed—by every decision made in the process of planning, typesetting and printing a collection of music.

Abstract

The genre of the *harmonia* (or humanist ode setting) presented printers with particular problems of mise-en-page. Because the settings tended to be quite short, while containing a lot of text, printers had to decide how to present them in a way that was easy to follow. Several different solutions were attempted: choirbook layout in folio, quarto, and octavo, and partbooks in oblong and upright octavo. The *Harmoniae poeticae* of Paul Hofhaimer were prefaced by a volume of encomia and memorial poetry, a circumstance which influenced the choice of format for the entire collection. The present investigation also examines the process of setting nested polyphonic type, and explains why this kind of type, cheaper than the full-staff type used by printers such as Attaingnant and Formschneider, may have proven attractive to a printer like Petreius, for whom music was only a relatively minor part of his total output.

*Free Papers*

A King, a Pope, and a War: Economic Crisis and *Faulte d'argent* Settings in the Opening Decades of the Sixteenth Century[*]

Vassiliki Koutsobina

Financial strain was hardly the exception in late fifteenth-century Europe. War was nearly continuous with major expeditions constantly mounted by important European powers. As a result, entire generations not only lived under the shadow of war but were also forced literally to pay for its immense expenses. In order to raise funds for their wars and maintain their rapidly emptying treasuries, rulers in this period instituted regular taxation. Literary sources from the late fifteenth and early sixteenth centuries provide an excellent record of people's concerns with the ill effects of war, the intense desire for peace, and the constant demand for currency. More specifically, turn-of-the-century French sources showcase a preoccupation with the topic of 'faulte d'argent' (lack of money) that reaches its peak shortly after 1510. Remarkable—albeit having so far escaped musicological attention—is the fact that during exactly the same period polyphonic settings of a presumably popular *Faulte d'argent* tune first emerge in the musical sources.[1] The present essay brings together a chronologically dense agglomeration of historical, literary, and musical testimonies related to the theme of 'lack of money' and explores the extent to which the political and economic landscape might have contributed to the genesis of the *Faulte d'argent* network of polyphonic songs.

At least three *Faulte d'argent* settings were composed in the opening decade of the sixteenth century or shortly thereafter.[2] Josquin des Prez's five-voice *Faulte d'argent*, which eventually became one of the most popular of his chansons, first appears under his name in AugsS 142a, an anthology compiled between 1505 and 1514.[3] The chanson

---

[*] Earlier versions of this study were read at the Medieval and Renaissance Music Conference, Utrecht, 4 July 2009, the Annual Meeting of the American Musicological Society, Indianapolis, 5 November 2010, and the 19th Congress of the International Musicological Society, Rome, 2 July 2012. I am particularly grateful to Prof. Edward Nowacki and Prof. Stephanie P. Schlagel for their helpful comments on an earlier draft. Manuscript citations follow those used in the Herbert Kellman and Charles Ham (eds.), *Census Catalogue of Manuscript Sources of Polyphonic Music, 1400-1550* (s. l., 1979-88). Sigla for print sources are those found in *Recueils imprimés XVIe-XVIIe siècles*, ser. B/1 (Munich, 1960) [RISM B1]. All translations are the author's except where otherwise noted.

[1] The *Faulte d'argent* tune can only be reconstructed from the surviving polyphonic settings since no such melody appears in the two central French chansonniers that preserve monophonic repertories (ParisBNF 9346 and ParisBNF 12744).

[2] For a comprehensive account of sixteenth-century chansons related to *Faulte d'argent* see Jacques Barbier, '*Faulte d'argent*: Fortune d'un thème littéraire et musical à la Renaissance', 3 vols. (Ph.D. thesis, Université de Tours, 1985) and Jacques Barbier, '*Faulte d'argent*: Modèles polyphoniques et parodies au XVIe siècle', in *Revue de Musicologie* 73 (1987), 171-202 at 183.

[3] Augsburg, Staats- und Stadtbibliothek, Ms. 2° 142a (*olim* Cim. 43; = SchlettKK #18). Modern edition by Luise Jonas, *Das Augsburger Liederbuch: Die Musikhandschrift 2° Codex 142a der Staats- und Stadtbibliothek Augsburg. Edition und Kommentar*, 2 vols., Berliner Musikwissenschaftliche Arbeiten 21 (Munich-Salzburg, 1983). Josquin's chanson survives in nine sixteenth-century manuscript and printed sources. See Peter Urquhart, 'Susato's *Le septiesme livre* (1545) and the Persistence of Exact Canon', in *Tielman Susato and the Music of His Time: Print Culture, Compositional Technique and Instrumental Music in the Renaissance*, ed. Keith Polk (Hillsdale, 2005), 172. Urquhart does not include the now lost *Livre de meslanges* (Paris, 1560) (not in RISM). Another possible testament to the chanson's popularity is the fact that Jean Richafort quoted *Faulte d'argent* in his Requiem mass for Josquin. For a rhetorical analysis of Josquin's five-voice

is placed amidst other Josquin compositions, while, a few folios later, a four-voice arrangement of the same tune opens a section of anonymous and textless settings. Another *Faulte d'argent* setting, this time by Antoine de Févin, appears in CambriP 1760, a manuscript associated with the French royal court and compiled between 1509 and 1514, thus absolutely contemporary with the Augsburg anthology.[4] As Lawrence Bernstein has convincingly demonstrated, Févin modelled his three-part arrangement upon Josquin's five-voice chanson.[5] Therefore, Févin's death date in late 1511 or early 1512 provides a *terminus ante quem* for both his and Josquin's settings.[6] The earliest source to provide the entire text underlaid in all voices is the chansonnier FlorC 2442, in which Josquin's song takes pride of place as the opening piece, while a four-voice homonymous setting by Nicole Beauvoys closes the anthology.[7] Howard Mayer Brown held the view that the four partbooks that comprise FlorC 2442 were copied in Florence between 1518 and 1527, but the manuscript's provenance and dating remain a matter of dispute.[8] By exploring the political, economic, and social circumstances surrounding the composition and dissemination of *Faulte d'argent* settings, this essay throws additional light on the origin and chronology of FlorC 2442.

Literary sources from the late fifteenth and early sixteenth centuries reveal four related poems starting with the line 'Faulte d'argent, c'est douleur non-pareille' (Figures 1-4). The earliest seems to be the ballade *Faulte d'argent, la douleur nonpareille*, copied c. 1483 on fol. 1 of a Ministry of Justice document by a financial clerk (Paris, Bibliothèque nationale, Ms. fr. 5727; Figure 1).[9] It consists of six eight-line stanzas that describe the miseries one has to face from lack of money. The inclusion of a ballade in a judicial document seems odd at first glance. However, Ms. 5727, assembled during Louis XI's reign, abounds in letters and applications of pleading grace for overdue debts.[10] More importantly for the present conversation, the ballade's strongly expressed views on the impact of lack of money on one's life and social relationships demonstrate how indispensable currency had become by the end of the fifteenth century.

---

setting see my dissertation 'Musical Rhetoric in the Multi-Voice Chansons of Josquin des Prez and His Contemporaries (c. 1500-c. 1520)' (Ph.D. diss., University of Cincinnati, 2008), 212-26.

[4] Cambridge, Magdalene College, Pepys Library, Ms. 1760. Facsimile edition by Howard M. Brown, Renaissance Music in Facsimile 2 (New York, 1988).

[5] Lawrence F. Bernstein, 'Josquin's Chansons as Generic Paradigms', in *Music in Renaissance Cities and Courts: Studies in Honor of Lewis Lockwood*, ed. Jessie A. Owens and Anthony M. Cummings, Detroit Monographs in Musicology 18 (Warren MI, 1997), 51-55.

[6] According to Bernstein, Josquin cannot have borrowed from Févin because the order of borrowing is out of sequence from the order of the events in the model, whereas Févin, borrowing from Josquin, incorporates elements of Josquin's polyphony in the precise order in which they appear. Bernstein, 'Josquin's Chansons', 53. Bernstein further connects the genesis of the five-voice chanson genre, of which Josquin's *Faulte d'argent* is one of the earliest examples, with the French royal court and emphasizes Josquin's contribution to the diverse character of secular polyphony at the court of Louis XII. Bernstein, 'Josquin's Chansons', 47-51, 55. I have elsewhere suggested that 'the popular monophonic melody known as *Faulte d'argent* either originated or was revived at the French royal court of Louis XII' (see Koutsobina, 'Musical Rhetoric', 217).

[7] Florence, Biblioteca del Conservatorio di Musica Luigi Cherubini, Ms. Basevi 2442 ('Strozzi Chansonnier').

[8] Howard M. Brown, 'Chansons for the Pleasure of a Florentine Patrician: Florence, Biblioteca del Conservatorio di Musica, Ms. Basevi 2442', in *Aspects of Medieval and Renaissance Music: A Birthday Offering to Gustave Reese*, ed. Jan La Rue (New York, 1966), 65-66. For opposing views regarding the provenance and dating of FlorC 2442 see fn. 43, 44, and 45.

[9] Marcel M. Schwob (ed.), *Le parnasse satyrique du quinzième siècle: anthologie des pièces libres* (Paris, 1905; repr. Geneva, 1969), 302. Schwob's edition is a selection of poems derived from ten different manuscripts, Ms. fr. 5727 being one of them. The boldface type in Figure 1 highlights recurring phrases in different *Faulte d'argent* versions and other related poems (see discussion below, especially Figures 2-4).

[10] Olivier Guyotjeannin and Serge Lusignan (eds.), *Le formulaire d'Odart Morschesne dans la version du ms BnF fr. 5024* (Paris, 2005), 88-89.

Faulte d'argent, la douleur nonpareille.	Lack of money, sorrow unequalled.
Le destourbier de tout esbatement,	The disturbance of all pleasure,
A povreté m'a donné accointance	It made me acquainted with poverty,
Parquoy je pers tout mon avancement.	This is how I lost all of my profit.
A moy deffault sens et entendement,	5 Now I lack sense and reason
Et de mon mal nully ne me conseille:	And no one advises me about my misfortune:
Car chacun scet que j'ay communement	Because everyone knows that I simply have
Faulte d'argent, la douleur nonpareille.	Lack of money, sorrow unequalled.
Tout mon maintien, semblant et contenance	My entire behaviour, appearance and air
Sont incertains, et de nul hardement.	10 Are uncertain, and without nerve.
Mes jeux, mes dicts sont prins en desplaisance.	My eyes, my words are taken by displeasure.
Quant je m'esbaz, je le foiz fainctement	When I find pleasure, I dissemble
Et tout me fault porter couvertement	And everything has to be done secretly
Et en grant dueil, **dont ce n'est pas merveille:**	And painfully, which is no wonder:
De tout cecy est cause entierement	15 Of all this the cause is entirely
Faulte d'argent, la douleur nonpareille.	Lack of money, sorrow unequalled.
Presque à tous ceux à qui j'ay eu fiance	To almost all whom I trusted
Ay remonstré mon fait secretement	I have secretly revealed my cause
Ausquelz j'avoye ma parfaicte esperance	From them I had the greatest hope
D'avoir secours et ayde aucunement.	20 To find some consolation and help.
Nescio vos m'ont dit tout plainement:	'Go away' they have told me plainly:
D'autres assez m'ont fait **la sourde oreille**.	Others pretended they did not hear.
Ainsi reboute mon cas villainement	So it rejects my case nastily
Faulte d'argent, la douleur nonpareille.	Lack of money, sorrow unequalled.
A mon besoing j'ay bien eu congoissance	25 While in need, I became well aware
Lesquelz du monde m'amoient parfaictement:	Of who the ones were that fully loved me:
Aucuns qui sont me font belle semblance,	Some of them show me their sympathy
Mais ne me font aucun secourement.	But do not offer any help.
Mon fait est bas; car tout finablement	My situation is pitiful; because finally
En dangier suis d'aler boire à la seille,	30 I am in danger of putting myself to an end,
Moy et tous ceulz qui ont semblablement	I and all those who similarly have
Faulte d'argent, la douleur nonpareille.	Lack of money, sorrow unequalled.
Riz, ditz et jeux mettray en obliance	Laughs, songs, and games, I will have to forget
Si *de quibus* ne vient prouchainement.	If cash does not come in immediately.
Tout, quant que j'ay, m'est baillé à creance.	35 Everything, if I have any, is given to me by credit.
Point d'argent n'ay, et en doy largement.	I have no money at all, and I am in great debt.
Pour dire vray, il advient bien souvent	To be honest, it often happens
Que disner n'ay, ne qui le m'appareille:	That I have nothing to eat or wear:
Par quoy je souffre impatientement	Which is why I impatiently suffer from
Faulte d'argent, la douleur nonpareille.	40 Lack of money, sorrow unequalled.
Se mon desir feult à mon ordonnance	If my desires obeyed my will
J'eusse des biens pour mon estorement.	I would have stored some wealth.
Mais, quant je puis, je foiz à ma plaisance	Instead, whenever I can, I satisfy my desires
Aucunes foiz plus que commandement.	Sometimes more than I can afford.
Fructus ventris en est le fondement	45 'The fruit of thy womb' lies beneath
C'est le soucy qui par nuyt me réveille.	It is the worries that wake me up at night.
Pour ce que j'ay continuellement	Thus I continuously have
Faulte d'argent, la douleur nonpareille.	Lack of money, sorrow unequalled.

Figure 1. Ballade *Faulte d'argent, la douleur nonpareille*, Paris, Bibliothèque nationale, Ms. fr. 5727, fol. 1 (c. 1483)

The *quatrain* set by Josquin is a humorous complaint on financial worries (Figure 2). Besides the opening line, this *quatrain* has two more common elements with the above ballade. Line 34 of the ballade reads 'Si de quibus ne vient prouchenement' and line 46 'C'est le soucy qui par nuyt me réveille'. The use of the Latin word 'quibus' for 'cash' cannot have been a coincidence, nor could the idea that financial worries can wake someone up in the middle of the night.[11]

Faulte d'argent, c'est dolleur non pareille.	Lack of money is sorrow unequalled.
Se ie le dis, las, ie sçay bien pourquoy:	If I say this, alas, I well know why:
Sans *de quibus* il se fault tenir quoy;	Without cash one has to remain silent;
Femme qui dort pour argent on l'esveille.[12]	A woman who sleeps will awake for money.[13]

Figure 2. Josquin des Prez, *Faulte d'argent*, text after FlorC 2442

A related seven-stanza chanson (Figure 3) was included in one of the earliest printed chanson-verse anthologies, published in Paris c. 1512.[14] Elements from the *Faulte d'argent quatrain* appear in stanzas 1 and 3. It is possible that the ballade served as model for both the seven-stanza chanson and the *quatrain* set by Josquin (see the boldfaced lines in Figures 1, 2, and 3). The chanson apparently was a success, since it was reprinted in two ensuing editions; the second of the two, dating c. 1515, actually celebrates *Faulte d'argent* as its opening piece.[15]

Faulte d'argent, c'est douleur non pareille.	Lack of money is sorrow unequalled.
Se je le dis, las, je sçay bien pourquoy:	If I say this, alas, I well know why:
Sans *de quibus* il se fault tenir quoy;	Without cash one has to remain silent;
Le temps le doibt, **ce n'est pas de merveille.**	No wonder why, it's a sign of the times.
Mes compaignons, a tous je vous conseille	My companions, an advice to all of you
Que ne prenez femme s'el n'a dequoy;	Do not take a wife if she does not have the means.
Raison pourquoy? Las, je la vous diray:	The reason why? Alas, I will tell you:
Quant elle dort, pour l'argent on l'esveille.	When she sleeps, she will awake for money.

Figure 3. *Faulte d'argent* (from *S'ensuivent plusieurs belles chansons nouvelles* [Paris?, c. 1512?]), stanzas 1 and 3

Another *Faulte d'argent* poem appeared in Pierre Fabri's treatise *Le grand et vray art de pleine rhétorique*, published in 1521 but written about a decade earlier.[16] Fabri's

---

[11] According to the *Dictionnaire du moyen français*, the Latin word 'quibus' meant 'avec quoi'. In the sixteenth century 'quibus' stood for 'cash'. Algirdas J. Greimas and Teresa M. Keane, *Dictionnaire du moyen français: la Renaissance* (Paris, 1992), 519.
[12] FlorC 2442, No. 1.
[13] Translation by Lawrence F. Bernstein, 'Chansons for Five and Six Voices', in *The Josquin Companion*, ed. Richard Sherr (Oxford, 2000), 397. I have substituted 'cash' for 'money' in line 3.
[14] The earliest printed chanson-verse anthologies have no indication of printer, date, or place. Brian Jeffery suggests they were published by the widow of the Parisian printer Jean Ier Trepperel during the period c. 1512-25. See Brian Jeffery (ed.), *Chanson Verse of the Early Renaissance*, 2 vols. (London, 1971-76), vol. 1, 20-22. The earliest extant print—which includes *Faulte d'argent*—is titled *S'ensuivent plusieurs belles chansons nouvelles* and Jeffery speculates a date not much later than 1512 (Jeffery, *Chanson Verse*, vol. 1, 21). For the complete seven-stanza chanson see Jeffery, *Chanson Verse*, vol. 1, 55-57. Later editions of the same poem reappeared in 1535, 1537, 1538, and 1543. See Howard M. Brown, *Music in the French Secular Theater, 1440-1550* (Cambridge, 1963), 218 No. 131c and Jeffery, *Chanson Verse*, vol. 2, 282 for the subsequent editions.
[15] Jeffery, *Chanson Verse*, vol. 1, 107 and 116-17.
[16] Pierre Fabri, *Le grand et vrai art de pleine rhétorique*, ed. A. Héron, 3 vols. (Rouen, 1890), vol. 2, 85.

poem unfolds in two stanzas, but, besides the opening line, there seems to be no further relationship with the other three texts (Figure 4).

Faulte d'argent, c'est douleur nonpareille.	Lack of money is sorrow unequalled.
Mourir m'en voys, et tiens tout seullement	I am going to die, and I only wish
Que je n'ay rien **fors la puce en l'oreille;**	That I had nothing but a burning desire;
Et tout me vient par deffaulte d'argent.	And everything happens due to lack of money.
Ie suis tout nud, aussi nud que le ver,	I am all naked, as naked as a worm,
Et n'ay sur moy ung poure abillemenet.	And I have no poor clothes on me.
Ie meurs de froit, et si n'est point yver;	I am freezing to death, even if it is not winter;
Et tout me vient par deffaulte d'argent.	And everything happens due to lack of money.

Figure 4. Pierre Fabri, *Faulte d'argent* (c. 1512; from *Le grant et vrai art de pleine rhétorique* [Rouen, 1521])

The concern with lack of money also figures prominently in the poetry of Roger de Collerye (1470-1536). No less than nine rondeaux incorporate the phrase 'Faulte d'argent', while references to metallic currency are omnipresent in Collerye's output ('or et argent' being a recurring expression).[17] It is no coincidence that the poet chose for himself the nickname 'Roger Bontemps'—that is, friend of good times, gaiety, and prosperity—whose eternal enemy is none other than Faulte d'argent. An interesting reference to the line 'Faulte d'argent, c'est doleur nonpareille' comes from a later source, François Rabelais's *Pantagruel*, first published in the 1530s. When describing the figure Panurge, Rabelais says that he suffered from a disease 'qu'on appelloit en ce temps là, *faulte d'argent c'est doleur non pareille*' ('called back then, *lack of money sorrow unequalled*').[18] Apparently, Panurge was coming of age at the turn of the sixteenth century, since he recounts how he was captured at Mytilene in 1502.[19] Thus it seems that Rabelais connects the *Faulte d'argent* topos with an early sixteenth-century context.

An important contemporary source mentioning the chanson *Faulte d'argent, c'est douleur nonpareille* is Pierre Gringore's *sottie*, *Le jeu du Prince des Sotz,* performed in Paris on 23 February 1512. The *sottie* is a satirical criticism on the conflict between King Louis XII and Pope Julius II during the period 1510-12 and thus reflects events absolutely contemporaneous with its time of performance. A basic knowledge and understanding of the political situation at the time is necessary in order to grasp the *sottie*'s content and importance as a record of historical events, and for understanding the emergence of polyphonic *Faulte d'argent* settings. The period 1510-12 marked the climax of the confrontation between Louis XII and Julius II, as a result of the pope's violation of the Treaty of Cambrai. This treaty was signed in 1508 by the allied forces of the French king (Louis XII), the king of Naples (Ferdinand of Aragon), the Roman emperor (Maximilian),

---

[17] The chansons are: *Au despourveu qui n'a la seulle bousche, Au pied du mur je me voy sans eschelle, D'ung tel ennuy que je souffre et endure, Faulte d'argent est douleur nonpareille, Le suppliant qui demande secours, Mon bon Seigneur, soyez le bien venu, Par accident je suis prins de froidure, Par ce temps cher mon corps est consumé, Trop asprement nécessité me maine*. Roger de Collerye, *Oeuvres de Roger de Collerye*, ed. Charles d' Héricault (Paris, 1855).
[18] François Rabelais, *Oeuvres complètes*, ed. Mireille Huchon with François Moreau (Paris, 1994), 272. Interestingly, Eustache Dechamps also refers to lack of money as a disease ('maladie') in his ballade *Maladie d'argent*: 'J'ay par cinq ans esté en maladie / Dont mire nul ne m'a voulu guerir / De pou d'argent, on maint homme mendie'; Eustache Dechamps, *Oeuvres complètes*, ed. Le Marquis de Queux de Saint-Hilaire, 11 vols. (Paris, 1876), vol. 5, 93.
[19] Rabelais, *Oeuvres,* 249 n. 7 at 1278.

and the pontiff (Julius II) with the purpose of forming a league against Venice, a threat to all involved. King Louis attacked the Republic of Venice in April 1509 and achieved an important victory at Agnadello. Following Louis's Venetian conquests however, the pope, fearing French expansionism in Italy, reconciled with Venice and replaced the League of Cambrai with a Holy League, this time against France.

To confront the pope's aggressive move, Louis announced a convocation of Christian leaders to take place in September 1511 in Pisa. The pope retaliated by calling an ecumenical council planned for April 1512.[20] The Pisa synod proved to be no easy affair, as the English, Spanish, and Italian cardinals remained faithful to the pontiff. France's ally Florence suffered the pope's wrath for allowing the council to take place in its territory and refusing to join the Holy League. Julius placed an interdict upon Florence, prohibited trade with the Levant, and arrested all Florentine merchants in Rome, seizing their goods.[21] At the same time, Florentine finances had fallen into chaos as a result of the fifteen-year Florentine-Pisan war, which finally ended in 1509 in favour of Florence.[22] To make matters even worse, a poor harvest leading to a severe shortage of grain in Pisa and the region of Lucca made it extremely difficult for the Florentine *Signoria* to provide food and lodging to the schismatic cardinals that finally gathered in Pisa for the council's first session, in November 1511. The *Dieci* (the Florentine Council of Ten), in urgent need of money to host the Gallican synod—and to prepare for a possible armed attack by the pope—placed emergency taxes on the clergy, which further infuriated Julius. Antonio Strozzi, Florentine ambassador to the Holy See, not only failed to persuade Julius to raise the interdict, but was further threatened by the pontiff: if the Ten did not remove the emergency taxes on the clergy, further actions would be taken against Florentine merchants in papal territories.[23] It was thus clear that the Florentine government was paying a high price for its long-standing alignment with France; the Florentines had to assure the pope of their filial obedience and, at the same time, the French of their loyalty.

On the French front, Louis's challenge to the head of Christendom could not pass without moral or political repercussions. No matter how easy it was in the case of the belligerent Julius, 'the warrior pope', to challenge the traditional role of the pontiff as peacemaker, people still respected the papacy. In order to secure moral support from the clergy, military aid by the nobles—who were growing reluctant to take up arms— and financial backing from the Third Estate, Louis turned to his court poets. As Table 1 demonstrates, throughout the Italian wars the *rhétoriqueurs*, poets in the service of the throne, had been producing literary works in prose, verse, or a combination of both in order to arouse the public's antipathy towards the Italian enemy cities and obtain military support for the French kings' campaigns. During the period 1510-12 the *rhétoriqueurs* responded once more by producing propagandistic works aimed at presenting the pope in as negative a light as possible and at justifying Louis's confrontation with the pontiff (Table 1c).

---

[20] Louis XII took advantage of the fact that the Council of Constance (1414-18) had decreed that general councils should be held every ten years, and Julius had failed to keep his word. Kenneth M. Setton, *The Papacy and the Levant (1204-1571)*, vol. 3: *The Sixteenth Century to the Reign of Julius III* (Philadelphia, 1984), 92.

[21] Setton, *The Papacy and the Levant*, 100.

[22] George R. Potter and Denys Hay (eds.), *The New Cambridge Modern History*, vol. 1: *The Renaissance (1493-1520)* (Cambridge, 1957), 362.

[23] Setton, *The Papacy and the Levant*, 112.

Table 1. Selection of polemical literature on the Italian wars of Charles VIII and Louis XII

a. In support of Charles VIII's expedition to Naples in 1494-95

Year	Author	Title
1494	André de la Vigne	La Ressource de la Chrestienté
1495?	André de la Vigne	Le Voyage de Naples

b. In support of Louis XII's Italian wars

Year	Author	Title
1500?	Pierre Gringore	Lettres nouvelles de Milan avec les regretz du seigneur Ludovic, for Louis XII's 1500 victory in Milan
1507	André de la Vigne	L'Attollite portas de Gennes, for Louis XII's 1507 victory in Genoa
1507	Jean Marot	Voyage de Gênes, for Louis XII's 1507 victory in Genoa
1509	Jean Lemaire de Belges	La concorde du genre humain, commemorating the signing of the Treaty of Cambrai
1509	Pierre Gringore	L'union des Princes, to justify Louis XII's impending Venetian invasion
1509	Jean Lemaire de Belges	Légende des Vénitiens, against the Venetians
1509	Jean Marot	Voyage de Venise, against the Venetians

c. On Louis XII's confrontation with Julius II

Year	Author	Title
1510	Pierre Gringore	La Chasse du Cerf des Cerfs
1511	Jean Lemaire de Belges	Le traicté de la différence des schismes et des conciles
1511	Jean Lemaire de Belges	Epistre du Roy a Hector de Troye
1511	Jean d'Auton	Epistre du preu Hector transmise au Roy Loys XIIe de ce nom
1511	Jean Marot	Epistre d'ung complaignant l'abusif gouvernement du Pape
1511	Pierre Gringore	L'espoir de Paix
1512	Pierre Gringore	Le Jeu du Prince des Sotz

References to the people, 'le gent populaire', in some of the above polemical works betray their authors' intent to reach a popular audience and, by justifying the king's actions, ultimately gain their support. The more caustic criticisms remained in manuscript form and thus circulated among a limited elite audience. As Jennifer Britnell points out, it is the works that do not overtly criticize the pope, and hence do not directly expose their authors to the danger of excommunication, that found their way to the printing presses and to general audiences.[24]

Of all the polemical literature concerning the Louis-Julius confrontation, Gringore's four-part drama *Le Jeu du Prince des Sotz* must have reached the widest possible public in

---

[24] Jennifer Britnell, 'Antipapal Writing in the Reign of Louis XII', in *Vernacular Literature and Current Affairs in the Early Sixteenth Century: France, England and Scotland*, ed. Jennifer Britnell and Richard Britnell (Aldershot, 2000), 45-47.

its double capacity as a written text and a staged presentation.[25] Performed on Mardi Gras of 1511, that is, on 23 February 1512, *Le Jeu* consists of a *cry*, a *sottie*, a *moralité*, and a *farce*. The two middle parts, the *sottie* and the *moralité*, directly relate to the antagonism between Louis and the pontiff. According to the general convention of *sotties*, characters appear under veiled names, all fools.[26] Thus King Louis becomes the Prince of Fools; Mère Sotte (Mother Folly) wears the clothes of the Church; and Sotte Commune represents the Third Estate (Table 2 presents the characters and the distribution of their lines).[27] Three fools, advisors to the prince, convene a session of nobles and prelates and advise the prince to retaliate against those who have been plotting against him. Sotte Commune's attempts to express her own concerns about the situation are met with indifference and contempt. Mère Sotte, that is, Julius, gathers the clergy and, through bribery, succeeds in securing their support to revolt against the prince. Although Mère Sotte launches an armed attack against the nobles, who insist on being loyal to the Prince, the Prince refuses to retaliate. At the end, the Sotte Commune realizes that it is actually Mère Sotte hiding under the church's robes, and everybody agrees that the entire conflict reflects the general madness of mankind.

Table 2. Characters by number of lines in Pierre Gringore's *Le Jeu du Prince des Sotz*

Character	No. of lines
Le premier sot	**90**
La Mère Sotte (Julius II)	**87**
La Sotte Commune (The people)	**86**
Le tiers sot	**77**
Le second sot	**57**
Sotte Occasion	45
L'abbé de Plate Bource	30
Sotte Fiance	29
Le Seigneur du Plat	27
Le Prince des Sotz (Louis XII)	**25**
Le Seigneur de La Lune	21
Le Seigneur du Pont Alletz	19
Le Seigneur de Gayecte	18
L'abbé de Frevaulx	16
Le Général d'Enfance	13
Le Prince de Nates	12
Le Seigneur de Joye	10
Croulecu	6

In her study of the political dimension in the works of the *rhétoriqueurs*, Cynthia Brown suggests that

> in the *Sottie du Jeu du Prince des Sotz*, Gringore seeks not only to justify the point of view of the French king and his allies in their fight with the Roman pontiff but to provide a

---

[25] The play apparently also triggered reactions far from Paris. The city council of Lyons authorized Florentine actors in residence there to produce 'certains jeux et farces en faveur et à la louange du pape' to answer the charges in *Le Jeu*; see Louis Petit de Julleville, *Répertoire du théâtre comique en France au moyen âge* (Paris, 1886), 362. It is noteworthy that the actors summoned were Florentine, perhaps a further indication of the stressful situation Louis's confrontation had caused to the city of Florence and, indirectly, of the relevance of FlorC 2442 to Florentine politics.
[26] For a study of the *sottie* and its conventions see Heather Arden, *Fools' Plays: A Study of Satire in the Sottie* (Cambridge, 1980).
[27] Boldface type in Table 2 indicates the most important characters of the *sottie*.

forum for the voice of the people whose concerns and interests are not always coincident with those of the French monarch. The opinion of the French Estate, which has rarely been expressed at length in other Rhétoriqueur compositions, is here given an equal airing with that of the king.[28]

Indeed, there are several outstanding features in *Le Jeu* that clearly project Gringore's intentions. First, the play's unusual length, 658 lines compared to an average of 375 lines, reflects the significance of the subject.[29] Most importantly, Sotte Commune's lines rank almost equally with those of Le premier sot and La Mère Sotte (see the distribution in Table 2). Moreover, instead of scattering Sotte Commune's lines between shorter, rapid dialogues, according to the general convention of *sotties*, Gringore allows her to break through with longer utterances to express her concerns about and objections to the situation. Sotte Commune speaks against the war and overtly complains about the already evident financial hardships (*Le Jeu du Prince des Sotz,* Sotte Commune, ll. 271-78):

Et! Que ay je a faire de la guerre,	Hey! What do I have to do with war,
Ne que a la chaire de saint Pierre	Or whether on Saint Peter's chair
Soit assis ung fol ou ung saige?	A mad man sits or a wise?
Que m'en chault il se l'Eglise erre,	What do I care if the Church errs
Mais que paix soit en ceste terre?	As long as there is peace in this land?
Jamais il ne vint bien d'oultraige.	Offending never has a good end.
Je suis asseur en mon village:	I feel safe in my village:
Quant je vueil je souppe et desjeune.[30]	I eat my soup and supper whenever I want.

As she also rightly observes, 'I am the one who always pays the bill at the end' ('Enfin je paye tousjours l'escot').[31] Indeed, there was a direct relationship between the people's tax money and the Italian wars, since the *taille* (the direct land tax on peasants) was the main resource for the upkeep of the royal army. It was also not uncommon that the king would sell administrative offices, first financial, later judicial, to newly rich bourgeois as a means to reduce royal debt.[32] In fact, the French troops had abandoned the northern border of Ferrara because they had not received their pay, and, since Louis denied a raise to the Swiss army, they, in turn, sided with Julius.[33] In the third part of *Le Jeu du Prince des Sotz*, a *moralité* titled *Peuple François, Peuple Ytalique et L'Homme obstin*é (that is, the pope), Gringore has the Italian people also forcefully express their concern with the economic crisis.

Gringore not only gives the Sotte Commune a central part in the play, but he also allows her to break into song. Strategically placed in the middle of the action, starting in line 320 of the 658-line play, the single song of Gringore's *sottie* is none other than *Faulte d'argent, c'est douleur non pareille*, 'Lack of money is sorrow unequalled'. The 1512 edition of the *sottie* provides only the incipit, which suggests that the song was already widely

---

[28] Cynthia J. Brown, *The Shaping of History and Poetry in Late Medieval France: Propaganda and Artistic Expression in the Works of the Rhétoriqueurs* (Birmingham, AL, 1985), 113.
[29] Arden, *Fools' Plays*, 43.
[30] Émile Picot (ed.), *Recueil général des sotties*, 3 vols. (Paris, 1904), vol. 2, 149, ll. 271-78.
[31] Picot, *Recueil général*, vol. 2, 168, l. 568.
[32] Potter and Hay (eds.), *The Renaissance*, 314-15.
[33] Picot, *Recueil général*, vol. 2, 132 n. 4. Earlier, on 13 February 1507, Louis had to promise double pay to the 4000 Swiss mercenaries he wished to employ for the attack of Genoa. Henry Lemonnier, *Les guerres d'Italie: La France sous Charles VIII, Louis XII et François Ier (1492-1547)*, L'histoire de France depuis les origines jusqu'à la Révolution, vol. 5, ed. Ernest Lavisse (Paris, 1903), 78.

known.[34] Whether its continuation was anything close to the text set by Josquin is difficult to ascertain; the verses immediately preceding the song incipit, however, offer valuable clues as to which of the possible versions was sung during this February performance:

Le Premier [sot]		
Commune, de quoy parles tu?	307	Commune, what are you talking about?
Le II		
Le prince est remply de vertu.		The prince is full of virtue.
Le III		
Tu n'as guerre ne bataille.		You have no wars or battles.
Le Premier		
L'orgueil des sotz a abatu.	310	The pride of fools has conquered.
Le II		
Il a selon droit combatu.		He has fought according to law.
Le III		
Mesment a mys au bas taille.		He had also lowered the taxes.
Le Premier		
Tu vient on rober la poulaille?		Did someone steal your hens?
Le II		
Tu es en paix en ta maison.		You have peace at home.
Le II		
Justice te preste l'oreille	315	Justice lends her ear to you.
[prepares rhyme]		
Le Premier		
Tu as des biens tant que **merveille**		You have so many goods that you can marvel
Dont tu peux faire garnison.		And of which you can make provisions.
Le II		
Je ne sçay pour quelle achoison		I do not know for what reason
A grummeller on te **conseille**.		They have counseled you to grumble.
La Commune *chante*		**The Commune** *sings*
Faulte d'argent, c'est douleur **nonpareille**.[35]	320	

    Lines 315, 'justice te preste l'oreille', and 316, 'tu as des biens tant que merveille', besides providing a political subtext on Louis's judicial and tax reforms, apparently foreshadow the song's rhyme and possibly individual verses. Both strophe 1 of the chanson text and Fabri's *Faulte d'argent quatrain* fit with the rhyme scheme, suggesting that it is highly possible that Sotte Commune sang one of these two *Faulte d'argent* versions.[36] Whether or not one of these continuations, or another one that has yet to be

---

[34] *Le ieu du prince des sotz et mere sotte. Ioue aux halles de paris le mardy gras. Lan mil cinq cens et vnze* (Paris, 1512).
[35] Pierre Gringore, *Le Jeu du Prince des Sotz,* ll. 307-20 (immediately preceding the *Faulte d'argent* song).
[36] For the possible continuations see Figures 3 and 4, respectively. With only the incipit written out and no further instructions, it remains unclear whether the actors would sing just the opening verse or the entire song. Common

identified, was intended, it is clear that Gringore uses a song on the *Faulte d'argent* topos to express the concern of the French people about the economic disaster of the impending war, which would jeopardize the two most important attributes that Louis XII stood for: *bon temps* (prosperity) and *paix* (peace).[37]

That the *Faulte d'argent* topos transcends the domain of entertainment to acquire political significance is also evident in another satirical work, written during the first Italian war led by Charles VIII. The farce *Faulte d'argent, Bon temps, et les trois gallants* is an outright criticism of the outcome of the war, which had deprived the French people of good times, as 'Bon temps' is held prisoner by the malicious female figure Faulte d'argent.[38] Three gallants open the farce, singing the well-known chanson *Bon temps, reviendra-tu jamais*:

Bon temps, reviendras-tu jamais	Good time, will you ever return
A ta noble puissance	To your noble power
Que nous puissions tous vivre en paix	So that we can all live in peace
Au royaulme de France?[39]	In the Kingdom of France?

In the course of the farce, the imprisoned Bon temps talks about the unpleasant consequences of the war, the levy of taxes, the paralysis of trade, and the subsequent impoverishment of the people. It is thus made explicit that Bon temps's suffering is the result of Lack of money (Faulte d'argent), which, in turn, is a consequence of the war: 'Que Faulte d'argent si le point / Velà pourquoy suis en prison' ('Lack of money is to blame / That's why I am in prison').[40] Indeed, at the end of the fifteenth century, the lack of metallic currency had become a pressing issue that affected all financial activity, especially commerce. In his study of the political and economic conditions in France at the close of the fifteenth century, Roger Doucet points out that,

> even governments had to seek the help of bankers, when their enterprises demanded the advance of large sums. Charles VIII's campaign in Italy was financed by loans granted by Italian bankers at Lyons… This emphasis on money, and the fact that it was indispensable in certain industries and in large-scale trade, mark the advent of capitalism in the economic life in France.[41]

An implicit concern with monetary issues is also evident in FlorC 2442, which Howard Mayer Brown suggested was compiled in Florence between 1518 and 1527 and presented to Filippo Strozzi by his alleged confidante Bernardo Rinuccini.[42] Brown's views remain a matter of dispute. Joshua Rifkin has proposed an earlier compilation time-frame, sometime between 1510 and 1515, and a French instead of a Florentine origin.[43] David

---

practice in farces indicates that the actors sang fragments of songs, usually written out. The surrounding verses in *Le Jeu*, however, suggest performance of at least an entire stanza.

[37] Among the many events that took place during Louis XII's first entry into Paris as king of France, an allegorical theatre at the Porte aux Peintres presented him as the keeper of 'Bon Temps' and 'Paix'. Cynthia J. Brown, 'Patterns of Protest and Impersonation in the Works of Pierre Gringore', in *Vernacular Literature and Current Affairs*, ed. Britnell and Britnell, 16-17.

[38] *Faulte d'argent, Bon temps, et les troys gallans* in Gustave Cohen (ed.), *Receuil de farces françaises inédites du XVe siècle* (Cambridge, MA, 1949), 379-84. See the discussion of the farce in Elisabeth Caron, 'Des *Esbahis* la sottie aux *Esbahis* la comédie: la formation et l'usurpation d'un théâtre national populaire', in *The French Review* 65 (1992), 725-26.

[39] Cohen, *Receuil de farces*, 379.

[40] Cohen, *Receuil de farces*, 380, ll. 97-98.

[41] Roger Doucet, 'France under Charles VIII and Louis XII', in *The Renaissance*, ed. Potter and Hay, 292-315 at 313-14.

[42] Brown, 'Chansons for the Pleasure', 55-56.

[43] Rifkin's dating appears in the *Census Catalogue of Manuscript Sources*, vol. 1, 236, without justification. Regarding the manuscript's origin see Howard M. Brown, 'Words and Music in Early Sixteenth-Century Chansons: Text Underlay in Florence, Biblioteca del Conservatorio, MS Basevi 2442', in *Quellestudien zur Musik der Renaissance I: Formen und Probleme der Überlieferung mehrstimmiger Musik im Zeitalter Josquins Desprez*, ed. Ludwig Finscher, Wolfenbütteler

Fallows suggested 'a date soon after 1510' and, based on 'the confident orthography of the French texts', compilation 'perhaps even in France'.[44] Louise Litterick accepted the early dating and proposed an origin in north-eastern France, possibly near Langres, where Ninot le Petit and Antoine Bruhier (the two composers best represented in FlorC 2442) were employed at the cathedral.[45] Even more importantly, the fact that the book contains only one chanson by Heinrich Isaac, who spent most of his life in Florence and chose the city as his permanent residence, points away from a Florentine origin. In all other sources of unquestionably Florentine provenance compiled between the 1490s and the composer's death, Isaac is significantly represented, and usually more so than Josquin.[46]

Some additional circumstantial evidence throws into relief the discrepancy between the manuscript's early repertory and Brown's dating and provenance. Although the binding, as Brown suggests, betrays its Florentine connection, this work might have been done after the manuscript reached Florence. One of Brown's main arguments interconnecting the manuscript's proposed Florentine origin and the late dating involves the use of several pages from a printed edition of Luigi Pulci's *Morgante*, published in 1500, to stiffen the covers of the three extant partbooks. According to Brown, 'the book must have been at least 20 or 25 years old before being discarded—a binder would hardly dismember a new book for such a purpose—and therefore, FlorC 2442 cannot have been bound before the third decade of the 16th century'.[47] Another likely explanation for Brown's otherwise valid observation, one that reconciles the early repertory of FlorC 2442 to a more plausible compilation date, lies within the recent turbulent history of Florentine politics. The last decade of the fifteenth century was one of the most controversial periods in the city's history. It was marked by the rise and fall of the fervent Dominican friar Girolamo Savonarola, above all remembered for his famous bonfires, on which large quantities of luxury goods, including paintings and books, were tossed. In 'Do penance', his first sermon of the so-called Haggai series of 1494, Savonarola addressed the question of money, profit-gaining, and superfluous luxuries: 'O you whose houses are filled with vanities and images and shameful things and evil books and the *Morgante* and other poems against the faith, bring them to me, to be burned as sacrifice to God'.[48] Thus Savonarola specifically targets *Morgante* as one of the items that ought to be discarded. In this context, and given the fact that the Strozzi family was pro-

---

Forschungen 6 (Munich, 1981), 122. Rifkin's proposal of a French origin appears in the transcription of the discussion that followed the presentation of Brown's paper during the conference.

[44] Josquin des Prez, *Secular Works for Four Voices: Critical Commentary*, ed. David Fallows, New Josquin Edition 28 (Utrecht, 2005), 141. Fallows's dating is based on 'repertory and context'.

[45] Unpublished papers presented at the American Musicological Society Toronto meeting in 2000 and the 2005 Medieval and Renaissance Music Conference in Tours. In an earlier essay the author had proposed the years 'c. 1510-15 or later'; see Louise Litterick, 'Who Wrote Ninot's Chansons?' in *Papal Music and Musicians in Medieval and Renaissance Rome*, ed. Richard Sherr (Oxford, 1998), 224-69 at 245. For a detailed exposition in support of the chansonnier's French origin and regional rather than royal character see her recent 'Out of the Shadows: The Double Canon *En l'ombre d'ung buissonet*', in *Instruments, Ensembles, and Repertory, 1300-1600: Essays in Honour of Keith Polk,* ed. Timothy J. McGee and Stewart Carter (Turnhout, 2013), 269-72, especially 270.

[46] Isaac was resident in Florence, albeit not continuously, from 1503 until his death in 1517. Had the manuscript been compiled in Florence between 1518 and 1527, as Brown suggests, it would most certainly have included more chansons by the composer. Recently, Giovanni Zanovello has presented sufficient evidence of Isaac's expanded professional network in Florence in the early years of the sixteenth century, which questions the received notion that Isaac's main residence before his final years was in the imperial lands. Giovanni Zanovello, '"Master Arigo Ysach, Our Brother": New Light on Isaac in Florence, 1502-1517', in *Journal of Musicology* 25 (2008), 287-317. The chanson included in FlorC 2442 is *Fillez vous avez mal gardé*.

[47] Brown, 'Chansons for the Pleasure', 58-59.

[48] Girolamo Savonarola, *Prediche soppra Aggeo, con il trattato circa il reggimento e governo della città di Firenze (1494)*, ed. Luigi Firpo, Edizione Nazionale delle Opere de Girolamo Savonarola (Rome, 1965), 19.

Savonarolan, it is not unlikely that the book that was dismembered by the binder of FlorC 2442 was one of the *Morgante* vanities that had been tucked away following the friar's exhortations. Within this context, it is well justified that a recently published book, and a lavishly illustrated one, was literally torn to pieces to provide bookboards for another book's covers.[49]

FlorC 2442 is a carefully planned anthology of French chansons, mainly four-part arrangements of popular monophonic tunes. The manuscript features seventeen French composers, all active in the opening decades of the sixteenth century, and the chansons are grouped together by composer. The inclusion of Josquin's *Plus nulz regretz*, composed to celebrate the signing of the Treaty of Calais, establishes 1508 as a *terminum post quem* for the manuscript. The three extant partbooks (superius, tenor, and altus) feature careful text underlay, and the orthography betrays the hand of a francophone scribe.

Framing the entire manuscript, as mentioned above, are two *Faulte d'argent* settings, Josquin's and Beauvoys's. Josquin's opening *Faulte d'argent* is the only five-voice chanson in the anthology. Brown sees the inclusion of these two settings as particularly appropriate, since *Faulte d'argent* is 'a sentiment most fitting for a member of one of Florence's leading banking families', that is, the Strozzis.[50] Similarly, Bernstein interprets the incorporation of the two *Faulte d'argent* settings as 'a gesture meant to honour the distinguished Florentine banking family'.[51] However, the only flattery involved with beginning a manuscript for a banker with a song about the *lack* of money would be that a celebrated composer, such as Josquin, composed it. Even if the compiler included Josquin's *Faulte d'argent* as a 'hit', the question remains of why would he conclude the collection with another *Faulte d'argent* setting by a lesser composer.[52] Furthermore, the penultimate song, Obrecht's *Tant que nostre argent dura*, also deals with the subject of 'lack of money'. Finally, could it be a coincidence that a few folios earlier appears a quodlibet, ascribed to Gaspart (van Weerbeke?), that combines fragments of the tunes *Bon temps je ne te puis*, *Adieu mes amours*, *Bontemps ne viendra tu*, and *Il est de bonne heure n*é, all replete with monetary allusions and references and thus inextricably related to the *Faulte d'argent* topos?[53]

The fragment from *Adieu mes amours*, Josquin's popular combinative chanson, in the above quodlibet would immediately activate an entire network of monetary intertextual allusions in contemporary audiences' minds. Composed in the 1480s, *Adieu mes amours* provides additional evidence of the indispensable need for cash that had come to put its seal on various types of offered services and exchanges.[54] The two different texts combined

---

[49] It is also conceivable that the manuscript was bound anew at the expense of Bernardo Rinuccini during the time Brown proposes (the third decade of the sixteenth century). This could also explain the difference between the watermarks of the original pages that contain the music (similar to but not identical with watermarks in use in the early 1490s) and the blank pages—possibly inserted later—before and after the music, used in Tuscany between 1529 and 1540. Brown, 'Chansons for the Pleasure', 59.
[50] Brown, 'Chansons for the Pleasure', 62.
[51] Bernstein, 'Notes on the Origin', 286 n. 28.
[52] This is actually the only extant composition ascribed to Beauvoys.
[53] The two *Bontemps* texts do not explicitly refer to money. However, the absence of good times was directly related to lack of money as the farce *Faulte d'argent, Bon temps, et les trois gallants* amply demonstrates. For different possibilities regarding the identification of 'Gaspart' see Litterick, 'Out of the Shadows', 272 n. 32.
[54] Josquin's motet-chanson *Ce povre mendiant/Pauper sum ego* could be grouped with the songs that display an earthly concern with material reimbursement for rendered services, although its texts do not directly refer to money. The superius and tenor text of the motet-chanson reads: 'Ce povre mendiant pour Dieu / Qui n'a benefice ne office / Qui ne lui vault ou soit propice / Autant porte que sur le lieu'. The contratenor text is taken from the Vulgate, Psalm 87:16: 'Pauper sum ego, et in laboribus a juventute mea; exaltatus autem, humiliatus sum et conturbatus'. David Fallows

in this chanson, a rondeau *cinquain* (Table 3, left column), and a bergerette (Table 3, right column), are tightly related in their prosodic details and poetic content.

Table 3. Superius and tenor/bassus texts in Josquin's *Adieu mes amours*

Superius	Tenor and bassus
Adieu mes amours, on m'atent;	Adieu mes amours, adieu vous command,
Ma boursse n'enffle ne n'etend,	Adieu je vous dy jusquez au printemps.
Et brief, je suis en desarroy	
Jusquez à ce qu'il plaise au Roy	Je suis en sousci de quoy je vivray.
Me faire avancer du content.	La raison pour quoy? Je le vous diray:
Quant je voy que nul ne m'entent,	Je n'ay point d'argent; vivray je du vent,
Ung seul blanc en main il s'entent,	Se l'argent du Roy ne vient plus souvent?
Qu'il faut dire sans faire effroy:	
	Adieu mes amours, etc.
Adieu mes amours, on m'atent;	
Ma boursse n'enffle ne n'etend,	
Et brief, je suis en desarroy.	
Ainsi qu'il vient il se despent,	
Et puis après on s'en repent;	
N'est ce pas, cela je le croy.	
Remede n'y voy, quant à moy,	
Fors publier ce mot patent:	
Adieu mes amours, on m'atent;	
Ma boursse n'enffle ne n'etend,	
Et brief, je suis en desarroy	
Jusquez à ce qu'il plaise au Roy	
Me faire avancer du content.	
Farewell my love, they are waiting for me;	Farewell my love, farewell I bid you,
My purse neither swells nor stretches,	I say farewell to you until the spring.
And in short, I'm in a bad state	
Until it pleases the King	I'm troubled about what I shall live on.
To give me some ready money.	The reason why? I'll tell you:
When I see that no one listens to me,	I have no money; shall I live on the breeze,
That is, when you've only got a halfpenny in your hand,	If the King's money doesn't come more often?
You have to say without making much commotion:	Farewell my love, etc.
Farewell my love, they are waiting for me;	
My purse neither swells nor stretches,	
And in short, I'm in a bad state.	
As it comes, so is it spent,	
And then you repent it later;	
Isn't that so? I think so.	
I see no remedy, for my part,	
But to make this announcement:	
Farewell my love, they are waiting for me;	
My purse neither swells nor stretches,	
And in short, I'm in a bad state	
Until it pleases the King	
To give me some ready money.[a]	

[a] Texts and translations after Howard M. Brown (ed.), *A Florentine Chansonnier from the Time of Lorenzo the Magnificent: Florence, Biblioteca Nazionale Centrale, Ms. Banco Rari 229*, 2 vols., Monuments of Renaissance Music 7 (Chicago, 1983), vol. 2, 274.

proposes that *Ce povre mendiant/Pauper sum ego* was composed in the first decade of the sixteenth century, while he dates *Adieu mes amours* to the mid 1470s. David Fallows, *Josquin* (Turnhout, 2009), 41 and 305.

Furthermore, the tune *Il est de bonne heure né*, also incorporated in Gaspart's quodlibet, appears elsewhere combined with texts directly related to the theme of lack of money. In Petrucci's *Odhecaton* it is paired with the texts *Amours fait moult tant qu'argent dure* and *Tant que nostre argent dure* (Table 4).[55] Its close intertextual connection to the *Faulte d'argent* topos is further made explicit in Willaert's later *Faulte d'argent* setting. In this six-voice arrangement, Willaert incorporates the *quatrain Qui a beau né* as a second part to *Faulte d'argent*:

Qui a beau né beuvra en la bouteille	Whoever is lucky will drink from the bottle,
Qui a argent sera le bienvenu	Whoever has money will be the welcome one,
Entre les dames tres bien entretenu	Among ladies, very well cared-for.
Pour vous ne dors jay la puce en l'oreille.	Because of you I cannot sleep, I burn from desire.[56]

Table 4. Texts of the Superius, Contratenor I and II, and Tenor parts of *Amours fait moult/Il est de bonne heure né/Tant que nostre argent durra*

Superius and Contratenor I
Amours fait moult tant qu'argent dure;
Quant argent fault, amour est dure,
Et dit tout franc à son amy:
'Puis que nostre argent est failly,
Allés querir aultre aventure'.

While money lasts, all love is fair,
When money's gone, all love looks bare
And it says frankly to its friend:
'Now that your pelf is at an end,
Go find yourself your next affair'.

Tenor
Il est de bonne heure né
Qui tient sa dame en ung pré
Sur l'erbe jolye.

How fortunate is he
Who has her on a lea,
Upon the grass.

'Ma tresdoulce amye,
Dieu vous doint bon jour!'
'Mon tres bel amy,
Dieu vous croisse honnour'
'Par ma foy, mon bel amy,
Je suis tout vostre et celuy
Qui ne vous faudra mye'.

'My sweetest queen,
God give you peace!'
'May God, dear friend,
Your grace increase'.
'On my faith my dearest friend,
I am yours—you can depend—
A faithful lass'.

Contratenor II
Tant que nostre argent durra,
Qui tantost fauldra,
Nous mesrons ioyeuse vie.
Or est nostre argent failly:
Adieu, mon amy,
Adieu, ma tresdoulce amye.

As long as our money lasts,
Which will be lacking soon,
We'll lead a joyous life.
And when our money is finished,
Goodbye, my friend,
Goodbye, my sweet lady.[a]

[a] Texts and translations after Brown, *A Florentine Chansonnier*, vol. 2, 271, 273. Although the text of *Il est de bonne heure né* does not directly refer to money, it belongs to a network of poems that certainly do, as *Qui a beau né* above. In *Le parnasse satyrique*, poem XCVII starts with the lines: 'Qui n'a point d'argent / De malle heure est né'. Schwob (ed.), *Le parnasse satyrique*, 188. *Il est de bonne heure né* provides a happy contrast to the pessimistic tone of *Amours fait moult* and *Tant que nostre argent durra*.

---

[55] Helen Hewitt (ed.), *Harmonice Musices Odhecaton A* (Cambridge, MA, 1942; repr. New York, 1978), no. 31.
[56] *Le cinquiesme livre contenant trente et deux chansons* (Antwerp: Tylman Susato, 1544) [RISM 154413]. Also in the *Mellange de chansons tant des vieux autheurs que des modernes, a cinq, six, sept, et huict parties* (Paris: Le Roy & Ballard, 1572) [RISM 15722]. For a modern edition of Willaert's setting see Charles Jacobs (ed.), *Le Roy & Ballard's 1572 Mellange de Chansons* (University Park, PA, 1982). There is an interesting connection between the last line of *Qui a beau né* and Fabri's *Faulte d'argent*, l. 3, which reads: 'Que je n'ay rien fors la puce en l'oreille'.

The idea that money is an indispensable factor for erotic success constantly emerges in fifteenth- and sixteenth-century literature. In the mystery *Le chevalier qui donna sa femme au diable* performed in 1505, that is, during Louis XII's reign, the theme of money's power over love's workings and social acceptance is central:

L'amour si vault quant argent dure;	Love is good while money lasts;
Mais, quant finance est faillye,	But once you go bankrupt,
A peine trouve on nulle amye.	You can hardly find a lover.
....	
Vous scavez que chascun deboutte	You know that everyone rejects
Les gens quant ilz n'ont **de quibus**.[57]	The men that do not have the means.

Considering the carefully planned organization of FlorC 2442, it is obvious that the inclusion of four settings on the subject of 'lack of money' and the lack of good times was unlikely to have been coincidental. In fact, it makes perfect sense considering the immense financial strain—for both France and Italy, and especially Florence—caused by Louis XII's Italian campaigns and his confrontation with the pope, and reinforces the views favouring a compilation date during Louis XII's reign. The selection of composers, all active at the turn of the sixteenth century, also indicates that the manuscript was prepared earlier than the date Brown proposed. By the third decade of the sixteenth century, when Brown suggests the manuscript was compiled, most of the chansons in FlorC 2442 were already outdated. Giving a single five-voice chanson pride of place possibly aims exactly at attracting attention to the anthology's novel character by including the latest development in secular writing, a chanson in the new medium of the five-voice expanded texture.

The issue of the manuscript's recipient also remains unresolved as recent literature has focused more on its provenance and dating. Brown suggested that FlorC 2442 was intended for a member of the Strozzi family on the basis of the crescent moons that decorate the corners of the leather covers, a tribute to the Strozzi coat of arms.[58] A problematic aspect of this suggestion lies with the fact that the half-moons on FlorC 2442 are single moons, whereas the Strozzi emblem features three crescent moons, usually interlocked. The covers of the account books of the Strozzis, as Brown reports, display single crescent moons as decorative details of the larger design in which the interlocked crescent moons dominate. It remains thus unclear whether the single half-moons on the cover of FlorC 2442 (one on each corner) represent the Strozzi emblem.

Nevertheless, since the case for a Strozzi recipient cannot yet be dismissed, some additional circumstantial evidence may illuminate alternative scenarios regarding the manuscript's owner. If FlorC 2442 was indeed presented to Filippo Strozzi, as Brown originally proposed, its central theme resonates better with his personal circumstances in the first decade of the sixteenth century than with his late years, when he had amassed a huge fortune. In 1508, Filippo decided to marry Clarice de' Medici, whose large dowry—Filippo's mother, Selvaggia, was hoping—would help compensate for the immense expenses the construction of the Strozzi palace had caused. Such a move, however, triggered a vigorous reaction from the entire family, as the Strozzis had a long

---

[57] *Le chevalier qui donna sa femme au diable*, in *Le Théâtre français avant la Renaissance: 1450-1550, mystères, moralités et farces*, ed. Édouard Fournier (Paris, 1880), 186.
[58] Brown, 'Chansons for the Pleasure', 62.

tradition of opposing Medici rule. When the news for Filippo's secretly kept intentions became public, the *Signoria* commanded him to pay a fine of five hundred gold florins and sentenced him to confinement in Naples for three years. His mother and brothers were forbidden to provide any financial or material aid to him.[59] Although in the end Filippo spent less than a year in Naples, this period was one of confrontations and financial stress. The theme of the manuscript resonates better as a gesture of sympathy during these hard times than as a gesture to honour a banker during a period of economic affluence (the late 1520s), as Brown had suggested.

An alternative possibility for the intended recipient of FlorC 2442 during the early years of the sixteenth century would be Antonio di Vanni Strozzi (1455-1523), a prominent lawyer who was appointed ambassador to Rome in 1511 by Piero Soderini, Florence's republican head.[60] Antonio was caught in the middle of the harsh economic negotiations between Florence and the pope during the Louis-Julius conflict. The contents of FlorC 2442 could be interpreted as an expression of sympathy and understanding for someone who was trying to ensure the viability of Florentine finances during a very unstable and sensitive time of the city's history. Antonio was in fact one of the most respected members of the Strozzi family. With the reinstatement of the Medici in 1512, he was singled-out as the best candidate to represent the family in the new governing body of the *Balìa*, instituted by the Medici.[61]

Although the views about the possible recipient of FlorC 2442 inevitably remain speculative until more evidence comes to light, they offer some additional information that has been neglected in musicological discussions. The literary record and circumstantial evidence strongly supports the views of FlorC 2442 originating in France in the first decade of the sixteenth century and reflecting the widespread concern with the scarcity of money. The manuscript then travelled to Florence and was offered to a patron at a time when the 'lack of money' topos resonated with the city's history and, possibly, with his personal circumstances.[62]

Historical, literary, and musical sources from the last decades of the fifteenth century and the early years of the sixteenth century provide ample evidence of the centrality of money, or rather lack thereof, in the political, social, and cultural life of France and Italy. Specifically, the *Faulte d'argent* topos emerges as a recurring theme in both musical and literary documents. In fact the earliest musical sources containing polyphonic settings of *Faulte d'argent, c'est douleur nonpareille* (AugsS 142a, compiled between 1505 and 1514, and CambriP 1760, compiled between c. 1509 and 1514), the earliest printed editions of chanson verse in Paris (c. 1512-15) incorporating and even

---

[59] Melissa Meriam Bullard, *Filippo Strozzi and the Medici: Favor and Finance in Sixteenth-Century Florence and Rome* (Cambridge, 1980), 57.
[60] Bullard, *Filippo Strozzi*, 46.
[61] Bullard, *Filippo Strozzi*, 69. Eventually, however, no Strozzi member was included in the government.
[62] The last line of the *quatrain* reflects the typical medieval misogynist notion of women's unbridled desire for money. This line would have made perfect sense to the Florentine recipient of the chansonnier, since the city of Florence had been issuing sumptuary laws since the early fourteenth century. These laws aimed at controlling extravagant expenditures and excessive display of luxury, especially by women; see Dora Liscia Bemporad, 'Hierarchy, Privilege and Luxury in the Florentine Sumptuary Law', in *Money and Beauty: Bankers, Botticelli and the Bonfire of the Vanities*, ed. Ludovica Sebregondi and Tim Parks (Florence, 2011), 81-92 and Ludovica Sebregondi, 'The Sumptuary Laws', in *Money and Beauty*, 191. It is possibly not a coincidence that the last line of the closing chanson, Beauvoys's four-voice *Faulte d'argent*, reads 'madame' instead of 'femme', that is, changes from a more generic terminology to specifically targeting the courtly female.

celebrating *Faulte d'argent* as opening song, as well as the famous performance of Gringore's *sottie* (1512) including a *Faulte d'argent* chanson as its central and unique singing number are all contemporaneous with the period of Louis XII's Italian wars, and in particular with his confrontation with the pope. The historical record indicates that within the crisis in political, social, and economic affairs, the subject of lack of money was a central one. The rich concentration of testimonies from the first two decades of the sixteenth century—especially when considering the scarcity of French sources from this period—suggests that the *Faulte d'argent* topos found fertile ground at the French royal court of Louis XII, prompting a vast array of musical and literary responses. The prominence of chansons on the subject of 'lack of money' in FlorC 2442 testifies to the political circumstances that surrounded the genesis and circulation of related musical settings in early sixteenth century France and Florence. The abundance of songs directly referring to money as a guarantor of happiness and erotic success (*Faulte d'argent, Tant que nostre argent durra, Amours fait moult, Qui a beau né*), as an essential means to lead a decent life (the ballade *Faulte d'argent*), or as a means to compensate for services offered (*Pauper sum ego, Adieu mes amours*) provides fertile ground for further research related to the changing economic landscape of modern Europe and the advent of capitalism.

Abstract

The French-Italian wars reached their peak with the confrontation between Louis XII and Pope Julius II from 1510-12. This conflict created a strain in the financial situation of France and its Italian ally Florence. During this crisis many of the *rhétoriqueurs* in royal service produced propagandistic works to support the king's cause against the pope. The same poets, however, also penned satirical works expressing the people's concern with the economic hardships accompanying a new expedition into Italy. The sharpest criticism emerges in Pierre Gringore's *sottie, Le jeu du Prince des Sotz* (1512), featuring the song *Faulte d'argent, c'est douleur non pareille* as its central piece. During the same years, polyphonic settings of this presumably popular tune first appear in musical sources (AugsS 142a, CambriP 1760). Two such versions form a pair that opens and closes FlorC 2442, and another two chansons on the subject of lack of money appear within that same collection. Given FlorC 2442's highly organized structure, it is unlikely that the inclusion and placement of the above chansons was haphazard. FlorC 2442's disputed chronology, provenance, and alleged recipient are thus examined against the crisis in the politico-economic affairs, during which the *Faulte d'argent* topos apparently found fertile ground, prompting a vast array of musical and literary responses. This historical approach strengthens the arguments for an early compilation date of FlorC 2442, situating it during Louis XII's reign, and it suggests that *Faulte d'argent* settings started life in association with events indeed characterized by 'lack of money'.

Research and Performance Practice Forum

Mechanical Carillons as a Source for Historical Performance: An Artistic Reconstruction of Seventeenth-Century Carillon Music Using Historical Re-pinning Books

CARL VAN EYNDHOVEN

Carillon culture blossomed as never before in the Low Countries during the seventeenth and eighteenth centuries.[1] An incredible amount of music, played by mechanical carillons or performed by carillonneurs, must have resounded every day in many towns in the Netherlands at that time. Yet, surprisingly few primary musical sources survive from the period to testify to that lively historical reality.[2] Only a few eighteenth-century 'carillon books'—manuscripts including the repertoire for manual performance by carillonneurs—are known today. In addition there are some 're-pinning books'—collections of arrangements (called *versteken*), usually including some technical instructions for setting the pegs on the barrel of the automatic carillon—which offer a glimpse of the seventeenth- and eighteenth-century carillon repertoire for automatic performance (see Table 1). Prevailing opinion sees the carillon books and not the re-pinning books as the only sources for research into performance practice.[3] However, several years ago I conducted a study into the performance of eighteenth-century repertoire, which revealed that re-pinning books not only give us knowledge about the repertoire, but that they can also be reliable sources for historically informed performance.[4] This insight led to the development of a new methodology that compares re-pinning and carillon books, and involves human performance of the *versteken*. This methodology functioned as a key element in my doctoral research, the aim of which was the artistic reconstruction of a seventeenth-century carillon book.[5] The reconstructions that resulted from my research do not, and cannot, claim to recreate musical objects that actually existed. Rather, I consider my recreations to represent *authentic possibilities*: possibilities that, through a combination of practice-based and more academic, source-based enquiry, accurately mirror the spirit of seventeenth-century carillon performance practice.

---

[1] André Lehr, *The Art of the Carillon in the Low Countries* (Tielt, 1991), 121-54.
[2] Lehr, *The Art of the Carillon*, 162-69 and 196-201.
[3] See, for example: Arie Abbenes and André Lehr, *De Gruÿtters Carillon Book* [facsimile of the original manuscript of 1746], (Amsterdam, 1971), Introduction, n.p.: 'These manuscripts [=re-pinning books] are of interest only as far as they show us the type of music which was provided for the hour-strike-tunes to be produced in a mechanical way at the quarter hours… For a deeper understanding of performing habits (…), we can only scan the authentic carillon compositions [= carillon books] of that period.'
[4] The results of this study were published in: Carl Van Eyndhoven and Peter Strauven (eds.), *Trillers, mordanten en schielijke loopen… Een artistieke reconstructie van de beiaardmuziek in de achttiende eeuw*, Cahiers van het IvOK 7 (Leuven, 2008).
[5] Carl Van Eyndhoven, 'A la recherche du temps perdu. Een artistieke reconstructie van de beiaardmuziek tussen 1600 en 1650 in de Zuidelijke Nederlanden op basis van historische versteekboeken' (Ph.D. diss., University of Leuven, 2012).

Table 1. Seventeenth- and eighteenth-century re-pinning and carillon manuscripts

Date	Source	Siglum[a]
Seventeenth century		
c. 1616-33	Re-pinning book of Hendrick Claes	F-Pn, Ms. néerlandais 58
1648	Re-pinning book of Théodore De Sany	B-Ba, No. 3814
1681	Re-pinning book of Philippus Wyckaert	B-Gar, Reg. 96.2
Eighteenth century		
1728	*Beÿaert. 1728* Theodoor or Clemens-Augustinus Everaerts	B-Aa, M. 25
s.d.	Re-pinning book of Georg Gottfried Aßmus	D-DSsa E 14 A 85/10, 85/11, 85/12, 86/1, 86/2, 87/1
1740-1804	Re-pinning book of Joannes and Amandus De Gruÿtters	B-MEjd, s.s.
1746	Carillon book of Joannes De Gruÿtters	B-Ac, Ms. 17761
c. 1755	Leuven Carillon manuscript I	B-LVu, BE/212934/PU/ELEWYCK/30
s.d.	Leuven Carillon manuscript II	B-LVu, BE/212934/PU/ELEWYCK/31
1769	Re-pinning book of Theodor Friedrich Gülich	PL-GDap 300, R/Pp, q9
s.d.	Re-pinning book of Paul Friedrich Knaack	PL-GDap 300, R/Uu, q9
1775	Re-pinning book of Theodor Friedrich Gülich	PL-GDap 300, R/Pp, q10 & 10a
1776-1816	Carillon books of Johannes and Frederik Johan Berghuijs	NL-DELFTa 191, Nos. 2-20, 21, 25
1780-85	Carillon book of André Dupont	F-SOM, Ms. 1691
1781	Carillon book of Frans De Prins	B-LVu, BE/212934/PU/ELEWYCK/115
1784	Re-pinning book of Johann Ephraim Eggert	PL-GDap 300, R/Pp, 45

[a] All sigla from RISM.

Research into Eighteenth-Century Performance Practice on Carillon

The pieces in the eighteenth-century carillon books raise many questions regarding performance practice. Sometimes, only a melody is notated. Occasionally the melody is accompanied by a bass line. In the Leuven carillon manuscripts and the carillon book of De Gruÿtters we also find harpsichord pieces by Joseph-Hector Fiocco, Dieudonné Raick, François Couperin, and others, often not as exact copies, but rather as transcriptions with changes based on the particular physical possibilities of the carillon itself (tessitura, chord reductions, tuning). One of the main questions these sources pose is: how faithful should a carillonneur be in regard to the very diverse notation of the pieces in these carillon books? The discovery of the carillon manuscript of Frans De Prins (1781) in 2003, was the impetus to address this question and to research, for the first time, the performance of eighteenth-century carillon music.[6]

---

[6] Van Eyndhoven and Strauven (eds.), *Trillers, mordanten en schielijke loopen*.

This research showed that the eighteenth-century carillon books do not include carillon adaptations that are to be faithfully played according to the musical text. They present practical notations that form a link between the original composition and the final performance on the carillon. Compare, for example, the original first measures of the *Andante* from Joseph-Hector Fiocco's *Pièces de clavecin*, op.1, of 1730 (Figure 1) with the transcription in the De Gruÿtters carillon book of 1746 (Figure 2). This comparison illustrates how De Gruÿtters adapted Fiocco's harpsichord composition to the requirements of the carillon: the key was changed from E minor into D minor (because of the meantone temperament of the Hemony carillon of Antwerp cathedral where he played), and the chords are reduced from three to two voices (making them playable by double pedals). The seemingly odd transition from bar 1 to bar 2 is a consequence of the very common lack of a low C♯ bell. Despite the notation, a carillonneur will most likely prefer to play the notes in the lower staff in bar 1 one octave higher than notated.

Figure 1. Joseph-Hector Fiocco, *Andante*, bb. 1-7 (*Pièces de clavecin…oeuvre premier* [Brussels, 1730], p. 14)

Figure 2. Joseph-Hector Fiocco / Joannes De Gruÿtters, *Andante*, bb. 1-5 (*De Gruÿtters Carillon Book* [Antwerp, 1746], p. 32)

The study also made clear that re-pinning books are important documents in the context of repertoire research, as well as unique sources of information on the performance practice of carillonneurs. Of particular interest to this research was the comparative analysis of works notated by Joannes De Gruÿtters in both his carillon and re-pinning books. Not unexpectedly, the repertoire compiled in De Gruÿtters' re-pinning and carillon books is rather similar. Moreover, it appears that the music he set on the barrel of the automatic carillon was very similar to what he himself played on the carillon. The eighteenth-century listener could easily confuse manual performance by the carillonneur with automatic performance played by the automatic carillon. This possibility is clear from a story concerning Joachim Hess (1732-1820) and Jacob Potholt (1720-82), both renowned organists and carillonneurs in, respectively, Gouda and

Amsterdam. They travelled to Delft to hear carillonneur Johannes Berghuijs (1725-1802) perform. Hess writes:

> ...en voorts op de markt komende, begint juist het speelwerk, waarnaar Potholt terstond met de uiterste aandacht dus begon te luisteren, mij intusschen vermakende, met het denkbeeld waarin hij was, dat namelijk Berghuis nu speelde, liet ik hem in dien waan, tot dat daarna de klok elf uren slaande, hij met des te meer verwondering, uit zijne dwaling geraakte. Nu begon Berghuis te spelen, met eene vlugheid, dat Potholt niet vlugger met zijne vingeren op het orgel, tegen zijne vuisten op het klokkenspel kon zijn.[7]

> ...and then just as we came on to the market, the automatic carillon started playing and Potholt immediately started listening to it with the utmost attention, meanwhile amusing me with the idea he held, namely that Berghuis was now playing; I left him in this delusion until, when the clock struck eleven, he realized his error with all the more amazement. Now Berghuis began to play with such quickness that Potholt with his fingers on the organ could not play faster than he [Berghuis] with his fists on the carillon.

This passage makes it clear that even professional musicians easily confused the automatic carillon with a live carillonneur. Hess's story gave rise to my hypothesis that, in the eighteenth century, the notation of the *versteken* matched the playing of carillonneurs. In contrast to the carillon books from which carillonneurs played, the *versteken* required the precise notation of all the notes (including, among other things, embellishments). Johan Fischer confirms this when he writes in 1738: 'De port de vois die men tusschen de nooten set, moet men altyt Considereren, als nooten die hunne waerdy hebben, want anders kan men se niet op de Ton steeken' ('The *port de vois* that one sets between the notes must always be considered as notes that have a value. Otherwise, we cannot place them on the barrel').[8]

Because of the precise notation, *versteken* are an important source of information for 'authentic' performance. Nonetheless, the re-pinning books must still be considered in their context: they provide important information about the musical text (which notes were played), but reveal little or nothing about the performance (how these notes were played); they inform us about important aspects of performance practice, such as which embellishments were used or the fact that sometimes short preludes were added, but say little or nothing about all the performance-related elements that are not included in the musical text. It is these aspects that make every performance unique and that make it clear that the search for authentic performance is not possible 'without creativity and musicality.'[9] In other words, an eighteenth-century *versteek* is not a recording of a performance but 'an analytical, indirect representation of the live performance.'[10]

On the basis of the hypothesis that the re-pinning books and automatic carillon music form a primary source of information for historically informed performance on the carillon, two complementary research experiments were set up that would ultimately culminate in the development of an entirely new methodology. In one experiment, a number of Joannes De Gruÿtters' *versteken* were set on the barrel of the carillon of Antwerp cathedral (sound reconstruction). In a second experiment, I myself played De

---

[7] Joachim Hess, *Over de vereischten in eenen organist* (Gouda, 1807), 75-76.
[8] Johan Philip Albrecht Fischer, *Verhandeling van de klokken en het klokke-spel* (Utrecht, 1738); facs. ed. Klokkengieterij B. Eijsbouts (Asten, 1956), 49-50.
[9] Ton Koopman, 'Authenticiteit in de historische uitvoeringspraktijk', in *Kunst & Wetenschap* 5 (2008), 11.
[10] David Fuller, 'An Introduction to Automatic Instruments', in *Early Music* 11 (1983), 164-66 at 165.

Gruÿtters' *versteken* in order to empirically determine whether or not they are actually playable on the carillon and to what extent they imitate a hand-played carillon performance.

I. *Versteken*: Sound Reconstruction

The first experiment examined whether automatic playing could indeed imitate the carillonneur to the extent that the distinction is hardly noticeable to a listener. To this end, a number of De Gruÿtters' *versteken* were placed, in part or in their entirety, on the Antwerp cathedral carillon, using the barrel of Jan de Hondt (1730) and the historical Hemony bells (1655/58). Listening from ground level, it was confirmed that confusing this automatic music with a performance by a carillonneur is indeed possible. The most significant difference between the two was the tempo of the music played by the barrel, which seemed rather slow by contemporary standards. However, tempo was the only parameter that could not be historically recreated. The carillon barrel of Antwerp cathedral is nowadays driven by a small electric motor, and not by a heavy weight as it was in the eighteenth century. In addition, the air brake speed regulator of the barrel was (and still is) adaptable with the use of small propellers that allowed the speed to be doubled. However, we do not know which of the propellers positions were used by De Gruÿtters. It can also be assumed that the tempi of performances by carillonneurs in the eighteenth century varied according to the type of carillon (heavy or light) and the suspension of the bells in the tower (open lantern or closed bell chamber).

II. Playing *Versteken* on the Carillon

After having determined that a listener could confuse music played by the automatic carillon with a manual performance by the carillonneur and that (to a certain extent) the playing mechanism imitates manual performance, the next logical step was to play the *versteken* by hand. The intention was to experimentally test whether the *versteken* not only created a general auditory approximation of hand playing, but also effectively imitated the techniques of manual playing. A *versteek* is in this respect not a 'recording' of a performance but a fixed, pre-programmed interpretation of a musical text. It will always remain identical in a given, unchanged context by means of the historical automatic carillon mechanism.

    The conclusion was that most of De Gruÿtters' notated *versteken* are playable on the carillon. Some passages are not easy to perform, (i.e., parallel thirds with large leaps, long passages in quavers in the bass, parallel sixths, broken chords in the bass or left hand), but passages such as these also occur in De Gruÿtters' carillon book, a fact which proves that they were also played by hand and were not solely reserved for the automatic playing mechanism.

III. Practice-based research method

All this led to a new methodology that analyzes, through practice-based research, the relationship between the pieces in the carillon books and the *versteken* of these works. This methodology is depicted in Figure 3.

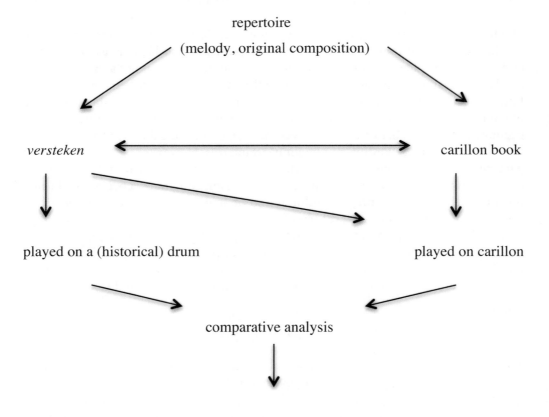

Figure 3. Diagram of a practice-based research method, comparing re-pinning and carillon manuscripts

As mentioned earlier, it was particularly relevant to my research that this methodology could be applied to the carillon and re-pinning books of one specific author, Joannes De Gruÿtters. The *versteken* confront us with his carillon interpretation (performance) of keyboard works by composers such as Couperin and Fiocco. These *versteken* show that musical texts associated with some pieces in his carillon book are not taken from fixed scores and that they leave a good deal of room for extemporaneous variation and melodic decoration.

    It appears that De Gruÿtters did not feel obliged to slavishly follow the original ornamentation of the works he copied. Embellishments of melody notes—mainly combinations of trills and mordents, respectively referred to by De Gruÿtters as 'tremblans' and 'pincés'—are sometimes added or omitted. The many variations of the bass line are remarkable. Also typical is the use of scale figures as ascending upbeats or as descending chord extensions. The frequent appearance of embellishments in the *versteken* undoubtedly reflects a practice which was also used while playing from the carillon books *ex tempore*. Adding an introduction is a practice that De Gruÿtters mentions in his *Regelement ofte manieren om alle trommels dienende tot beijaert spelen te verst[eken]*.[11] To avoid empty bars on the barrel, he advises filling them with a prelude. Some passages notated in equal quavers in the carillon books are rendered by De Gruÿtters in the *versteken* in dotted rhythms. This practice could indicate a written form of 'inégalité'. The *versteek* of Couperin's *La Bourbonnoise* indicates that De Gruÿtters in all likelihood played the notated quavers in this piece unevenly (Figure 4). But it is not clear whether he did so in the ratio 3:1 (the notated dotted rhythm of the *versteek*) or in a milder form that he was unable to realize on the barrel for technical reasons. This same finding can be extended to embellishments: a human player could play them with a level of complexity that went far beyond what was possible even on technically advanced barrels, such as the one in Antwerp cathedral.

Research clearly showed the importance of the *versteken*: they imitate a performance practice within the boundaries of the technical possibilities of the barrel and the automatic playing mechanism. In this way, the *versteken* provide insight into the musical text and give practical information on its rendition.

Research on Seventeenth-Century Performance Practice on Carillon

It is clear that insight into the relationship between re-pinning and carillon books is of pivotal importance to the reliable reconstruction and artistic execution of eighteenth-century carillon music. Since the only material from the seventeenth century known today are re-pinning manuscripts (see Table 1), my doctoral research investigated how the seventeenth-century carillon repertoire could be reconstructed and performed on the basis of these *versteken*.

The research focused on two re-pinning manuscripts from the first half of the seventeenth century: those of Hendrick Claes (c. 1616-33) and Théodore De Sany (1648).

I. The Re-pinning Book of Hendrick Claes

Hendrick Claes was from Mechelen. On 25 July 1616 he married Anneken Ingels in the 'Sinter Goelen tot Brussel' church (Cathedral of St. Michael and St. Gudula). Anneken Ingels was probably related to the *Engels* or *Inghels* family, a well-known dynasty of watchmakers which had been established in Mechelen since the mid sixteenth century, and which worked together with numerous bell founders.

The manuscript of Hendrick Claes is a remarkable mixture of instructions on the production of tower clocks, personal notes, invoices, poems, and sixty-three musical pieces. There is no doubt that the pieces in the manuscript are *versteken*: this fact is evident from indications such as 'por la demieure' (for the half hour) and the indication of the number of barrel bars at the ends of pieces. It is also clear from the *versteken* that

---

[11] Joannes De Gruÿtters, *Regelement ofte manieren om alle trommels dienende tot beijaert spelen te ver[steken]*, Antwerp, City Archives, Inventaris Oude Muziek M. 25.

Figure 4. Opening of François Couperin, *La Bourbonnoise. Gavote*: original, carillon-arrangement, and *versteek* compared
a. François Couperin, *La Bourbonnoise. Gavote*, bb. 1-5 (*Pièces de clavecin. Premier Livre. Premier Ordre* [Paris, 1713], p. 13)

b. François Couperin / Joannes De Gruÿtters, *La Bourbonnoise*, bb. 1-5 (*De Gruÿtters Carillon Book* [Antwerp, 1746], p. 18)

they were intended for use on a small carillon with nineteen bells. All the pieces fit within a diatonic scale from c to e'', with two extra chromatic tones, $b\flat$ and $b\flat'$. On fol. 51 Claes presents the medieval and Renaissance system of hexachords, adding numbers that match the position of tones in the gamut. These numbers also appear at the ends of the *versteken* staves. Apparently they were intended to assist a person who could not read notes (Claes himself?) in putting the correct pegs in the correct barrel holes.

The *versteken* in the Claes manuscript can be broadly classified into three types: liturgical *versteken* (24), fantasias (4), and *versteken* of dances and songs (35). Claes presents *versteken* for all the major holidays of the liturgical year in no particular order: Advent, Christmas, Shrove Tuesday, Lent, Palm Sunday, Easter, Ascension, Pentecost, Corpus Christi, Marian feasts, feasts of Martyrs, All Saints. One liturgical *versteek*, of the sequence *Mittit ad virginem* (fols. 41v-42r) for the Feast of the Annunciation states the name 'Racquet' at the end. Charles Racquet (1597-1664) was a Parisian organist and composer.[12] Four secular *versteken* also mention the name Racquet: *Balet de madam* [*C'est trop courir les eaux*] (fol. 76r), *Ballet* [*Speme Amorosa*] (fols. 76v-77r), *Ballet* [*L'innamorato*] (fols. 77r-77v), and *Corante* [*Ballet de la Reine*, 1606] (fol. 77v). Aside from these five examples, there are no further direct references to the original sources of Claes's *versteken*.

The liturgical *versteken* are based on plainchant cantus firmi. The cantus firmus is almost always presented first in a single-line form, then followed by one or more versets. This single-line presentation is also found in the work of De Sany and enhances

---

[12] François-Pierre Goy, 'Une source inattendue pour l'œuvre d'un des Racquet: Le Manuscrit de Hendrick Claes, Paris, Bibliothèque nationale, Ms. Néerlandais 58', in *Revue de Musicologie* 80 (1994)1, 97-113, esp. 97, 103-4.

c. François Couperin / Joannes De Gruÿtters, [*La Bourbonnoise. Gavote*], bb. 1-4 (*De Gruÿtters Re-pinning Ms.*, fol. 46r) the recognition of the plainchant melody. After the monodic presentation of the melody, Claes limits himself, with a few exceptions, to two-voice, homo-rhythmic arrangements, with the plainchant usually in the lower voice (Figure 5).

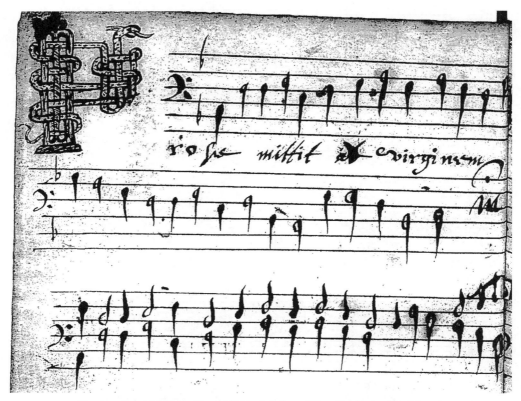

Figure 5. Hendrick Claes, Prose *Mittit ad virginem* (*Claes Re-pinning Ms.*, fol. 41v)

Claes's secular *versteken* are largely based on contemporary French repertoire. The four fantasias are presumably reductions of works originally for keyboard or lute. They are mainly written for two voices, with an occasional third voice to flesh out the music. This feature might indicate that the original compositions on which these *versteken* were based were written for three voices. The other secular *versteken* are mainly adaptations of dances, *airs de cour*, and excerpts from *ballets de cour*. This repertoire is clearly of Parisian origin, but was also well-known in the Netherlands.[13]

The overview of the *versteken* from the *ballet de cour* repertoire indicates how contemporary Claes's adaptations for the automatic carillon were (Table 2).[14]

---

[13] Goy, 'Une source inattendue', 102.
[14] For the dates of these *ballets de cour*, see David J. Buch, *Dance Music from the Ballets de Cour 1575-1651: Historical Commentary, Source Study, and Transcriptions from the Philidor Manuscripts* (New York, 1993), 75-91.

Table 2. Overview of Claes's versteken from the repertoire of the ballet de cour

Versteken by Claes (c. 1616-33)	Ballets de cour
Ballet du Roy	*Ballet des Nègres*, 1601
Courante la Bohémienne (La Montmorency)	*Ballet des Boesmiens*, 1606
Courante Sarabande	*Ballet de la Reine*, 1606
Courante la Durette	*Ballet de la Reine*, 1606
Ballet de M. de Vendôme	*Ballet à Cheval*, 1610
Robinette	*Ballet de Robinette*, 1611
Ballet de Madame (C'est trop courir les eaux)	*Ballet de Madame* or *Triomphe de Minerve*, 1615

Two *versteken*, *Speme Amorosa* and *L'innamorato*, are taken from Gastoldi's popular *Balletti*, which were first printed in Venice in 1591 and were very famous in the Netherlands, where they even appeared in Dutch translation.[15] Claes's attribution of these *versteken* to Racquet suggests that he based his versions on keyboard adaptations by the latter. Also included are familiar dances and songs (emanating from a variety of sources): *Bourée d'Avignon*, *Volte de tamboer*, *Courante l'Espagnole*, *J'ai vu le cerf*, and *C'est une jeune fillette*. Usually, the secular *versteken* are adapted in a standard way: single-line presentation of the theme followed by a repetition with modest harmonization in which the theme is repeated in a different octave or varied with diminutions (Figure 6).

Figure 6. Hendrick Claes, *Set une iune filette* [*C'est une jeune fillette*] (*Claes Re-pinning Ms.*, fol. 68r)

---

[15] Rudi Rasch, 'The *Balletti* of Giovanni Giacomo Gastoldi and the Musical History of the Netherlands', in *Tijdschrift van de Vereniging voor Nederlandse Muziekgeschiedenis* 24 (1974), 112-45.

II. The Re-pinning Book of Théodore De Sany

The manuscript of De Sany contains a total of fifty-nine *versteken*. In his dedication to the magistrates of Brussels, De Sany describes the repertoire in general terms as: 'alle hymnissen voor alle feestdaeghen ende tijden des geheel jaers, midtsgaeders eenighe andere musicale stucken' ('all hymns for all holidays and times of the whole year, together with some other musical pieces').[16] The two indexes added by De Sany divide the *versteken* into two groups. The first index (forty-six *versteken*) includes 'alle Himnissen ende geestelÿcke liedekens, dienende voor het veranderen van alle Feestdaegen des Jaers' ('all hymns and spiritual songs, for the changing of all holidays of the year').[17] These are *versteken* for the hour and the half-hour, based on plainchant cantus firmi, and spiritual songs such as *Een kindeken is ons gheboeren*. Unlike Claes, De Sany ordered the pieces in his re-pinning book closely following the calendar of the church year. De Sany's book includes a significantly greater proportion of liturgical and religious music than that of Claes: 80%, compared to Claes's 38%. The second index (twelve *versteken*) contains 'alle de musickaele stucken die gemaeckt zÿn, om d'orlogie te veranderen buÿten alle feestdaegen' ('all the musical pieces that are made to change the clock outside of the holidays').[18] It includes ten secular pieces: madrigals, chansons, dances, and songs, mainly of Italian origin and clearly pre-dating Claes's contemporary French secular repertoire.

Most *versteken* are based on instrumental and vocal works which De Sany follows quite literally. Adaptations are usually made because of the technical limitations of the barrel rather than the musical possibilities of the automatic carillon. Concordance research and comparative analysis make it possible to determine the original composition and/or composer of some of the *versteken*. For some composers, the *versteken* of De Sany represent exciting expansions to their known oeuvre. For example, De Sany mentions the name 'Turnhaut' by the *versteek* of *Tantum ergo* (fol. 49v). This *versteek* is undoubtedly based on an (unknown) organ verset or motet by either Geert van Turnhout, whose works were still included in the register of St. Gudula at the beginning of the seventeenth century, or Jan van Turnhout, a musician connected to the Brussels court (Figure 7).

De Sany's liturgical *versteken* based on plainchant cantus firmi adopt the strict contrapuntal procedures of vocal polyphony. The other *versteken*—the secular repertoire, the religious *versteken* based on *Cantiones natalitiae,* and some *versteken* that De Sany uses for church holidays (i.e., *Le Bergemaska, J'ai vu le cerf,* and *Den lusteluycken maÿ*)—are more reminiscent of new developments in seventeenth-century keyboard music. In the liturgical *versteken*, the plainchant cantus firmus is almost always played monodically, followed by a contrapuntal treatment that De Sany calls 'het dobbel'. The origin of three of these liturgical *versteken* can be determined with certainty: *Pange lingua* (fols. 51v-52r), *Ut queant laxis* (fol. 54r-54v), and *Ave maris stella* (fol. 58r-58v) are based on organ compositions by Jehan Titelouze (c. 1563-1633). Titelouze's pieces are included in his *Hymnes de l'Église pour toucher sur l'orgue, avec les fugues et les recherches sur leur plain-*

---

[16] Brussels, City Archives, No. 3814, fol. 3r [B-Ba, No. 3814].
[17] B-Ba, No. 3814, fols. 86r-87r.
[18] B-Ba, No. 3814, fol. 88r-88v.

Figure 7. Théodore De Sany, *Tantum ergo*, bb. 1-10 (*De Sany Re-pinning Ms.*, fol. 49v)

chant, published in 1623 by Ballard in Paris. The other liturgical *versteken* are likely also based on organ compositions. In this sense, De Sany's liturgical *versteken* indirectly refer to the rich organ culture of the southern Netherlands.

Four Christmas *versteken* find their origin in the *Cantiones natalitiae* repertoire. This repertoire gained ever greater popularity during the seventeenth century in the southern Netherlands, and included, among others, the songs *Een kindeken is ons gheboeren,* and *Laet het ons met herten rÿne*. According to Rasch, it was precisely the seventeenth-century automatic carillon that promoted the spread of this repertoire.[19]

The hymn section also includes three *versteken* on the very popular song *Den lustelycken maÿ* (of which many sixteenth-century contrafacts with religious lyrics are known), and two *versteken* on *Maria schoon*, a song that became increasingly popular in the course of the seventeenth century.

De Sany includes two chansons and two madrigals in the secular *versteken* (Table 3). Also included are a number of dances and songs (*Almande de St Nicolas, Pavanne d'Espaingnie, Une jeune filiette dormant a son jardin*, among others) which are also likely based on keyboard pieces.

---

[19] Rudolf Rasch, *De Cantiones natalitiae en het kerkelijke muziekleven in de Zuidelijke Nederlanden gedurende de zeventiende eeuw,* 2 vols. (Utrecht, 1985), vol.1, 288.

Table 3. Chansons and madrigals in the re-pinning book of De Sany

Versteek by De Sany	Original composition
Susanne un jour à4 (fols. 68v-69r)	Didier Lupi II (c. 1510/20-after 1559), *Susanne un jour*
Bon jour mon Ceur à4 (fols. 69v-70r)	Orlandus Lassus (1532-94), *Bonjour mon coeur*
Si tanto Gratiosa (fols. 70v-71r)	Giovanni Ferretti (c. 1540-after 1609), *Sei tanto gratioso*
Donna Croudele (fols. 71v-72v)	Giovanni Ferretti (c. 1540-after 1609), *Donna Crudel*

The re-pinning books of Claes and De Sany lead us to conclude that the liturgical repertoire as a whole is expressly present in the automatic carillon music of the southern Netherlands. Sometimes this repertoire is supplemented with spiritual songs such as the *Cantiones natalitiae*. The secular repertoire shows greater variety, ranging from older works of Italian origin to contemporary French items. The re-pinning books contain both traditional melodies that had acquired the status of 'evergreens' and contemporary '*airs à la mode*'.

Carillon Intabulations in the Seventeenth Century

The practice-based research into the Claes and De Sany books (playing the *versteken*) confirmed the conclusion reached with De Gruÿtters's re-pinning book: *versteken* do not copy a particular playing technique, but rather present an imitation of a performance practice. Along with practice-based research, primary documentary sources relating to carillon repertoire and performance practice were also collected and studied for my research. These sources include archival documents, travel diaries, journals, and pamphlets. Only rarely in these sources do we find mentions of specific works. An interesting exception is Vincenzo Giustiniani's reference to Palestrina's madrigal *Vestiva i colli* in his *Discorso sopra la musica* (1628): '…e l'istesso Madrigale ho sentito in Anversa suonare nel campanile della chiesa principale con le campane, e quello che suonava aveva, il libro davanti, e toccava li tasti, come s'usa ne gli organi, e l'istesso mi dissero che s'usava in Bolduch et in altri luoghi del Brabande e di Fiandra.' ('I have heard the same madrigal on the bells of the campanile of the principal church in Antwerp; the player has the book in front of him and touches the keys as though he were playing the organ. I was told that this madrigal is put to similar use in 's-Hertogenbosch and other places in Brabant and Flanders.').[20] From Giustiniani's account it appears that *Vestiva i colli* was played on the carillon in various locations in the early seventeenth century.

The fact that carillonneurs played madrigals and motets is also mentioned in a request for a pay raise submitted to the Antwerp city government on 31 December 1590 by Jan Rieulin [Reolin], the carillonneur of the city's cathedral from 1584 to 1631: 'Gheeft te kennen Jan Reolin, clockspeelder der kercke van Onse-Lieve-Vrouwe, hoedat hy tot dienste ende eere derselver kercke ende stadt, hem nyet en laet verdrieten dagelyckx te studeren ende grooten arbeyt te doene om alle musicale stucken, soo motetten als liedekens, in tabulatura over te setten ende te spelen.' ('Jan Reolin, bell player of the church of Our Lady, makes it known how he, in service and honour of this same church

---

[20] Quote taken from Vincenzo Giustiniani, 'Discorso sopra la musica de' suoi tempi [1628]', in *Le Origini del Melodramma*, ed. Angelo Solerti (Turin, 1903), 98-128 at 127.

and city, does not mind studying daily and making a great effort to play and copy in tablature all musical pieces, such as motets and songs.')[21]

From De Sany's re-pinning book and documentary sources mentioned above, it can be concluded that carillonneurs, in the first half of the seventeenth century in the southern Netherlands, made intabulations for both the automatic carillon (*versteek* intabulations), as well as for their own performance (carillon intabulations). Carillon intabulations are characterized by two major concepts: reduction, involving thinning the polyphonic texture; and by extending the sound with embellishment. De Sany's *versteek* intabulations are examples of how these intabulations were realized despite the technical limitations of the barrel. When carillonneurs played intabulations, they undoubtedly added embellishments that had not been included in the *versteken* because of the technical limitations of the automatic chiming system.

Reconstructing the Carillon Music of the Seventeenth Century

The conclusions of the *versteken* research and the documentary sources formed the basis for reconstructing the carillon music of the first half of the seventeenth century in the southern Netherlands. This reconstruction was mainly realized by making adaptations of *versteken* for manual performance and by re-creating carillon intabulations. These two practice-based methods will be illustrated by means of an example.

I. Adaptation of the Versteek on *Ave maris stella*

Although no known sources can confirm this assumption, it seems plausible that seventeenth-century carillonneurs adapted *versteken,* possibly *ex tempore*, for their recitals. With this hypothesis in mind, I adapted, amongst others, De Sany's *versteek* on *Ave maris stella* for carillon performance. De Sany's *versteek* is itself adapted from an organ work by Titelouze. Detailed comparison of the *versteek* with Titelouze's original score shows that De Sany reduced the number of notes, thereby creating greater textural transparency. The reduction is rather random, without any regard for voicing, and is often motivated by the available number of hammers per bell and the corresponding repetition rate of the notes. The smallest subdivision of De Sany's barrel was the quaver. De Sany either omitted the semiquavers from the original, or converted them into new quaver motifs. Titelouze indicates no particular embellishments, and states in the preface to his edition that he leaves this matter to the discretion of the performer.[22] There are also no embellishments in De Sany's *versteek*. Considering the relevance of embellishments to the performance of Titelouzes work, this omission might be explained by the division of the bars on the barrel (the smallest value being the quaver). It is very likely that embellishments were added during hand-played performance by carillonneurs, as was also expected of organists.[23]

---

[21] Quote taken from Godelieve Spiessens, 'De Antwerpse stadsbeiaardiers. Deel I: 1540-1650', in *Jaarboek 1993-1994 van de Provinciale Commissie voor Geschiedenis en Volkskunde* (Antwerpen, 1994), 5-97 at 78.

[22] See Jehan Titelouze, *Hymnes de l'église pour toucher sur l'orgue. 2ᵉ édition, 1624*, facs. ed. Marcel Degrutère (Bressuire, 1992), 'Au lecteur'.

[23] On embellishments in Titelouze, see Edward Higginbottom, 'Jehan Titelouze, c. 1563-1633', in *The Musical Times* 124 (1983), 571-73.

My carillon adaptation further reduced the voices to two above the cantus firmus (Figure 8 and Example 1).

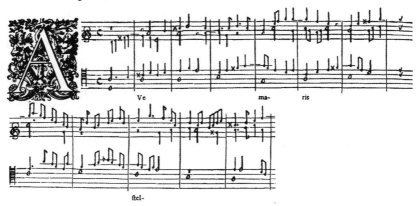

Figure 8. Opening of Jehan Titelouze, *Ave maris stella*: original and *versteek* compared
a. Jehan Titelouze, *Ave maris stella*, bb. 1-12 (*Hymnes de l'Église* [Paris, ²1624], fol. 18v)

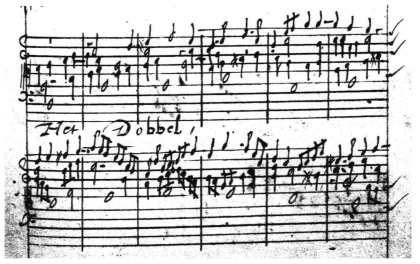

b. Jehan Titelouze / Théodore De Sany, *Ave maris stella*, bb. 1-12 (*De Sany Re-pinning Ms.*, fol. 58r)

Example 1. Jehan Titelouze / Carl Van Eyndhoven, *Ave maris stella,* Adaptation for carillon, bb. 1-13

II. Carillon Intabulation of *Bonjour mon coeur*

The intabulation technique De Sany employs in his *versteken* offers a starting-point for making similar carillon intabulations. De Sany's intabulation techniques include reducing the polyphonic voices, adding diminutions, extending chords, and, occasionally, adding (cadence) embellishments.

In De Sany's *versteek of* Lassus's chanson *Bonjour mon coeur* the four voices are occasionally reduced to three. He maintains the bassus and superius and elegantly diminishes these voices with passing notes, auxiliary notes, and scale figures (Figure 9). The occasionally decorated middle voices fill out the chords following the harmonic scheme of the original. De Sany also fills in gaps produced by long notes with broken chords and embellishments. This practice is clear from comparison of the cantus and bassus of Lassus's original with De Sany's *versteek* (Example 2).

Figure 9. Orlandus Lassus / Théodore De Sany, *Bonjour mon coeur*, bb. 13-24 (*De Sany Re-pinning Ms.*, fol. 69v)

Example 2. Orlandus Lassus (2-4) / Théodore De Sany (1-3), *Bonjour mon coeur*, bb. 1-13

Example 2. continued

Example 3. Orlandus Lassus / Carl Van Eyndhoven, *Bonjour mon coeur,* Intabulation for carillon, bb. 1-12

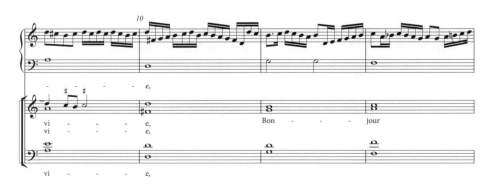

In addition to De Sany's *versteek* of *Bonjour mon coeur*, I also studied the practice of playing divisions which was commonplace among organists and lutenists in the Low Countries. Extensive divisions can be found in the works of among others Peter Philips, Pieter Cornet, John Bull, and Emanuel Adriaenssen. Through imitation of their technique and style, I developed a vocabulary of idiomatic carillon divisions which I used to re-create a carillon intabulation of *Bonjour mon coeur* (Example 3). The next step was to play this intabulation on historical carillons that have copies of seventeenth-century keyboards to find out how the music could be performed on an instrument whose key-depth is twice as great as that of a modern keyboard. I learned that such a difference of key-depth not only results in a totally different attack of the hammer on the bell, but also requires a nuanced approach of tempo.

III. Authenticity of the Artistic Reconstruction of Seventeenth-Century Carillon Music

The playing of both the historical *versteken* and all the intabulations I had re-created was one of the most important criteria for evaluating the reliability of my artistic reconstruction of seventeenth-century carillon music. It is important to note that 'practice as research' was an essential part of the methodology of my Ph.D. project. This artistic reconstruction differs from a musicological reconstruction; when the objectivity of scientific research reaches its limits, the subjectivity of the artistic research continues.

Conclusion

Comparative study of re-pinning and carillon books not only broadened our knowledge of the carillon repertoire, but also provided new insights into performance practice. That study gave rise to a new methodology that originates in the observation that *versteken* imitate the playing of the carillonneurs, and thus form an important source of information about performance practice. Both documentary sources and De Sany's *versteek* intabulations demonstrate the common use of intabulation by seventeenth-century carillonneurs, allowing polyphonic vocal works to be performed on the carillon. Carillonneurs thus imitated a practice that was common among players of keyboard and plucked instruments, without, however, developing a genuinely idiomatic carillon playing style. My doctoral research, in which playing the *versteken* was a key method, allowed me to reconstruct this practice and has resulted in 'authentic' performances of the repertoire played by seventeenth-century carillonneurs.

Abstract

> The remarkable development of the carillon in the seventeenth century, culminating in the magnificent instruments of François and Pierre Hemony, contrasts sharply with the lack of primary musical sources that testify to the music that must have been performed on that instrument. Three seventeenth-century re-pinning books, of pieces to be set on automatic carillon drums, offer a glimpse into the carillon's repertoire at this time. No seventeenth-century carillon music books for manual performance are preserved. The prevailing opinion sees the carillon books, and not the re-pinning books, as acceptable sources for research into performance practices. However, examination shows that re-pinning books can be reliable sources for historically informed performance, and allow the artistic reconstruction of a seventeenth-century carillon book.

Contributors to this Issue

Jane Alden is Professor of Music at Trinity College, Dublin. Her research addresses musical notation and visual culture in the medieval and modern eras, manuscript production and patronage, reception history, and experimental music. She has published a monograph with Oxford University Press entitled *Songs, Scribes, and Society: The History and Reception of the Loire Valley Chansonniers*, an edition of the known works of Johannes Delahaye, and a number of articles on medieval and historiographical topics.

Vincenzo Borghetti is Ricercatore in Music History at the University of Verona. His research interests are centred on Renaissance polyphony and early-twentieth-century opera. He is coauthor of *Il bacio della Sfinge: D'Annunzio, Pizzetti e "Fedra"* (Turin, 1998), and his essays and articles have appeared in *Early Music History, Acta musicologica, Imago Musicae, Yearbook of the Alamire Foundation,* among other publications.

Oliver Huck is Professor of Musicology at the University of Hamburg, where he is also director of the 'Manuscript Cultures in Asia, Africa and Europe' graduate school in the Centre for the Studies of Manuscripts (CSMC), and Dean of the Faculty of Humanities.

Vassiliki Koutsobina holds a Ph.D. in musicology from the University of Cincinnati. Her research focuses on musical rhetoric in the chanson repertories of Josquin des Prez and his contemporaries and has appeared in *Early Music* and *Tijdschrift van de Vereniging voor Nederlandse Muziekgeschiedenis*. She has presented papers at meetings of the American Musicological Society, the International Musicological Society, and the Medieval and Renaissance Music Conference. Dr. Koutsobina teaches at Hellenic-American University in Athens, Greece. She is currently completing a monograph on sixteenth-century French chansons that were specifically composed as responses to pre-existent songs.

Grantley McDonald is a post-doctoral fellow in the department of musicology, Universität Salzburg. He holds doctoral degrees in musicology (Melbourne, 2002) and history (Leiden, 2011). His research has been distinguished with prizes from the Australian Academy of the Humanities (Canberra) and the Praemium Erasmianum Foundation (Amsterdam). Previous positions include postdoctoral fellowships at the Herzog August Bibliothek (Wolfenbüttel), Centre d'Études Supérieures de la Renaissance (Tours), KU Leuven, and Trinity College Dublin. He is author of *Marsilio Ficino in Germany, from Renaissance to Enlightenment: a Reception History* (Geneva, 2015), and *The Politics of Biblical Criticism in Early Modern Europe: Erasmus, the Johannine Comma and Trinitarian Debate* (Cambridge, 2015). He is also active as a performing musician.

Thomas Schmidt-Beste is Professor of Music at the University of Manchester. After holding positions in Heidelberg, Urbana, and Frankfurt, he was appointed as Chair in Music at Bangor University in 2005 and came to Manchester in 2012. His main areas of research are music and musical sources of the fifteenth and sixteenth centuries and German music of the late eighteenth and nineteenth centuries (Mendelssohn and Mozart in particular). He is the director of the AHRC-funded research project 'Production and Reading of Music Sources, 1480-1530'; other current projects include a book on texture and timbre in nineteenth-century chamber music and an edition of Mendelssohn's *Reformation Symphony*.

Carl Van Eyndhoven graduated in organ and music pedagogy from the Lemmensinstituut, Leuven and carillon from the Netherlands Carillon School. He holds a Ph.D. in seventeenth-century carillon performance practice from the University of Leuven and is vice-dean for research at the LUCA School of Arts.

Hanna Vorholt is an Anniversary Research Lecturer in the Department of History of Art at the University of York, and co-investigator of the AHRC-funded research project 'Production and Reading of Music Sources, 1480-1530'. Her research focuses on illuminated manuscripts and on the representation of Jerusalem in the medieval West. Before moving to York in 2012 she held positions or fellowships at the Max Planck Institute for History (Göttingen), the Fitzwilliam Museum, Cambridge University Library, the British Library, and the Warburg Institute.

Plates

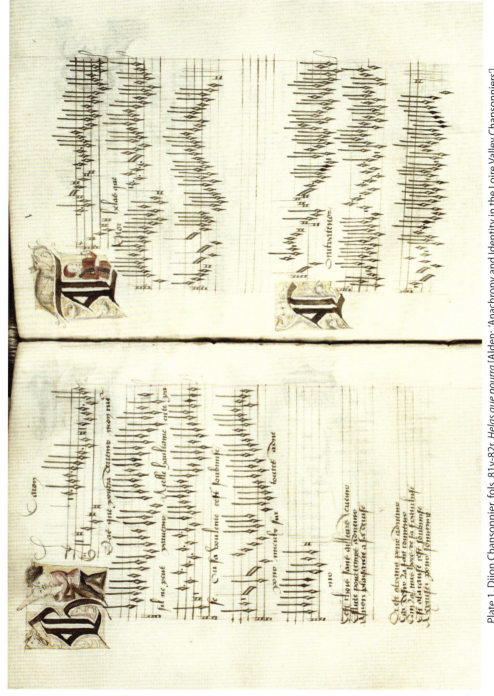

Plate 1. Dijon Chansonnier, fols. 81v–82r, *Helas que pourra* [Alden: 'Anachrony and Identity in the Loire Valley Chansonniers']

Plate 2. Laborde Chansonnier, fols. 20v–21r, *Puis que si bien* [Alden: 'Anachrony and Identity in the Loire Valley Chansonniers']

Plate 3. Jan Coessaet, Opening Session of the Parliament of Mechelen in 1473 (ca. 1587), Stedelijke Musea Mechelen, inv. S/615; photo copyright Dries Van den Brande [Alden: 'Anachrony and Identity in the Loire Valley Chansonniers']

PLATES ■ 131

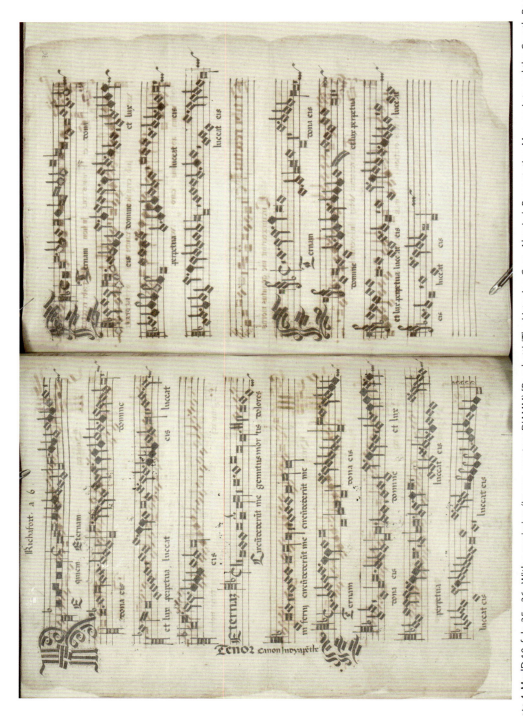

Plate 4. ModD 10, fols. 35v-36r. With permission (image courtesy DIAMM) [Borghetti: 'The Listening Gaze: Alamire's Presentation Manuscripts and the Courtly Reader']

Plate 5. JenaU 3, fols. 29v–30r. With permission (image courtesy DIAMM) [Borghetti: 'The Listening Gaze: Alamire's Presentation Manuscripts and the Courtly Reader']

Plate 6. BrusBR 228, fols. 1v–2r. With permission (image courtesy DIAMM) [Borghetti: "The Listening Gaze: Alamire's Presentation Manuscripts and the Courtly Reader"]

Plate 7. BrusBR 228, fol. 1v, detail. With permission (image courtesy DIAMM)
[Borghetti: 'The Listening Gaze: Alamire's Presentation Manuscripts and the Courtly Reader']